I0725403

DRIVEN BY DRAGONBLOOD

BLOOD BORN 3

LYNN BURKE

Copyright © 2025 by Lynn Burke

All rights reserved.

Editor: Katherine McIntyre

Proof Reader: Deborah Peach

Cover Artist: Golden Czermak / FuriousFotog

Model: Robert Kelly

This is a work of fiction. Names, characters, places, and incidents are the product of the author's imagination or are used fictitiously, and any resemblance to actual persons, living or dead, business establishments, events, or locales is entirely coincidental. This book is copyright. No part of this book may be reproduced in any form except for the inclusion of brief quotations in a review or article, without written permission from the author.

No generative AI was used in the writing of this book or the creation of its cover. No part of this book may be used as data for 'training' any large language model or as part of any machine learning or neural network architecture.

Visit Lynn's website at https://authorlynnburke.com/ for a comprehensive list of titles, free reads, trope guide, and printable reading list.

DRIVEN BY DRAGONBLOOD

Driven by instinct, I leave the seclusion of my ancestral home to find my fated mates. With my isolated upbringing, I naïvely thought my journey toward completion would be simple.

However, shifting winds complicate my flight.

The cunning voice that my beta hears lands him in a psychiatric ward, leaving me no hope of freeing him without exposing the secret that humans are not the only sentient beings on earth.

My alpha battles his inner darkness, living a life of strict self-control to prove his sanity. He seeks out yet rejects the truth of our connection, shattering my dreams.

When a court order grants my beta his freedom, a moment of passion breaks down all barriers between us. Yet, without our alpha, we remain unsatisfied.

In our struggle to claim what is rightfully ours, fate reveals itself to be even more cunning.

Our alpha's dragon asserts dominance over his human side, speaking into being what cannot be broken. We find ourselves caught in flames that threaten to destroy every-thing he has fought to achieve.

Will our alpha embrace his destiny, or will his humanity keep the three of us from finding the wholeness we have all been desperately searching for?

CHAPTER I
PRIMROSE

The scent of rain lay heavy on the wind, sighing through the trees over my head. Laughter rang out from the children on the playground across the grass from where I slumped on the hard ground, knees pulled to my chest.

Picnic tables sat between me and the laughing youngsters, families with loved ones packing up what was left of their lunches they had enjoyed in the fresh air now threatened by an incoming storm.

Two people lay on a blanket a few feet from me, cuddling each other as though they didn't have a care in the world about what went on around them. Let the winds blow, the downpour soak them. They lived in a bubble of perfection where nothing could touch them.

Sighing, I tore my gaze off the lovers.

Two photographers hurried a couple in wedding attire back toward a waiting limo, their smiles almost as bright as the warm winter sun that had been taken over by clouds a few minutes earlier.

Sweetness from nearby flowers wafted past my nose, and

I breathed them in deeply as I'd been doing since flying southward enough that the snow-covered Tetons were nothing but a distant memory. I'd hunted for my fated mates by air in dragon form for days on end, anticipation of a sense of connection that would lead me toward my alpha and beta, but no such feelings had swept through me while in flight. And I'd stretched my wings wide and soared over the entire state of Arizona.

Defeat had sent me permanently to the ground a couple of weeks earlier, and I'd taken on my human form, hoping that mingling with people more closely would allow me to find the connection I yearned for. But so far, I'd been unlucky, which caused my heart to wilt in my chest. At least I wouldn't run out of funds anytime soon, thus being forced to return to the mountains.

On the day I had turned eighteen, my human grandmother had added me to her bank account, one richly donated to by my grandpapa, who had recently found out I existed. A debit card allowed for motels and hotels, much less accommodating and comfortable than the cavern I'd grown up in, even if the amenities of my childhood home were severely outdated.

And the noise…

Engines, radios, humans chattering—vastly different than the solitude of Grand Teton and the quiet wildlife interested only in surviving.

Thunder rumbled, and I lifted my face skyward, hugging myself a little tighter. Darker clouds lay on the horizon, promising cleansing rain to the arid land and sustenance to the thirsty plants struggling to survive the dry winter.

But the people enjoying the unseasonably warm afternoon in the park didn't seem to care about the danger on the horizon.

My loneliness sharpened while watching parents and

children as well as lovers being affectionate with one another.

Soft touches.

Kind words.

Secretive smiles.

Sweet kisses like those shared by the couple on my left.

I wanted those same interactions but had no experience or knowledge of how to go about finding such things.

For the first time in my twenty-two years, I began to question how my grandmother had raised me. She'd kept us cooped up in the mountains, far from civilization and others who might seek to harm us. I'd been sheltered, hidden away, and now, tears stung my eyes over all I had missed out on.

Even though fated mates awaited those with dragonblood in their veins, I could have experienced a fuller life, such as school with my peers and perhaps even a tender young love or a first crush, even if it wouldn't have lasted for my lifetime.

At least I would have been better equipped to deal with the humans now surrounding me, those without inner voices my dragonblood gift would have allowed me to communicate with.

The ache in my chest hurt almost as much as it had on the morning I'd buried my grandmother beneath stone and dirt. Returning to our cavern home alone that afternoon had been brutal, but I felt an absence of connection now more than I did that day, among people who had purpose and a reason for living. They had others they looked to for either nurturing or partnership, while I was a single star in my life's sky, attempting to prohibit darkness from overshadowing my heart and mind.

A tear slid down my cheek as the first pattering of rain hit the leaves above me, and my next inhalation caused a shudder to wrack through my huddled body.

The people around me, lovers included, scrambled to gather their belongings, rushing toward the safety of their vehicles while I sat alone, the heavens opening up faster than I'd expected. I couldn't be bothered to move from where I sat, chest cracked wide, throat swelling shut, and eyes releasing the sorrow inside me.

Within a matter of minutes, I was once more alone, without a trace of humanity left behind except for a bit of trash beneath one of the abandoned picnic tables.

No more laughter.

No more smiles.

No more gentle caresses or chaste press of lips for me to envy.

Rain and cloudy skies surrounded me, a mirror of the heaviness upon my shoulders.

Sniffling, I tilted my head down, forehead on my knees, hugging myself tighter.

I'd fled the comforts of home even though I'd never truly felt a sense of belonging in the Teton mountains. An urging deep inside, the whispering of my inner dragon, had insisted it was time to fly and seek out our fate. I'd left my newly met grandpop, Dolyn, behind with his alpha and female in the cavern of our ancestors, where they would mate and raise a family. Having seen their love and how they belonged to each other, I wanted nothing more than to experience the same. The thought of returning to the Tetons alone and having to witness their happiness made my stomach twist.

But where else would I go?

Stay.

My throat tightened as my inner dragon attempted to soothe my emotions. She'd been as silent as my human half for days on end, overrun by thoughts of despair.

"And do what?" I whispered aloud, since no one was around to accuse me of being mad from talking to myself.

Seek.

"That's all we've *been* doing," I stated, straightening to swipe my arm over my wet eyes even though rain continued to batter my face.

My dragon half went quiet once more.

The feeling of urgency that had sent me flying south through the winter winds to the warmer southern state had calmed to where I barely felt a hint of my dragon's assurance we were in the right place.

So why didn't I sense my mates?

Were they even of lesser blood than Grandpop's alpha and female that I couldn't perceive or communicate with their dragons? I was a Blood Born with the rare ability to hear all inner beings of those with dragonblood in their veins. Even the most minuscule from those I'd come into contact with on the few times Grandmother and I had gone into town for supplies before her death.

But it seemed no such creatures inhabited the southern-most parts of Arizona.

Perhaps I'd missed my fated mate by a mere mile. Flown past where they resided, their supernatural halves unknown or somehow hidden away from their consciousness. What if both my alpha and beta had managed to suppress what they didn't understand, burying their true self deep enough our souls couldn't call to one another as, according to the ancient texts I'd studied, fated mates ought to be able to do?

I lifted my face once more, eyes closed.

Rain sluiced through the branches overhead, soaking through the old-fashioned, large shirt and the long skirt that flowed around my ankles while I'd walked listlessly across the park in search of a sense of belonging. The material would stick to my legs now, clinging and itching, reminding me how much I hated the restriction of clothing.

North.

I sniffled but didn't bother attempting to wipe the wetness from my face. "We can't return to what used to be home," I whispered, my heart aching for my mates.

The canyon.

Heaving a sigh, I straightened my legs, shoulders still slumped. "What about it?"

Let us soar over its beauty once more.

A huff of sad laughter escaped me. Thanks to Grandpop sharing his ability to cloak our true selves, my inner dragon had released and been able to fly during daylight hours, invisible to the human eye. Diving deep into the reaches of the Grand Canyon, shooting skyward in a rush of wind, rolling and tucking my wings to glide above the winding river at its base, was almost as pleasurable as winding through the peaks of the Tetons.

I had been in this form for far too long.

Standing, I stretched my back, filling my lungs. Three steps took me from beneath the semi-shelter of the tree, exposing me to the full force of the elements. Wind and rain buffeted me, whipping the soaked skirt around me.

But a torrential downpour didn't compare to my stubbornness or my beast's strength.

My mind's desire to cloak myself from sight blinked me from visual existence. I removed the sodden clothing from my body and stuffed it into the drenched duffle bag I carried everywhere before straightening once more.

Communicating with my inner dragon came as easily as breathing, and the shift rippled through my physical body like a bend of light, morphing my human form into that of a pale golden dragon, the same color of my waist-length hair, scales, spines, and all.

Front claws of our left foot wrapped tight around our duffle, and we launched into the stormy sky, our grief-filled roar masked by the thunder rumbling around us.

We will locate them.

My human half held no such hope but gave over to the dragon side, a powerful flap of golden wings sending us into the dark sky. We shot through the rain, northward toward the canyon.

More than anything, we yearned for happiness.

But all we had learned thus far in our travels was that heartache proved much easier to find.

CHAPTER 2
JAXON

Wind whips through my hair. I can barely breathe from the air blasting against my face—but I can't keep the grin off my face. Plummeting to the earth causes my heart to race. My muscles too tense. Elation swells in my chest and even makes my dick hard.

I can fly.

I can fucking fly!

The ground rushes up to meet me, but tingles erupted along my spine. Wings sprout from my back. Instinct has them spreading wide, catching wind, gracefully arcing me upward, toward freedom rather than splattering to my death—

I gasped, pulse pounding in my temples as reality slammed into my brain, ripping me from my favorite dream that had been on repeat in my head for as long as I could remember.

"Goddamnit," I muttered, readying to stretch and reach for my throbbing cock—

Couldn't move.

"The fuck?" I lifted my head, blinking weariness from my

eyes even as familiar scents flooded my nose and made my breath hitch and hair stand on end.

I wiggled my hands and toes. All four limbs were lashed down to a bed. A white gown covered me from neck to knees, my morning wood creating an obscene tent. A shift of my backside made the plastic sheet beneath me crinkle.

"No, no, no," I whispered as the truth weighed on me, causing me to sink powerlessly into my restraints regardless of how my heart raced and legs twitched in desire to escape.

My dick remained hard, uncaring of our predicament, throbbing and letting me know nothing but the gown stood between its heated flesh and the air.

I glanced around the room, my sparse surroundings, the stark white walls, the scent of bleach in the air, the lone window with its bars to keep me prisoner—

Lockwood.

Fucking Lockwood. Again!

What goddamned fuckery had I gotten up to this time that my parents had shipped me out over three hours from home into the middle of nowhere?

Snickering echoed in my mind, and I scowled, cursing at myself under my breath. I'd been well on my way toward proving I wasn't a nutcase so my parents wouldn't keep sending me away.

Wait.

I jerked my head up, straining my neck to see past the tenting of my gown. Wiggled my toes again—toes *not* covered by a cast. Legs bare. No pins sticking out, no bandages, or evidence of fresh wounds. Just a jagged scar from the time I'd leaped off a building while high as a kite.

"Oh, thank fuck." I huffed a laugh, half-mad with relief even while adrenaline crashed through my entire body, making me feel as though I could rip through the straps tying me down to the hospital bed.

My paternal grandmother had been schizophrenic and, thinking she could fly, had thrown herself off one of the south rim viewpoints of the Grand Canyon long before I'd been born. Unfortunately, I seemed to inherit the inner voice that promised me wings would sprout from my back if only given a chance. Yeah, I wasn't right in the head, and then when I'd become too much for my parents to handle, they had sent me to an expensive boarding school so they wouldn't have to deal with their defective son.

The first time I actually listened to the voice though, I'd ended up with a shattered leg and, a few too many surgeries later, could pretty much run like a normal guy my age. I would never be a medalist in the hundred meters at the Olympics, but as long as I could chase the ladies and be the best lay of their lives while getting my rocks off, I deserved gold.

I took stock of my body now, relaxing as I realized I was whole—and obviously still healthy. No searing agony ripped through me, leftover from a surgery to repair the damage I'd caused a body I'd believed indestructible thanks to drugs I knew better than to touch.

But I'd been weak. Lonely as fuck, worse than normal, even though part of my daily affirmations included reminders that I didn't need anyone, that I was stronger on my own. Letting people into your head and heart only weakened a man.

Take my parents—the ones who were supposed to love me unconditionally and have my back.

Yeah, right.

They'd abandoned me countless times, the final being Christmas break this year. Rather than have me home from my senior year for the holidays, they jetted overseas on some lovely vacation, dining at five-star restaurants while I'd sat alone in my dorm, eating takeout.

The return of my so-called friends and their readiness to party after break had led us all down a path toward sure trouble and possible destruction.

Well, me, anyway. I was the only one of us who'd ever gone to the roof of our dorm, ready to leap off, believing I could shoot into the sky like a goddamned bird.

Just like Gramma—

"No." I shook my head at my inner voice's insistence, ridding my thoughts of her. I was *nothing* like her.

More snickering sounded between my ears, but I pretended to ignore it like I always did. Wished I could do the same with my throbbing balls.

Obviously, the madness I attempted to hide had reared its head while around others, but someone or something had stopped me. I'd been lucky last time I did a swan dive off a roof that I only shattered bones in my right leg rather than cause my head to splat like a watermelon dropped to the sidewalk.

I wracked my brain, filtering through haziness to remember what had gone down. There had been liquor. A couple of shared joints—one had been laced with a funky substance. Had I hallucinated? Memories flashed through my head like murky shadows.

Stumbling upstairs.

Laughing like the Mad Hatter.

Howling into the sky like I was a werewolf or some shit.

A straitjacket

Sweet darkness finally quieting my consciousness that was louder than most humans'.

"Moron," I muttered to myself, wishing I could scrub my hands through my hair and try to rip it from my scalp.

I'd been so close to full independence. A few months away from graduating, but even better, not long before I turned eighteen, when I would have complete freedom from the rule of my parents, who didn't give a shit about me.

Having visited this lovely—*not*—place before, I expected a ninety-day stay with shit food, therapy, and playdates with fellow inmates who stared and drooled or threw violent tantrums regardless of the drugs they had shoved down their throats.

At least I didn't have a roommate. Maybe I would manage to get some sleep—

The familiar squeak of a cart came from out in the hallway, and I glanced toward the solid white door with its small square of unbreakable glass. A pause in the noise assured me the orderly had stopped. Sure enough, a beep sounded, and my room's door swung open to allow a sweet-smelling morsel over the threshold.

My dick didn't care about being caught straining toward the ceiling. It had a brain of its own, and exhibition was its kink, especially when it came to pretty ladies.

I grinned at the face I recognized from my last stint in Lockwood, the only good thing about being behind Lockwood's walls. "Nurse Yum Yum."

She snickered, shaking her dark head, cheeks pink as she glanced over my restrained form. "Yano," she reminded me while I fought off the need to thrust into the air, desperate for a touch from one of the few people in this joint who hadn't stared at me like I was some deranged criminal.

"I don't know," I said smoothly, checking her out from cleavage to Crocs in her blue scrubs, my backside shifting restlessly as pre-cum smeared between my cockhead and the gown. "Still looking as delicious as ever."

Nurse Yano rolled her eyes and wheeled the cart closer while I stared up at her face, loving how I unnerved her. How she couldn't keep her gaze from flitting to the tent above my groin. I flexed my cock every single time, expecting a wet spot had appeared, considering how much I leaked.

She bit her lip while putting the cuff on my arm, glancing once more at where I ached.

"Naughty girl," I whispered, and she cleared her throat, pretending to be all professional and shit.

I'd tried to get into her panties when I'd last been locked up in this shithole, but with me being underage…fuck. I was *still* too young. But in three months—

"No," she stated firmly, and I huffed as she pumped the cuff full of air.

Same as last time, I was a caged animal being poked at, but at least she didn't hold a needle.

"You're no fun," I muttered with a pout that included puppy dog eyes.

"Because you're jailbait."

I smirked. "I won't tell if you won't."

"Behave, Jaxon Denham."

A snicker, both internally and from my own lips, sounded. Serious mental illness ran in my family, but I *wasn't* mad. That inner part of me I shared space with was fulfilling. Felt right. Peaceful even while mostly chaotic. I called the fucker—whatever it was—my beast, which suited him just fine. "You know me better than that."

She listened briefly to my blood pressure before retrieving my meds and a small cup with a straw. "Head up."

"Oh, it's *up*, all right."

Another eye roll and shake of her head set my grin in place, but I was a good boy, sticking out my tongue.

Two pills.

A long pull on the straw, and I swallowed the lukewarm liquid that tasted like tap water.

Ugh. Gross.

"Were you high again?"

Nurse Yano and I had been chatty when I'd last visited her workplace, and since being on her good side afforded me contraband in the form of caramel hard candies during my last stint, I filled her in on what I could remember while she finished doing her nurse duties in taking care of me—just not in the way I'd have preferred.

"You need to stay away from the drugs, Jaxon."

"Don't I know it," I grumbled, tugging on my wrists' restraints, twitchy with the need for freedom. "Can I get these off?"

"Doctor Holliday will be in to see you since you're awake. It's his decision to make."

"That old fart is still here?" I asked, not looking forward to the probing of doctors attempting to make sense of my brain with endless questions and demands to talk about my dreams of flying.

I'd always hated zoos as a kid.

Even more now that I was caged up like an animal.

"He's one of our best." Nurse Yano patted my forearm, all motherly and shit. "Three months," she reminded me, trying for a firm look, but I saw the truth behind her professionalism, which gave me something other than my prison to focus on.

"Can you help me out before you go? Pretty please with a big juicy cherry on top? Hell, I'll even throw in a couple of chocolate bars once I'm finally free of this place for good."

She pressed her lips tight but managed not to check out my raging boner again.

"I'm already so damned close—just a brush of fingertips, and I'll shoot off like a goddamned rocket." I pumped my hips upward, but she managed to ignore me.

Nurse Yum Yum reached into her pocket, the crinkling of a wrapper making my mouth water. "Open up."

I did so without argument, releasing a low, sensual moan as the taste of caramel slid over my tongue.

"Three months," she stated with a twinkle in her eyes before turning away.

I enjoyed the sweetness making my mouth water and the swell of her ass in her scrubs as she moved toward the door, the squeaky cart wheel grating on my nerves. "Promise?"

She didn't answer before locking me in once more, and I lay back, determined to enjoy myself this time around.

The woman had almost caved last year. I could wear her down.

Need.

My dick bucked on its own, and swallowing the lush taste of caramel, I groaned, rubbing my ass against the crinkling mattress cover beneath me. Coming untouched was something I fucking loved. The out-of-control ache, the desperation for friction, the agony of my taint pulsing without fingers or a mouth on me just fucking did it for me.

Need.

I closed my eyes at the insistent word in my head and gave over to my favorite fantasy.

A blonde goddess with curves like a train track, hair draping over her lush backside. Thick thighs, spread and inviting. She would stick her finger up my ass, play with that patch of nerves that always made me shoot off like a geyser whenever I felt the desire for a little something extra.

Wet warmth would welcome me home. Tight heat clutching at my thrusting shaft, desperate for me to breed her.

"Fuck yeah," I murmured around the hard candy in my mouth, the slight friction of my gown rubbing over my leaking slit more than enough to get me there.

Her teeth on my neck. Fingernails breaking skin.

Delicious fucking violence, sweet pain to send me—

"Fuck!" I jolted against my restraints, spurting cum all the fuck over my pulsing dick and groin. Curses continued to spill with every shot of spunk, and I shuddered, loving the pain of release without a firm grip on my shaft. The agony of denied true fulfillment.

Goose bumps rose over me, like bubbles attempting to break free from skin.

I finally stilled, my heart racing, lungs sucking in air.

Cum leaked over my relaxing balls, down my taint, to drip onto the bed.

"Shit." I lifted my head. There was no denying the wetness of the white gown and how it now clung to my softening dick.

Snickering echoed in my ears, and I shook my head at myself while crunching what was left of the candy between my teeth.

Doc Holliday knew I was a horny fucker from my last stay in Lockwood.

No biggie.

My smile faded along with my arousal that had been sated for the time being.

Yeah, I would be eighteen soon, but what if my parents somehow managed to keep me in the loony bin? What if the doctors deemed me unsafe to live among the people who didn't have really fucking loud inner voices that constantly got them into trouble or attempted to embarrass them by leaving messes for anyone to see?

I was desperate to travel my own path toward wherever the fuck I belonged. Make mistakes. Learn and grow as every other young adult was allowed to do. I deserved the right to become my own man, figure out who and what I was.

And my secret longing that I hated but couldn't help? Finding someone who would love me. Accept me. See the value in my life and want me for more than just my rocking body that fucked like a god.

Ask my past hookups about the validity of that statement.

Escape.

"Wish we could," I muttered, pulling against my restraints again even though I had personal knowledge such a thing wasn't possible.

Lockwood was tighter than a virgin asshole, and no amount of lube would get me where I wanted to be.

Outside its walls.

Need.

"We're not going anywhere. Gotta be patient."

I snorted at my attempts to soothe the agitation inside me. Patient, I was not. A wild animal better portrayed who I was at my core. Instincts dictated my actions more often than not, life-threatening at times, but maybe someone understanding would collar me. Tame the beast, so to speak.

I snorted at my pipe dream.

First off, I had to get out of here in order for that to happen, and second, that meant I definitely needed to stop talking to myself.

I glanced at the camera up in the corner of the ceiling. Yeah, the first rule about showing you weren't off your rocker was to act like every other supposed normal person on the planet.

Closing my eyes, I waited for Doc Holliday's visit and the chance to prove my sanity.

My inner beast found that fucking hilarious.

CHAPTER 3

PATRICK

Hands on hips, I stared up at the pull-down ladder and its frayed string hanging overhead.

I'd been back home for going on six months, and while I'd managed to clean out Dad's—now *my*—house, I'd yet to tackle the attic. Dad had been a pack rat, and I couldn't begin to imagine, nor did I want to, the mess I would find beneath the eaves.

"It's not going to get done on its own." I pulled on the string, unfolding the wooden stairs. The apparatus shifted as I climbed, groaning beneath my weight like the sky did outside with its constant rumbles of thunder. Regardless of their weakness, the stairs allowed me entrance into the chilled space that smelled like mothballs and stale air.

Rain slashed at the roof attached to the exposed beams above me and dirty windows on either end of the attic that didn't allow enough light for me to see. Had this storm hovered over the apartment building I'd moved out of back in Boston, rather than the Arizona two-story house I'd been driven to make my own, we would have been knee-deep in snow. As it was, the weather was warmer than normal, giving the parched earth some much-needed water.

I pulled on another string above my head, this one attached to a bare bulb. Pale yellow light attempted to dispel the gloom.

Floorboards creaked beneath my feet as I surveyed the hoarded mess around me. Dust motes tickled my throat, causing me to cough while taking in the boxes of who the fuck knew what, old pieces of furniture, and odds and ends Dad had most likely picked up at estate or yard sales.

Green bins of Christmas decorations from when Mom had still been alive stacked on my right, faded boxes with peeling masking tape on my left. *Patrick* was written in black marker, Mom's curved loops easily recognizable to me, even though she'd been gone for over a decade, thanks to aggressive breast cancer. A couple of dead flies lay on the top box, and feeling I had too much in common with their dried-out husks, I flicked them from sight.

Through meds and years of study, I'd gained control over my unstable mental health and had learned to hide the madness inside me from the world. And even though I'd received my doctorate in psychology and treated patients for over a dozen years, I continued to fight for a sense of belonging, a way to fill the dark void inside me that sometimes made me question my sanity.

As far as everyone in my life was concerned, I was normal —whatever that might actually be.

I'd had an easy, middle-class childhood with decent enough role models as parents and no serious trauma. Our small family had enjoyed family meals at the scarred oak table down in the kitchen. Christmases beside the artificial tree standing upright alongside the bins on my right, the fake branches covered in balls and tinsel from whenever Dad had last managed to wrangle the thing to the living room for the holiday season.

There'd been no emotional torment, no wounding event that had hindered my growth into adulthood. But a restlessness that felt like a separate entity lay buried deep inside me. I'd gone into psychology to figure out what was wrong with me but hadn't ever gotten a clear diagnosis. I wasn't sure what to make of it other than to consider myself a driven person, always seeking out the next task to execute and goal to attain.

However, no matter how much I accomplished, a sense of lacking remained, and I strove every day to rid myself of its clutches.

A flash of lightning lit the dim attic for a split second before thunder rumbled loud enough that the house shook around me. We needed the rain desperately, but the weather matched my mood.

A little gloomy. Overcast, a complete lack of sunshine.

But what else was new?

I had hoped moving back and opening a practice of my own would give me what I'd spent two decades searching for in Boston, whatever that might be. Nothing satisfied or filled the emptiness in my soul that drove me toward fulfillment of some sort.

My savings dwindled, so I'd put in an application at the mental institution that had been built here in town a couple of years ago, while working on my plans to rent office space on Main Street. While my location finally felt right, the deficit inside me remained.

I needed…something.

Getting laid always took the edge off for a short while, and it had been some time since I'd last had a woman beneath me. But no one ever felt like they belonged.

Turning my thoughts toward cleaning out the attic, then

heading into town to find a willing partner for the night, I reached for the closest box. I unpeeled the tape, keeping its flaps closed, and pulled up short.

Hesitant, I fixed my eyes on the leather-bound journal atop countless others, my brain quieting while my insides strained to reach out and relive the past I'd buried, as innocent as it had been. I'd forgotten about the memories I'd written—and had asked Mom to toss them out with the trash when I'd packed up to leave home for college.

She'd been stubborn to a fault, never one to listen, so I should have expected to find these still around, collecting dust.

My hand shook as I reached for the final diary of the childhood I'd left behind when I'd driven eastward.

The spine cracked as I leafed through the thick pages that had cramped writing filling every bit of space. Mostly ramblings about girls, sports, and grades, but some of the secrets I'd kept from everyone, parents included, lay inside the warped pages.

All children had imaginary friends—but mine had been too real. Held substance. Carried on full conversations with me. I'd been in seventh grade when I'd first heard the word schizophrenia, but that mental disorder didn't match the darkness that billowed like smoke inside me, as if a separate being was held captive inside my body.

As though the discovery of my old written words had zapped me like a defibrillator, heat came to life in my core, spreading outward until my limbs tingled.

My back itched.

Feet grew restless.

Teeth clenched, I tossed the diary into the box, my gut like lava, but my mind set on ridding myself of this part of me for good as I thought I'd done years earlier.

"I am in control," I stated my life's mantra through

clenched teeth and carted both boxes of my old ramblings downstairs.

The awareness of something *other* from my childhood lingered, unbothered by the repeated words that helped me silence the madness and envision it behind walls that no voice could penetrate.

I coaxed flames to life in the fireplace that had only ever seen action on Christmas Eve.

Fed my past to the gold and orange flickers above embers that glowed red.

One by one, the diaries disintegrated into ash, forever gone from existence. But the strange consciousness beneath my breastbone remained, alive and needy, threatening to erupt and devour my humanity.

Jaw set, I strode upstairs to get ready for a night on the town, tiny and somewhat backward as it might be compared to Boston. A shower rid me of dust and filth from having cleaned all day, and crisp jeans and an ironed button-down made me feel semi-normal again, even though I felt anything *but*.

Two hours later, I stumbled back through my front door, a fiery redheaded woman attached to me like a leech. She smelled like flowers, and her mouth tasted like hope. Attraction at first glance had prompted me to initiate, chemistry enough that my sleeping dick had shown interest in someone for the first time since returning to Arizona.

She agreed to take things to my place.

And here we were, both of us halfway to drunk, fucking on my living room floor.

A hissing built in my ears, like a whispered admonishment that I was making a mistake, but I buried myself in the warmth of the woman's welcoming arms, deciding she would do just fine. Might even be worth keeping around for a while. Maybe we could grow together. Find a new beginning of our own, one where the hollowness that haunted me wouldn't seem as stark—or dark.

She could be my sunshine, I decided once I lay gasping in her soft hold, her fingers sifting through my hair, her long legs still wrapped around my waist.

Yeah, this could work, I told myself.

The hissing went silent, but I didn't trust that so-called imaginary friend from my past hadn't reawakened and planned on sticking around.

CHAPTER 4

PRIMROSE

Three Months Later

"Looking for crazies, huh?" The old woman peered up at me from the park bench with watery, blue eyes, not a hint of an inner dragon within her whispering to me.

I smiled, having learned over the months that pure humans responded better to kindness than the anger her words simmered to life inside me. "Some people's inner thoughts can take on a mind of their own. Not everyone who hears voices has mental issues."

She snorted, lips pressed in a tight line, and glanced around the small park, the first of many such areas I'd explored while traveling in an ever-widening circle around the Grand Canyon. Leaves had burst from branches after their winter sleep, the promise of a new beginning, and gifted me a renewed hope that had dwindled over what seemed like a long winter.

I'd learned in my travels that older humans were full of stories—gossip, lore, and truth. Weeding through the fantastical proved harder for me, especially since I hadn't spent much time around others in my childhood. I'd also found that while the older generation didn't mind answering questions like the younger did, they had similar people skills like my own—almost nonexistent.

At least having lived in isolation for so long, I had a reason for my behavior should anyone pose a question about my inability to converse as well as others.

But being immersed in the human world over the previous four months had earned me knowledge of their ways, better forms of communication—mainly knowing when to keep my thoughts to myself—and how to dress so as not to draw unwanted attention, like the old-fashioned clothing I'd brought from Wyoming had earned me.

"What do you want with people like that, anyway?" the gray-haired woman asked, peering up at me from where I towered over her. "They're the sickos who take guns into schools and blow themselves up for their religion."

"Have you heard any good gossip lately about people hearing voices? Do you know anyone personally?" I forced myself to ask—*again*—rather than storm off for reasons she would never be able to fathom, ones that a recluse like me understood perfectly well.

Another snort of sarcastic laughter shook her shoulders. "All kinds of crazies like that over at Lockwood."

"Lockwood?"

"Hospital for the crazies out in the middle of nowhere."

I'd never once considered that humans would lock up people who claimed to hear voices to the extent I did, and I was far from mentally unstable. While my forehead furrowed over the woman's assumptions, a lightness roused in my chest that I didn't dare trust. I smoothed down my blouse with shaking hands. "Can you tell me where this Lockwood is located?" I asked while leaning toward her, my breathlessness betraying my rising hope.

Wrinkled hand waving toward the west, where she said a small town lay buried near the rim of the Grand Canyon with hardly a population worth mentioning. "Plenty of them crazies you're looking for over there."

Flutters woke in my belly, causing my limbs to tingle with the need to shift and escape her ignorance. But she was human and knew nothing about Blood Born and the inner beasts that might be mistaken for madness.

"I appreciate your time," I told the old woman, rather than turn on my heel without offering a good day.

She hummed beneath her breath, and I took the dismissal for what it was, happy to leave her behind.

Old duffle clutched tightly in my hand, I hurried toward a line of trees and the privacy they would afford me for a quick shift, since flight would get me to the next town faster than any rented car.

My inner dragon purred at the possibility that one of the two I searched for might be at this Lockwood. That I might finally feel the draw of our mates, the stirrings of desire only they would be able to sate. My alpha and beta, the two I would need to procreate and rebuild the dragonblood line on earth, might be closer than I'd imagined. While I longed for the physical hunger my grandpapa experienced with his fated mates, I had yet to meet anyone, human or dragonblood, who could make my body burn, yearn for my first sexual encounter.

Warmth stirred in my core, and a sense of calm settled over me.

Even though we had soared over that area before and hadn't felt any connection drawing me toward the earth, I had no choice but to follow the lead gifted to me.

Once out of sight of the small park, I cloaked myself and readied to fly, taking care to pack my clothing away as I always did before shifting into my true form.

Invisible to the human eye, I soared through the warm, spring air, breathing as deeply as always, hoping for a hint of the scents that would bring my body to life. The ragged cliffs and ancient openings in the earth lay below to my right in muted tones of red, brown, and gray, the deepest parts still hidden in shadow from the rising sun—a different beauty than the snow-capped mountains of my home, but no less stunning.

A small town nestled along a snaking, two-lane highway, so we banked slightly and drew closer, our dragon sight allowing us to focus in on buildings and cars easily. No hint of male dragonblood floated on the breeze from my height, so we circled until we located what must be the hospital the watery-eyed woman had spoken of.

Stark white and sprawling, the building was surrounded by a metal fence topped by razor-sharp wire. It looked more like a prison than a safe place for those with supposed mental health issues or disabilities to reside.

Seeing no other towns on the horizon, and even though no pull of awareness enticed me to land, we did so on the town's outskirts, near a rundown motel.

Once shifted into my human form, I hid amongst the fauna, uncloaked, and pulled on my leggings, a bra—something I'd hardly worn while living in seclusion and hated with a passion—and a long-sleeve tunic that fell to mid-thigh. My favorite ballet flats, easy to tear through should I need to shift in a hurry, pinched more than I would have liked, and I told myself I would spend my days naked once fate allowed me to live in privacy with my mates.

I breathed in the soothing scents of spruce and juniper from the surrounding trees, and finding no hint of dragonblood in the air, I headed to the motel to reserve a room for the night and possibly longer, depending on what I did or didn't find. Belly still fluttering, I stowed my duffle bag away in my room and started off in the direction of Lockwood, which the motel's owner had assured me I had properly located from above.

The purr in my head accompanied my light steps through town, past a cafe of sorts, a used car dealership, a small grocery store, and various other businesses that kept the community afloat.

Turning a corner brought Lockwood into sight, the three-story building the largest in the area by far and no more inviting than it had been from the sky.

My steps hurried as I approached, gaze roaming over the landscape and exterior, desperate for a glimpse of the ones who belonged to me.

Because they had to be here. I couldn't handle any more disappointment, couldn't imagine having to—

Yessss.

A shiver slid over my skin, causing goose bumps to erupt and heat to pool low in my belly. My head swiveled toward the hospital's closest wing as a sense of dragonblood, delicious and enrapturing, tangled with my mind and made my heart race.

This was the draw I'd been searching for, the feelings I'd read about but had almost given up hope of ever experiencing for myself.

Beta.

Swallowing against the thickness growing in my throat, I nodded an agreement with the creature inside me I trusted fully. Surely, she would be more aware of the Blood Born behind bars than my human half would be.

I eyed said bars on the windows, anger stirring over the fact one of my mates would be held against his will.

My dragon growled in my chest, and I bit my lip to keep it contained as humans approached me on the sidewalk. I didn't bother forcing a smile or replying to their greetings, my focus flitted from window to window along the hospital's wing, wondering which separated me from my beta.

I'd been mistaken to believe finding my mates would be easy. Even more so that connecting them wouldn't require work other than simple introductions and being led by instinct to bond and live happily ever after.

I threaded my fingers through the chain-link fence holding me at a distance, allowing my dragon to take over my wandering gaze since her instincts far outshone those of my human form.

Energy rippled over the mostly-empty parking lot on the other side of the fence, the tether of dragonblood calling to dragonblood leading up to the second floor…third window from the building's end.

He is there.

"Yes," I whispered my agreement with my inner dragon, the draw strengthening enough I could almost feel it like a physical caress across my fingers. Tingles rose to life between my thighs for the first time, and I gasped at the luscious dampness, the slight pulse of need for my mate to fill the emptiness inside me.

Biting my tongue against the whine building in my chest, I stared at his window as the sun warmed my face.

Did he sense me as I did him? Did he communicate with his inner dragon to the extent he knew who and what he truly was?

I clutched at the fence, unmoving except for the gnawing

of my lip as questions plagued me and the minutes slipped past. What if the voice had driven him to insanity? What if the ability to think rationally, to understand the truth of his circumstances, lay beyond his grasp?

The energy between us strengthened with every passing minute, and I focused on finding a way to save my beta from those who wished to keep him from my side.

CHAPTER 5

JAXON

The first time I'd sat on Doc Holliday's couch in his office, the box of tissues on the small table between us had mocked me. Every scratch of his pen had made me want to snap the damned thing in two, and while I still hid my other half that always begged to come out and play, I no longer resented the doc or hated the months I'd been locked up.

I'd been on my best behavior this time around, even with Nurse Yum Yum, who continued to eye me like an ice cream sundae whenever she was working and making her rounds. Sure, I flirted—what healthy eighteen-year-old wouldn't when a woman showed interest?

But I kept my hands to myself. Behaved, like she'd insisted on from day one, while gifting me candy for being a good boy, because freedom awaited.

The appeal I'd sent to the court system had come back in my favor, and since my three-month mark in the joint had come and gone, I would be released. Add to that fact I'd turned eighteen two weeks prior and my parents were no longer my keepers, they didn't get to dictate how I would live my life. It was Monday morning, and in forty-eight hours, I would once more have access to my small trust fund and the freedom to seek out my destiny.

Which sure as fuck wouldn't be in Phoenix.

The drive inside me to get started, the desire to find my place in this fucked-up world, owned my thoughts. Not my dick, but what else was new?

Doc Holliday had assured me I would be free to walk the fuck out of here, and I'd never been more grateful for a shrink in my life.

"We have our final meeting tomorrow at ten," he told me, shifting through some papers atop his desk.

I sat still, hands in my lap, even though every atom in my body vibrated.

Escape now.

"I'll have your belongings and the key to your apartment that I've procured for you. You'll be free to leave of your own accord on Wednesday and start your new job next Monday."

I wasn't keen on bagging groceries, but it would keep me busy and hopefully out of trouble until I got my personal shit in order and decided on a real course of action. I hadn't gotten the chance to graduate like a normal kid, but nothing about me had ever been "normal". I would get my GED someday and figure out the rest later.

Doc Holliday leaned onto his desk, his old face a wrinkly mess but eyes kind. "Are you sure you're ready to be on your own, Jaxon?"

Yessss.

"Yep," I answered with a firm nod. "And I appreciate all your help in finding me a place to stay."

"It's nearly an hour from here and isn't much, just a studio apartment above a garage."

"It'll be *mine*," I insisted, the promise of freedom so

damned sweet my mouth watered. I was used to being on my own since people always left when times got tough.

Not alone.

Doc Holliday stood and rounded his desk, holding out his hand and giving me something to focus on other than the voice inside me that never shut up.

I leapt up to my feet and clasped Doc's hand with a firm grip. "Thanks again."

"I'm sure you'll be counting down the hours—"

"Got that right," I muttered.

"But try to get some rest, young man. I'll see you in the morning for our final session together."

Less than forty-eight hours until I could walk out of here a free man.

My new roommate snored like a madman, keeping me from that rest Doc Holliday had insisted I get. But even without the man enjoying his slumber beside me, I wouldn't have been able to sleep.

Energy-like vibrations lighting up my body had plagued me all day and still caused twitches to wrack through me. I swore wings stretched beneath the skin on my back, ready and willing to burst from my muscles and bones in order to get me the hell out from behind these bars.

Yessss.

My mind was fucked, just like Gramma's had been—no fucking doubt.

Problem was, I didn't *feel* mad. Rational in every other way, I struggled to make sense of *him*, the thing inside me that loved to whisper mischievous ideas, naughty thoughts about the opposite sex, and other tempting shenanigans that always ended up getting me into trouble.

I punched my pillow and groaned as my cock took interest in who the hell knew what. When my beast side was in the mood to fuck, my body responded. Horny fucker didn't care which hole a female offered release in, but neither of us had yet to find real satisfaction nutting inside someone.

Blessed with my asshole father's good looks and my mother's smile, I didn't have any trouble getting laid—another of the reasons my parents had sent me off to an all-boys school. Couldn't lock my cock in my pants when it lusted to dip into a slick, tight pussy.

At least I'd learned to keep the voice to myself. Not sharing his inner mutterings aloud had kept me pretty much on the safe side for years. It was the damn joint I'd shared with a couple of friends my sophomore year that had landed me on a ledge, high as a fucking kite, sure I could fly like one, back in January.

At least my heart still beat, and I now had a chance to navigate my way through this life.

If I could get some damned sleep!

I clenched my eyes shut, wishing the snorer on the bed behind me would shut the fuck up already. His mouth rumbled on every inhale—and exhale. Growling, I squinted at the clock. 12:10 in the goddamn morning. Soon, I wouldn't have to put up with shitty roommates, shitty food, and this shitty mattress anymore, never mind the lumpy pillow beneath my head.

A shiver licked over my skin, and my cock bobbed as though someone had feathered their fingertips along its length.

"The fuck?" I grumbled quietly, grabbing myself beneath the sheet.

The hospital preferred we sleep clothed, but fuck that. I couldn't stand restrictions while I lay in bed. Resting wouldn't be an option until I blew the load simmering in my balls, though, so I stroked, wondering at the unusual abundance of pre-cum easing my movements. I'd always been a leaker, but holy shit, the oozing from my slit made for one delicious glide up and down my shaft.

Blonde hair and caramel-colored eyes...

Grinning, I dove into my favorite fantasy, imagined my golden goddess on her knees, mouth wide open, begging for my cock on her salivating tongue. One night with her, and I would be ruined for life.

Own.

Breed.

"Oh, fuck yeah," I groaned, fucking up into my fist at the thought of doing both to her.

There would be no more countless, faceless women clutching at me while I rocked their worlds. My golden goddess would be lush, curves for days, perfect for plundering with my insatiable cock.

Sweet on our tongue.

Tight around our shaft.

"Fuck..."

My balls seized, and I shot my load down her imaginary throat—into my waiting hand. I breathed heavy from hardly any exertion and muttered a few curses. I'd never shot off so damn quick in my life.

Tingles still raced over my skin for the fiftieth time that day, but not the creepy ant-like feels a lot of my fellow *inmates* experienced. Didn't mean the docs hadn't tried to force meds on me like the others when I'd first arrived. I'd been medicated unwillingly before, and those were the times I *did* feel mad.

The lack of that being's presence in my head was *not* normal.

One arm thrown over my forehead, I rolled to my back, my softening dick and a shit ton of spunk in my other hand. I would leave a nice mess on my sheets for housekeeping, but I didn't give a fuck. It was what they were paid for.

Another wave of...*whatever the fuck it was*, slid along my body, pulling my eyelids open. I peered through the dark at the barred window on the other side of my noisy-assed roommate. Hardly any moon hung in the sky, so pure darkness coated the inky expanse beyond.

She's leaving.

I blinked and frowned. "Who the fuck are you talking about?" I muttered, taking care to barely move my lips in case anyone watched, but the voice inside remained silent. Moments later, that weird energy vibe faded, but another hour passed before I drifted off to sleep.

I sauntered down the hallway for my last therapy hour with Doc in Lockwood *ever again* if I had any say.

Good man.

Yeah, I agreed with my beast, grinning around a yawn. Hadn't slept worth a shit, but tomorrow I would be out of the psych ward, in my own goddamned bed.

The carpet beneath my bootied feet kept my footfalls quiet, and I soaked in the stillness, loving the lack of constant noise like in the hospital's other wings. It didn't smell like bleach in here either. I filled my lungs—and stumbled to a halt as the scent of smoke and sex flooded my lungs, twitching my dick to full wakefulness.

Yessss.

The fuck?

Brow furrowed, I glanced around, but the hallway was empty. Doc Holliday's office door stood open a few feet in front of me, releasing more of what seemed a lot like pheromones to me.

Need.

My feet moved on their own, but I tucked my upright dick beneath my pants' stretchy waistband while walking. Thank fuck for long shirts.

I pulled up short on the office's threshold, but Doc Holliday's desk chair sat empty. That smell, causing blood to throb through my groin, intensified. "Doc?" My voice, ragged as hell, half-squeaked his name, and I cleared my throat, hating that I sounded like a pubescent kid.

A gorgeous man I'd never seen before came into view from the left, a stack of files in his hands, and I soaked in the sight of him. A tall drink of water on a hot-as-fuck day, he made me thirst like mad. Black slacks, white button-down shirt open at the neck, checkered vest...wide shoulders and scruff with a spattering of gray. He had hair a tad too long for a professional, a strong nose, and dark blue eyes, which he attempted to hide behind dark-rimmed glasses...

Alpha.

What the fuck ever, but the dude was hot. As. Fuck. Made me leak like a motherfucker. He also smelled so damn delicious I wanted to crawl to him and lick him from big toes to the tips of his ears, hopefully ingesting some of that delicious scent wafting off his skin along the way.

Want.

I huffed a laugh, but shouldn't have been surprised my dick—more like *I*—was bisexual.

Fuck.

Yeah, no kidding. Let the shenanigans begin...

"Who the hell are you?" I asked, stepping over the threshold, ready to get *this* show on the road. The beast inside me moaned his agreement.

The man frowned, gaze sliding quickly over the hospital-issued scrubs as I stopped in my tracks and struggled not to squirm beneath his perusal. "I'm Doctor Patrick Macaire."

His low voice sent shivers over my skin, causing a riot of goose bumps to erupt.

The fucker inside me whimpered, belly-up.

I attempted to swallow a rush of saliva while tearing my gaze off the guy to glance around the office. "Where's Doc Holliday?"

"He had a heart attack yesterday afternoon."

"Shit." I jerked my focus to the new guy, tension of a not-so-pleasant sort tightening my gut. "Is he okay?"

Doctor Macaire shook his head, lips pursed. "It happened quickly—there was no suffering."

"Goddamnit." I clenched my jaw, my emotions torn between grief for the one who hadn't thought I was crazy and my raging hard-on begging me to crawl toward the stranger in front of me.

"Jaxon Denham?"

"Yeah," I managed to say past the thickness in my throat, even though my name on the man's lips made my inner beast beg for attention.

"Why don't you have a seat?"

Instinct sent my body to the chair, and I slumped down enough that I could rest my head against the cushioned back. Throat aching, I tracked the new doc's movement around the desk, my focus dropping to his tight ass.

His ass was worthy of my worship. A ripe peach, juicy enough to make any mouth water. I wanted a little nibble.

Should I cry over the loss of Doc Holliday or grab my cock and beg the new doctor to let me ease its ache?

What the actual fuck?

I clenched my eyes shut to keep from doing a goddamned thing, wondering what the hell was going on—and what that meant for my soon-to-be-had freedom tomorrow morning.

The new doc sat, the chair squeaking slightly beneath

him. "I'll be taking over for Doctor Holliday until the board hires someone to replace him full-time."

My eyes opened on their own as though needing their fill of the sexy man since this would be our first and last session.

He immediately dropped his gaze to the desk, but the man seemed anything but weak. The energy around him stated commanding. In charge. Domineering and possessive.

A shiver slid along my spine.

"I'm outta here tomorrow," I stated, letting him know shit had been set into motion that I refused to have someone stop, no matter how sexy they were or how much my body and inner beast yearned to stick close—preferably impaled on his dick.

My asshole clenched at the thought, my dick bucking against my waistband.

Jesus, I needed to get laid.

Doc Macaire's lips didn't move, but I swore a whisper—and not my own inner voice—groaned with displeasure over my leaving his presence.

Want.

Yeah, no shit, Sherlock, you already made that clear.

My balls throbbed even as my eyes stung, while I stared at Doctor Macaire as he rifled through the file left in front of him. He jotted down a note or two on the inside cover, the silence oppressive. I wasn't about to mention the voice I heard, pushing me to beg the doctor to let me suck him off or fill my ass with his dick and cum. I would never get out of Lockwood if I spoke those desires I'd never experienced before—and definitely didn't hate.

His brow furrowed across the top rim of his sexy as hell glasses.

"Problem, Doc?" I asked.

He heaved a sigh, laid his pen down, and seemed to gather

his thoughts, reining in the displeasure pinching his face before meeting my gaze.

Energy rippled between us, hot and more potent than any sexual attraction I'd ever felt. Talk about a moth to the fucking flame.

My dick was wet—big surprise—and the voice inside me went quiet as though holding its breath, on edge and ready to fall to its knees.

A part of me actually *did* want to stay longer, find out what it was about the new doctor that drew me in like a kid to a candy store with the most mouthwatering bins of caramels.

"You're leaving tomorrow," he stated what he must have found in my file, eyes closed off to whatever he was thinking or feeling. If the latter was even *half* of the arousal swirling in my blood, the man had to be rock-hard.

"Yeah," I rasped, my need obvious as fuck.

He seemed the sort of man who could subdue and collar the damned beast—give me something to focus on other than the madness inside me.

I swallowed against a needy groan, my usual flirty smirk nowhere to be found.

Doctor Macaire settled back, hands still on his desk as though using it to stabilize his inner thoughts. "What will you do?"

"Doc Holliday helped me land a job. I start Monday." I swallowed again, my balls and backside aching. The desire for violence like last night rushed through my system again, causing a crash of adrenaline and a yearning I'd never felt before. I wanted this man's hands on me. Hurting me. Loving me.

Jesus, I wasn't right in the head.

"He, uh, found me a small apartment, too," I whispered, fingers digging into my thighs so I wouldn't grab my junk.

"Who is paying for it?"

None of his damn business, but he'd read my file and knew my dad and mom made sure I got the best of care, the best of everything—except acceptance and love—up until I'd turned eighteen.

"I've got savings."

"Do you have access to it?"

"I do now, and it's all mine. Parents can't touch it." Thank fuck my asshole grandfather had made sure of that before he dropped dead of an aneurysm.

Doc Macaire nodded absently, while glancing away and shifting his own ass on the chair at the same time I did, as though he, too, sported a hard-on that was desperate for a man's grip.

Yessss.

"What?" I asked, sure the word had been hissed out loud.

"Hmm?" He returned his piercing stare on me that made my asshole clench.

"Did you whisper something?"

The doctor's brow furrowed again, but that didn't lessen the intense need radiating between us.

"Never mind." I attempted to toss out a crooked grin, the one that usually got me into a girl's panties, but he didn't so much as twitch. "So yeah, I'm going to start my new life, the one my parents stole from me. I was a kid with a big imagination, you know?" My laughter sounded forced to my own ears. "I had a hard time keeping my head out of the clouds and feet on the ground."

"Literally."

My grin faded as I struggled to hold the doctor's shuttered gaze. "Yeah, but I was high. Being stupid."

"And the time before that, two years ago?"

I shrugged, even though the itch to jump off every edge sometimes *took* me to the edge before my brain caught up with reality, and I stopped myself. "What kid doesn't want to be Superman?"

The silence stifled, the click of Doc Holliday's clock on the wall like a gong with every passing second, heightening my lust to jerk off, fuck, or leap from the goddamn ledge of the closest building.

"You're going to be all right out there on your own? No parents? No roommates?"

I nodded. "Absolutely."

A few more seconds of breath-holding anxiety, and he pulled a card from the top drawer. He scribbled something on it and held it out atop the desk. "I live a few blocks from here. If you ever need anything—"

I leaned forward, my fingers grazing his as I took the card.

Fire raced up my arm, settling in the pit of my stomach, deliciously warm and intoxicating, causing my inner beast to whimper again. I bit down hard on my lower lip to keep the noise contained, as my balls tightened to the point of pain.

Doc Macaire's scruff twitched as though he clenched his jaw, and I studied him for a brief moment, wondering if he'd experienced the same thing I had. He cleared his throat. "This is for you." He slid an envelope across his desk, not bothering with handing it over like he'd done with the card.

Guess he hadn't liked our skin touching nearly as much as I had.

I grabbed the envelope and clutched it tightly to my chest, expecting it contained the key to my apartment and copies of the legal paperwork that allowed me to leave tomorrow. Glancing at the clock, I saw our time was far from over, but it seemed the new doc didn't have anything else to say.

I stood, soaking in Doc Macaire's quick glance down over my scrubs and obvious bulge before he quickly glanced away. "So that's it?"

Lips pressed tight, he nodded.

"Guess this is goodbye," I said.

Stay.

No fucking way.

The doc didn't stand to see me out. Didn't speak another word.

Every step that distanced me from his desk, out the door, and down the hallway stretched thin the strange energy I'd felt until I got to the cafeteria for breakfast, and it disappeared completely.

The beast mourned, and my balls ached.

Strangely, my heart doubly so.

CHAPTER 6

PATRICK

I'd gotten a call last night from the board at Lockwood, inviting me to join their staff on a part-time basis. Three days a week for now, with the possibility of going full-time, was the offer, and since my current load of clients at the office I'd opened across town barely made a dent in the bills starting to pile up, I'd thankfully agreed to fill in.

Yet another reason to get out of the house and away from the discomfort I'd left behind this morning. But that issue could wait.

Something much more disturbing now occupied my thoughts.

I tore my focus off the door that had shut behind Jaxon Denham, taking him from sight—but not from mind. I hovered on the edge of a storm, the impending change crackling like lightning, shooting electrical charges over my skin, the same as when his fingers had grazed mine. My scalp prickled, and I sat rigid in my chair, my palms sweating.

The boy reminded me too much of myself for comfort.

Like me, he'd heard voices as a kid, and according to his

file, the fact he wouldn't shut up about them while a young-ster had landed him in psych ward after psych ward. At least I had learned to keep silent after my first stint in a bleach-scented, white room when I'd been seven and had met the doctor who had set me on a path toward healing through medication and meditation. Doctor Sorino had been my hero and the reason for my career choice.

My heart had shattered when I'd learned, while in my senior year of college, following in his footsteps, that he'd crossed a serious line with a patient, lost his license to prac-tice, and was criminally charged with grooming and sexual abuse—with a minor.

He had nose-dived off the pedestal I'd placed him on, and I'd set my hero worship aside, my focus turning from becoming a man like him to helping those like me.

I'd been nothing but careful in all my years directing patients through their mental processes and behavior, prescribing medication when needed.

But Jaxon stirred up the whispering in my mind Doctor Sorino had taught me to keep under lock and key. I'd learned how to build a wall around whatever the darkness in my soul was until all evidence of its voice had no longer existed. While in high school, I had weaned myself off the pills that had given me a semblance of so-called normalcy, but the bricks stacked against the strangeness in my conscience had begun to crumble since seeing those old writings from my childhood three months ago.

Meeting Jaxon had sent a shiver of unease up my spine, loosening my hold over whatever it was dwelling inside me that had reawakened after finding those journals. He also made me question my sexuality and how I had never once been attracted to another male. He was so young that the word pedophile came to mind, even though I knew he was of legal age.

My dick didn't agree he was off-limits—damned near jail-bait like that patient had been to Doctor Sorino all those years ago when he'd given in to temptation.

Stomach turning, I grimaced and shifted on my seat.

I would *not* allow a similar situation to land me behind bars, no matter how badly I lusted to taste the young man's mouth and explore every inch of his body. The earthy scent of Jaxon's skin beneath the hospital's allotted soap still lingered in the enclosed office, filling my nose and causing my balls to tighten against my groin regardless of the disgust roused by Doctor Sorino's transgressions.

Deeply bowed, Jaxon's top lip had created enticing images in my head of shoving my dick so far down his throat he would gag. I wanted his greenish-blue eyes watering as he attempted to take every inch of me due to desperation for a belly full of cum.

A hissing sounded between my ears, and while alarm skittered through my mind, something about the entire exchange and my body's response felt...right. As though a path had opened in front of my feet, one I needed to follow with my usual drive to accomplish any task set before me.

"Fuck." I shifted my weight from one hip to another, trying to work through the various aspects of my current life and how to succeed in keeping from falling into temptation —and possibly fill the hollowness in my chest I weirdly felt sure Jaxon would.

My hand soothed over my left pec without thought, but the ache for so much more remained.

The suggestion that a person couldn't be happy with others until they were with themselves hadn't proven true in all my years of counseling patients. I'd met dozens of people who had found their soulmates, their person, who had helped them find healing and contentment.

I wanted the same, which was perhaps what had made me

trust too easily in the past, setting my heart at a woman's feet in the hopes she would offer me whatever I lacked that caused my unrest in life.

I thought of my current situation, the unstable girlfriend I'd been putting up with for too long. A match made in heaven, we were not. She had refused my aid for months, and I was done trying to fix her brokenness that did jack shit in soothing the need for *more* that had grown inside me since I'd returned home.

Thoughts of tossing her out, boxing up her shit, and changing the locks had occupied my head for over two weeks, and the idea of replacing her in my bed with an alluring man forbidden to me caused heat to rush through my blood.

Yessss.

My eyelids slammed shut, and I cursed over the hiss that had become vocal, the word distinct. My heartbeat raced, my twisting stomach tightening to rock.

"I am in control," I stated through gritted teeth, hands fisted atop my thighs to stop them from shaking—and shoving down my slacks to sate the raging lust Jaxon's proximity had awakened inside me.

Perhaps it was time to start wearing briefs rather than going commando like I preferred.

I imagined his slender but muscular body kneeling before me, soulful eyes an intoxicating shade of the sea filled with need as he stuck out his tongue, begging to taste me. Dark, wavy hair, the perfect length to clutch while he choked—

"Fuck." I rubbed a hand over my short beard and stretched my neck side to side.

So, this was what a temptation that even the most stoic professional would struggle to ignore was like. The boy was a patient, even if not for long, and still forbidden, no matter the craving he'd roused inside me.

There was no doubting my body's response to the young man, assuring me I'd experienced some sort of sexual awakening. While I didn't give a shit about labels when it came to whom a person loved, I'd never felt drawn toward males before. There was no denying the attraction between us, the potent chemistry that had swarmed the room upon his arrival. I hadn't questioned him being as hard as I was—I swore I could smell his want wafting past my nose while I fought to keep from drawing him deeper into my lungs.

But not him—not that...*kid.* Even if he wasn't jailbait age, messing around with a soon-to-be ex-patient would be frowned upon in my line of work.

My life's motto echoing in my ears and lips in a thin line, I set my mind on ignoring the unrelenting stiff dick in my slacks. I pulled the next file from atop the twenty or so high stack and covered up the one that drew me in like a carrot dangled just out of reach.

Couldn't. Touch.

Thank fuck Jaxon Denham would be gone in twenty-four hours without another scheduled visit to this office. Best to let him fade from my memory and figure out my next step toward fulfilling the emptiness inside me.

The first being ridding myself of the baggage at home that I never should have picked up in January.

A Dear John letter sat on the kitchen table rather than a drunk girlfriend when I arrived home.

The weight of having to end things with her and kick her out slid off my shoulders like an avalanche, and I cracked open a beer, sucking it down in hopes to cool the heat still racing through my blood.

Twice while making myself familiar with the hallways of

Lockwood, I'd run across the reason for my groin's discomfort. He'd taken note of me from afar as well, his sexy grin making my dick throb for a good, hard fuck. The hollowness had grown in my chest as well, aching and alarming with every hour, intensified by those brief glances. Regardless of my determination to focus on the patients being entrusted to my care, I found myself drifting toward darker desires I'd never experienced before.

Jaxon, tied to the posts of my bed, his back marked with lashes from a flogger. Satisfaction coursed through my blood at the thought of marking his skin, burying my aching shaft deep in his ass, and claiming him as mine.

"Christ." I clunked the empty beer bottle onto my kitchen counter and leaned forward, grasping the edges with a white-knuckled grip. Arousal coursed through me, hot and potent, making my balls seize.

Head hanging and eyes closed, I attempted to slow my breathing, but every inhale reminded me of the young man's alluring scent. All day, the memory of him had tormented me, caused my skin to pebble, and the lust for release drove me toward madness.

But now, I was in the privacy of my own home, where lines could be crossed mentally without anyone but myself being the wiser.

"Fuck it." Trembling with barely suppressed need, I freed my straining length, hissing as I wrapped my hand around it. Copious amounts of pre-cum welled on the head, easing the downward slide of my hand. I grunted, hips thrusting to fuck my fist as I imagined sinking deep into Jaxon's tight heat.

I could smell the muskiness of our fucking, his scent, even though this was only a fantasy I would never allow to come to fruition. His greedy groans filled my ears as I tore off my dress shirt and held it close, ready to capture my release.

Evidence of my weakness—

Teeth clenched, I worked myself hard and fast, my sac tightening, the base of my spine tingling. I wanted the boy with a fierceness I didn't understand—as though he was already mine to dominate, mine to pleasure. Mine to love.

Yessss.

The darkness whispered past my defenses, and my climax hit like a tidal wave.

Cum shot from my shaft in thick spurts, curses accompanying every pulse of my balls that soaked my shirt. Spunk overflowed and splattered on the floor as I gasped for air, body twitching, almost convulsing with my release that went on far longer than usual.

It had only been a handful of days since I'd last gotten off, but once finished, the amount of cum soaking my shirt and floor alarmed me.

It was…unnatural.

Exactly as my draw to the boy was.

Brow furrowed and lips parted in attempts to fill my lungs and slow my heart rate, I balled up my shirt and set it on the counter, leaning once more to grasp its edge. Head bowed, I stared at the mess at my feet.

I'd rather see the globs drip from Jaxon's puffy, red asshole.

"Jesus." I choked on an unhinged laugh.

"What the fuck?"

I clenched my eyes shut at the slurred voice stating the question on the tip of my own tongue. I'd been so lost in my lust, I hadn't heard Jessie let herself into the home I'd thought she'd left for good.

"Jerking off in the goddamn kitchen over my letter?" She snorted, pulling my focus toward where she stood in the doorway. She weaved on her feet, her eyes bloodshot and hazy, voice slurred as usual. "You're a sick fuck, Pat."

Fuck, I hated that nickname, but she didn't lie.

The truth of why a mess of my seed lay cooling on the floor could never be made known to her, so I let her believe what she would.

I straightened, tucking my spent dick away, the after-effects of my climax still making me feel shaky and light-headed. "You're drunk."

"As a skunk!" She laughed and shuffled toward the table, slamming her bony hip on one of the chairs. "Goddamnit," she muttered, kicking the offending piece of furniture and almost falling over before plopping her ass onto the seat.

Lips pressed tight, I turned my back on her and grabbed some paper towels to wipe up the mess I'd made. "I thought you weren't coming back," I shared what I'd been thrilled to learn. Her leaving had kept me from having to pull the plug on yet another failed relationship.

"Yeah…didn't plan on it, but I've got no other place to go, you know?"

I did—but Jessie was no longer my problem. She'd ended things between us, and no way would I be swayed into letting her stay.

"Call your sister," I stated, firmly squatting to wipe my cum off the floor.

"I'm not calling that *bitch*," Jessie muttered, her voice muffled.

I glanced up to find her head buried in her arms folded atop the table. This wouldn't be the first time she passed out cold, seated like that.

I tossed the drenched paper towels in the waste can, letting her stay put rather than carry her to the couch with a bucket close by like I'd done a lot in the previous few months.

"Fuck this." I strode into the entryway and rifled through

her handbag for her cell phone. Her sister answered the third time I tried calling.

"The fuck you want?" she growled.

"It's Patrick. Your sister is passed out at the kitchen table and needs a place to crash."

"She's there, isn't she? Put her in your goddamn bed."

And I'd thought Jessie was a bitch. "She broke up with me and is no longer welcome here." I clipped each word with finality, barely managing to keep from raising my voice.

"Well, I'm not coming to get her."

"Then she's sleeping out on the front porch."

"Bastard."

My pulse throbbed in my temple, causing an immediate headache. "She's the one who left a letter saying she hated me, didn't want to stay one more goddamn night under the same roof as me. Need I go on?"

"She was probably drunk when she wrote it—you know how she gets. Just let her sleep it off there. She'll be all over your dick in the morning, and everything will be fine."

The hell it would be. "Come get her, or I'll have the cops remove this trespasser from my home."

"You wouldn't dare." Her voice betrayed her question.

"Twenty minutes, or I'm making that call." I hung up, more than ready to have the authorities rid me of Jessie for good.

My ex snored, and I left her in the kitchen, while heading upstairs to see if she'd left any personal belongings behind.

I walked into my bedroom to find she hadn't packed up one goddamn thing after writing that letter. I gathered the essentials she would need to get started in her new life without me. The rest would have to wait.

A few minutes later, Jessie's sister cursed me out when I yanked the door open one-handed to her knock, my arm beneath Jessie's shoulders keeping her upright while she struggled to make sense of the world.

"Grab her shit," I ordered her sister, nodding toward the suitcase in the entryway. "I'll pack up the rest of her belongings and put them on the porch for her to pick up tomorrow once she's sober," I said while settling Jessie in the passenger seat. My ex's head slumped to the side, and she started snoring. I clipped the seatbelt around her and shut her in.

Tight-lipped, her sister stalked around the car, slammed the driver's door behind her, and tore out of my driveway without a damned word.

"Good fucking riddance," I muttered, sinking onto the top stair leading to my porch that faced the sinking sun.

Silence cloaked the evening, but my mind refused to quiet. Twinkling blue-green eyes and a flirtatious grin full of promise flashed through my memory, reigniting my lust for Jaxon and the desire to explore what he'd woken inside me.

The hiss whispered through the back of my mind, causing a shiver to slide down my spine, but two slow, measured breaths, and I envisioned shutting the door on the prison of my childhood insanity.

Shaking my head, I stood and strode inside, focused on ridding my home of every trace of Jessie.

If only erasing Jaxon from my mind would be as easy.

CHAPTER 7
PRIMROSE

For two days, I stood outside the chain-link fence and watched Lockwood's quiet lawns and parking lot as people came and went. My beta's energy meandered from wing to wing, sometimes switching floors, staying in one area for an hour or so before returning to his room.

The window with its bars keeping him from me angered both me and my inner dragon, but unless we wished to wreak havoc on the hospital and reveal to humanity that they weren't the only sentient beings on the planet, I was powerless to act. More than anything, the histories I'd read deep in the Teton's cavern home instructed me on remaining quiet—secret. The Blood Born had been brought to the edge of extinction due to fear and anger from the humans, and with how bigotry appeared to rule the land now more than ever, I knew better than to let my instincts rule over my better sense.

But the drive deep inside me to free my beta and claim him as my own crouched in tensed readiness, muscles quivering, causing my skin to shiver.

The first night, my beta's energy had flooded me with spine-tingling heat, causing a desperate desire to ignite in my core. Wetness had smeared between my thighs, and no amount of rubbing them together eased the ache to mate. To be bred.

Need.

"I know," I whispered since no one walked the sidewalks as night shadowed the arid land around me. I stood invisible to the naked eye, gaze once more glued to my beta's window, fingers hurting from grasping the fence before my nose.

My mouth watered to taste him—his mouth, his seed, the sweat on his skin.

Did he feel the same draw of mate calling to mate? Was he unable to sleep as I'd been the evening before and again tonight? I'd returned after sundown because a sensitivity throughout my body refused me rest. Impatience had me back at Lockwood, every stitch of clothing chafing my skin. I longed for nudity, or even better, to have my beta as my blanket, his weight heavy and welcome atop mine.

Desire rushed through me, settling in my core. My breaths came quickly as my heart fluttered in my chest.

Free him.

"We can't without revealing ourself," I insisted, my voice a whine when firmness would have better kept my dragon in check. Never had I felt such an internal war with myself, newly awakened arousal against better judgment. "Surely, Grandpapa would insist we wait for the right opportunity. Destiny has led us here to the one meant for us. We must trust fate to bring us together."

Sneak in—follow the humans.

I glanced away from my beta's window to the front entrance that was now locked up tight for the night. There would be no coming or going by staff or visitors until midmorning.

Cloak him. Remove him from their clutches.

Nibbling on the inside of my lip, I considered my dragon's suggestion. Invisibility granted me the ability to enter areas prohibited to the public, and I didn't question the energy linking us together would allow me to easily locate him.

But what if he didn't sense what I did? What if he questioned my being there and insisted he hold my hand so I could hide him from sight and lead him to freedom?

What if he *fought* me?

Didn't *want* me?

An ache split through my chest, cracking my emotions wide open. Wetness seeped over my eyes, making the sight of his room watery, unfocused.

Swallowing hard, I swiped my forearm over my face, my fingers entwined with the metal fencing as though its solidity kept me strong in the face of conflicting desires. The unknowing was torture, causing pain to radiate through my body. I couldn't tell where it began or if it would ever end.

Closing my eyes, I rested my forehead against the barrier denying me my mate and partial fulfillment. The throb in my heart mirrored the unrelenting yearning between my legs. My breasts were heavy, nipples tight and tingling.

I needed my beta's touch—

His energy grew restless as though he'd woken and sensed my desire.

Breath held, I tightened my grip on the fence, gaze glued to the bars of his prison.

Beta.

I swallowed hard as he came into sight, whimpering along with my inner beast.

A dim exterior light beneath my mate's window allowed me to better appreciate his naked upper body, but even with my dragon sight, I couldn't make out the color of his hair or eyes. He turned his head side to side as though he was aware of the supernatural connection between us, seeking me out in the dark night.

Various thoughts swept through my head, but I remained still. Invisible. Having no knowledge of his mental state or awareness of his true self, I couldn't risk showing myself to him and having his inner dragon take over—if he possessed such strength. Shifting to his true form while inside such a building would bring it crumbling down around him.

Breath held, I noted his strong nose and full lips, a square jaw I wanted to lick and nip with my teeth as he thrust into me. A rush of wetness seeped from me, preparing the way for my mate to pierce through my maidenhead.

My beast moaned, the noise leaking past my human lips.

My beta's head swiveled toward me as though he'd heard, his gaze settling on where I stood.

Breath held, I counted my pulsing heartbeats throbbing in my ears. The rush of heated blood sounded louder than any storm, stronger than any winds buffeting the mountain peaks back home.

Shift.

"We cannot." I choked on the words, willing the golden scales that wished to burst over my skin to remain hidden. Teeth gritted, I stared at our beta, wanting him yet requiring him to move from my sight to keep my instincts from owning my human form.

His hand moved over his body as though in open defiance of my need for him to lessen temptation. The flare of heat in the energy linking us burned brighter. Did he touch himself? He propped his forehead on the window, shoulder hunched as though in pain, and again, I fought my inner beast's yearning to break free of my human form, tear through the fence and walls to release my beta mate—

His form stiffened, head tipping back.

Goose bumps erupted over my skin.

Touch.

Lower lip between my teeth, I released one hand from its hold on the fence and slid my fingertips down over the front of my leggings, finding warmth and wetness. I was also swollen, the nub at the top of my slit hardened and sensitive to the feathered touch of my fingertips. I gasped at the new sensation, my hips bucking on their own as though he thrust into me, burying against my womb.

Heat exploded like a blinding light through the energy between us, capturing my entire being up in a euphoric race to the stars. I cried out, unable to keep my lips sealed as wave after wave rippled through my body, pulsing my core where his hard length ought to be.

Teeth gritted, I barely managed to stay in human form as my first ever release burned through my blood. My womb ached for pulses of his seed in an attempt to breed me as fate intended.

Alpha.

The reminder we needed more than one mate to fulfill our destiny eased the sweetness of my climax, slowly settling reality over me like a heavy cloud.

I gasped for breath, my stare on the window as my beta shuddered.

I could imagine his groan, sensed the same weakness in my legs. Wetness coated my leggings, the sweet scent of my cum rising to fill my nose. Would he like how I smelled? Want to taste me there?

Another pulse of raw lust spasmed through my inner walls, and I whimpered, shuddering and sagging against the fence, gaze unmoving from the window and the Blood Born kept from me.

Stillness lay over my mind, the urgent yearning having been eased for the moment. But my need for him would return, stronger now that I'd experienced a small taste of what mating would be like.

My beta's hand settled on the window as though reaching for me, causing my eyes to sting and throat to tighten.

He moved away from sight a moment later, taking a part of my heart with him.

Tomorrow.

"Yes," I agreed, forcing my legs to stiffen and hold me upright when I desired to sink into my beta's arms and experience true fulfillment. Having gotten a hint of what the connection would feel like between us on a deeper level, I no longer questioned whether he would choose me or not, given the chance. Together, we would seek out our alpha and claim him—this time without hindrance. We three would become one in heart, mind, and soul.

Fate wouldn't allow for anything else.

CHAPTER 8
JAXON

At two AM, I jerked awake, so damn horny my dick actually ached. Like, fucking *hurt*. First thing I would do on getting out of here would be to bury myself between a willing woman's thighs and get some goddamned relief.

Thoughts of Doc Macaire flitted through my brain, and I reimagined that woman between us—fucking hell, did that make my blood sing.

Twice, I'd seen him from afar after our meeting, and both times, I swore he'd sunk a hook into my mouth and reeled me in like a helpless fish on his line. He would gut me. Devour me. Fuck me good and hard, demanding I come around his cock untouched.

But distance and having him gone from my sight eased the lust for him that hadn't relented even though I'd gotten myself off once already in order to fall asleep. My light blanket, stiff from the dried cum I'd wiped off my hand and abs earlier, was bundled at the foot of my bed.

And here I was again, throbbing with an intense need to

climax, my dick leaking like a faucet beneath the top sheet covering my nudity.

The hell was wrong with me?

I rolled to my back and stroked myself from tip to root.

A shiver like the night before made me pause, and my gaze flicked to the dark window.

She's here.

Fuck the snoring roommate and my raging hard-on. I climbed out of bed and tiptoed across the room, my dripping dick leading the way.

Darkness coated the land outside the window, but a small exterior light on my left between floors illuminated the flower beds below. Giving over to my instincts, I let my gaze wander where it would—and ended up staring hard at the chain-link fence across the parking lot. No one walked the sidewalk beyond, and no one lingered close by in the early morning hours, but I swore someone watched me from that exact spot.

Goose bumps rose across my skin as though they drank in the sight of me, and I found my palm smearing over my oozing slit. I wanted to shoot off with a blast, but forced myself to go slow, languid strokes up and down every straining inch jutting up from my groin. My cockhead swelled, so goddamn sensitive beneath my grip that I cursed with every tease of my thumb before fucking into my fist again.

Heat licked over my skin from my toes clear to my scalp, tingling and intoxicating. My breaths heightened, and my pulse beat heavily in my ears.

The snores faded behind me as I focused on the fence and that strange energy I'd been feeling on and off for almost two days that was similar yet different from Doc Macaire. Whatever it was calling to me from outside, I wanted to bathe in it.

Submerge myself until I couldn't breathe without it filling my lungs, flooding my system.

The hairs on my body rose to stand on end.

My balls tightened in readiness, my taint on the verge of spasming.

Need.

"No shit," I whispered, restless with readiness to erupt.

The beast inside me groaned, and I leaned my forehead against the glass pane, hardly eased by its cool surface. My imagination flitted to the golden goddess of my dreams, and heat swelled inside me to the point I swore my insides burst into flames.

Our female.

I had no fucking clue what the voice meant, but I fucking *felt* it. A knowing—a drawing— slithered through the glass and iron barrier in front of me like a cord winding its way around my soul.

I imagined wrapping myself around my goddess alongside Doc Macaire, drowning in a sea of submission and acceptance. Lust and love.

My balls erupted, and I bit down on my lower lip, head tipping back and eyes closing, as I shot into my fist, every spurt of spunk causing a shudder to weaken my knees until I sagged against the window frame.

"Holy fuck," I whispered, glancing over the mess I'd made. It was like I hadn't come in weeks. "Shit."

I glanced outside, sure I'd given someone a show.

I just wished I could see who it was.

Our female.

Alpha.

Whoever—*whatever*—stood beyond Lockwood's fence, it sure as hell wasn't Doc Macaire, who'd been named as such by my beast earlier in the day.

"The fuck, man?" I asked, but the voice went silent, fading to the back of my mind along with the energy from outside.

Was I hallucinating?

I placed my hand on the glass, keeping out the night air and possibly the scent of my supposed female.

Ours.

Goddamned right she was, but my goddess was a figment of my imagination.

No.

"I'm having one hell of a dream."

No.

Fucking insistent voice…I wasn't right in the head.

Hell, maybe I was sleepwalking, and none of this was true.

Snorting at myself, I turned away, creeping across my room to retrieve the soiled blanket at the foot of my bed for yet another load of spunk. Cleaned up and cock sated for the moment, I crawled back onto the hard mattress, reminding myself that come morning, I was out of here.

I imagined her waiting for me. Arms open, golden tresses shifting in the breeze, amber eyes promising she was as enamored with me as I've been with her since I first saw her in my dreams.

Maybe Doc Macaire would walk me out and we would meet the woman together.

A deeply rumbled purr-like sound settled in my chest, and I closed my eyes, willing sleep to take me so the hours would pass quickly.

I stepped outside into the spring sunrise, my stomach full of crappy cafeteria breakfast, a bag of my belongings in hand, and a grin on my face even though I stood alone. Doc

Macaire hadn't shown up to see me off, and I was basically tossed out by the administration without further instruction.

My parents hadn't been in the lobby, nor were they waiting for me in the parking lot, thank fuck. They had been informed of my release, but even if Mom and Dad had been here, I didn't have any intention of speaking to either of them ever again.

They'd rejected me time and again, so why bother pushing for the love I longed for, yet they denied me at every turn?

I glanced at the fence I'd stared at the night before while busting the nut of the century, but the surety of some invisible force watching for me to exit the hospital the second visiting hours started for the day was absent. Regardless of the faint fall of my heart, my smile remained as I strode down the paved entrance and exited Lockwood's manned gate.

I was a free man—and it was time to do whatever the fuck I wanted.

But I sensed I would need my golden goddess and a stoic, domineering doctor in my bed to truly live.

For a solid fifteen minutes, I stood on the sidewalk and waited, scanning my surroundings—waiting. No one seemed to take note of me, no one cared I was newly released. No one approached, caught, or held my gaze.

No ripple of energy from the previous two nights from *her* licked at my skin, and my grin slowly faded as disappointment settled over my shoulder, turning my gut to rock.

Had I imagined the sensations of whatever the fuck it was calling out to me with potent lust? Perhaps the dry spell toyed with my brain, causing me to see and sense things that weren't real.

Like the wings beneath the skin on my back.

No.

Lips pursed, I closed my eyes for a moment, breathing deeply until my lungs ached with the need to expel the air.

Reality lay before me, *not* in the recesses of my mind where the voice whispered shit that got me into trouble.

I turned my back on where I would have bet money someone had watched me last night, away from Doc Macaire's place of employment, and headed toward a small cafe that promised real coffee, not the shit served in Lockwood's cafeteria. Order placed, I retrieved my cell phone Nurse Yum Yum had charged for me overnight, as well as one of the caramel candies she'd tossed into my bag. Since I was determined to start my life over, I deleted every message thread from before I'd been hospitalized.

Eventually, my so-called friends from down in Phoenix had stopped reaching out to me, and since the group was nothing but a further opportunity to get into trouble, I erased their contact info as well.

As for Mom and Dad—neither had texted nor called. Not even to inquire about my plans now that I'd been released.

Why the fuck did stabbing pain knife through my chest? I didn't *want* them in my life.

Jaw clenched, I checked the bus schedule, accepted my coffee from the barista, and exited the building.

My gaze wandered to the fence once more. No one stood watching my window.

Unable to accept I had imagined every second of last night, I told myself I would catch a ride back to Lockwood after dark.

She would be here—I had nothing to fear. Returning for a chance at feeling the energy I did from Doctor Macaire only added to my determination. Every step away from the hospital took me farther from the memory of the connection I'd experienced with him as well, and before I'd gone two blocks toward the bus station, it shimmered away from my mind, like a springtime breeze, forever breathing life into my soul—and yet tearing apart the beast inside me.

Go back to him.

"Not fucking happening," I muttered, even though I longed to beg Doc Macaire to take me, claim me in every way a dominant could. Becoming involved with a shrink, however hot, couldn't be good for my newfound freedom. Closeness would bring a desire for truth between us if my inner voice's whispered words of claiming and submission were true.

The beast would reveal himself, prove my madness even though I would insist I was sane as fuck.

I would land behind lock and key again, deemed insane and a threat to my own safety.

Which, yeah, that last part I could see—but as long as I avoided substances that weakened my resolve, I would be fine.

I sulked through the hour ride to the larger town in the south, and no flicker of energy furrowed my brow as the assurance I left behind something extremely important once more twisted my stomach.

I walked the few blocks to my apartment Doc Holiday had helped me contract for the next year, my mind focused on the hope of finding *her*, and my feet dragged with despair like a pouting child over the loss of *him*.

The lease had already been signed, the deposit and first month's rent paid. Key in hand, I climbed the exterior stairs to the studio apartment above my landlord's garage. A small deck offered me a place to relax while watching future sunsets, something I'd often enjoyed when not locked up in a sterile room like a lunatic.

While the place was small, it offered me more than my parents' large home ever had—freedom of choice to be me.

Fly.

"No fucking way, dude," I muttered out loud now that there was no one to see me talking to myself. "I don't want to end up back in Lockwood—don't care how hot that doctor with the sexy whiskers and longer hair is."

The memory of the man stiffened my cock, and I groaned while dropping my bag to the floor and taking a look around. A queen-sized bed, a small, round kitchen table, fridge, stove, loveseat, and old TV awaited me. Not much, exactly as Doc Holliday had said, but more than enough.

Rent included all utilities, cable, too, and I sprawled on the too-small couch, clicked on the TV, and watched an hour of ESPN because I could.

I wanted a warm, willing woman, but not just any leggy blonde with big tits I could suck on, an ass I could pound into if she allowed. I longed for my golden goddess—and Doc Macaire. Patrick.

Yessss.

To be between them, him fucking me while I fucked her, our bodies in synchronized motion. Of one mind, of one soul, our hearts beating in time, our climaxes rippling through the energy connecting us, soaring us to the stars.

I'd never known such thought-consuming need.

Fly.

Go find her.

Teeth clenched against the itch in my shoulder blades, I chose, instead, to take a hot shower and jerk off with a fierceness I didn't understand. My balls refused to erupt until I squeezed them to the point of pain, the memory of Patrick's face, his dark blue eyes shadowed by those goddamned reading glasses, pushing me over the edge.

The quiet of the apartment ate at me, and even though I had no wish to return to the hospital, I missed the mingling people and Nurse Yum Yum. Those three months had passed she'd insisted on—but I didn't get the sendoff I'd assumed she'd meant. Instead, I received a stern talking-to about behaving and a handful of sweet caramels to remember her by.

The problem with freedom, I found within a couple of hours after leaving Lockwood, was a loneliness I was all too familiar with and hated with a passion.

Heaviness weighed on me, and I sat back down on the couch, brow furrowed and stomach once more like a rock. The beast inside me lay quiet, but I could feel its emotions reflecting my own.

CHAPTER 9

PRIMROSE

The exhaustion of staying out until the middle of the previous two nights kept me abed until close to ten the next morning. Heart racing and a small smile on my lips, I readied for the day to meet my mate, taking care to cleanse myself thoroughly. Freshly showered and hair gleaming, I walked to the hospital a few minutes before noon.

For the first time in my life, my knees weakened from the shots of adrenaline my human body insisted on releasing whenever I thought of my beta. We would soon be together, never again to be separated. Together, we would locate our alpha.

But in the meantime, I would finally find out what kissing felt like, what a man's physical touch did to a woman, and he would teach me all of the sexual positions I had read about in some of the racier books in my family's massive library deep in the bowels of my ancestral home.

Warmth sprang to life between my thighs, and I wondered again over the power of my first orgasm. How much better would it be with him rutting between my legs?

While I knew enough to expect some pain, I looked forward to giving myself to him with the fierceness of a dragon.

I made my way down the sidewalk, cloaked and invisible to the humans I passed. My smile faded as I neared the hospital without the expected tether of energy radiating from the eastern wing. Alarm skittered down my spine, and my inner dragon held her breath along with me, with every step bringing us closer to Lockwood.

The gate remained closed as usual, but with people constantly coming and going through the daylight hours, slipping past once it opened to allow a car entry was easy. Hesitant steps took me closer to the front doors, the lack of awareness of my beta causing a riot of questions in my mind.

Had he been hurt and sedated? Became violent and attempted to escape, causing the doctors to medicate him?

Or was he no longer here…

I'd planned to sneak into my beta's wing, slipping past the first doctor to enter his room, and wait until they exited before announcing myself.

I expected my beta would need a lot of explanation for the sudden appearance of a woman he would doubtless feel a connection to, and I planned on honesty, hiding nothing, hoping he would be able to read the truth within my eyes of who and what we were to each other.

While I'd never had to cloak anything bigger than a duffle bag clasped to me, I hoped to adjust to rippling my capabilities through our clasped hands so we could walk out as easily as I would enter.

I bounded up the front stairs, skirting two people exiting to slip past them through the automatic doors into the reception area, and still no hint of my beta's energy reached toward me. The air smelled of bleach and a sickening odor that reminded me of food but didn't tempt my mouth to water. Nose wrinkled, I scanned the entryway, hoping for my mate's senses to flood over me. Surely, if he'd been medicated and was unaware, I would still be able to smell him with my dragon's heightened senses I called forth.

Nothing teased at my nose or enticed me deeper into the hospital's bowels.

My inner beast whimpered her concern, an echo of the ache in my heart.

I turned toward the eastern wing where he'd been imprisoned, my steps a little more sure even though I feared what I might find. The third door from the end of the hallway stood open, a cart with cleaning supplies parked beyond. I pulled up on the threshold to find a man in white humming beneath his breath and balling up linens he'd removed from the closest mattress where its bed stand sat empty.

A few personal belongings lay on the one beside the far bed, pristinely made with tucked edges and taut blankets.

I stepped back as the man drew near, but lifted my nose to breathe in the scent of the linens he carried past me and tossed into the hamper on his cart.

Yessss.

The scent of my beta's cum wafted past, filling my lungs. Musky and sweet—and insanely arousing. My knees went weak as wetness roused to life in my core.

Still humming, the man walked off, pushing his squeaky cart, and I slipped into the room he hadn't locked behind him. No physical trace of my beta remained, but I felt certain the stripped mattress had belonged to him.

Had he been given his freedom?

Hurrying back into the hallway, my mind raced and heart beat faster thanks to another shot of adrenaline through my system.

I'd only just found my beta—I couldn't lose him so quickly.

Driven by need, I rushed toward the reception area.

Tension riddled my body, hands fisted at my sides, and tears stinging my eyes as I stood before the receptionist's desk. Stairs led down and up in the back wing, and double doors on my left allowed entrance into the western wing.

From my outside strolls, I knew another building connected to the far side of that wing. Inhaling until it hurt didn't reveal a hint of my beta, only more of the sickening smells from the cafeteria, which my nose led me to believe lay straight ahead. Regardless of that part of the hospital's stench, I began my mission of traversing the entire campus, combing through every room in search of what belonged to me.

I started beyond the receptionist, first and second floors, then the basement area, my hope slowly sliding toward despair with every passing second.

Next, I entered the western wing, performing the same type of sweep, often having to wait what seemed an eternity to enter the doors leading to various public rooms. TVs, game tables, couches, and dozens of people, including two males with inner dragons whispering to me as they stared out windows, blank eyes revealing empty souls. A dark-eyed female jerked her head toward the door when I slipped inside, but not feeling my beta's presence, I fled before two seconds passed and our dragons could communicate with each other.

My shoulders sagged and my feet dragged, but I wouldn't leave without searching every last room. While quite a few had been locked—bedrooms included—I didn't need to do more than sniff at the doorjambs to know if my beta lay within.

An archway led into the second building, one with carpet and a hushed atmosphere as though more peaceful than the other areas.

A sudden rush of a scent that reminded me of home, of

brimstone deep within the heart of the mountain, caused me to stumble. I tilted my head back in attempts to fill my lungs better—but the deliciousness in my nose abruptly vanished from the air. Shivers skittered over me, pebbling my skin even though I swore I'd imagined what I had smelled.

Alpha.

My core thrummed to life, my pulse tripling in time even though I questioned my senses.

Alpha.

Inner dragon's insistence flooding my heart with hope, I strode forward in search of another whiff of brimstone.

Both of my mates were in the same building? Had they already met? Were they together as a couple? A pang twitched my stomach, and I wondered at the word jealousy, something I had never experienced before.

While I would be happy knowing they had each other while fate waited for them to find their female, I regretted the time I might have missed out on.

My instincts took me up a set of stairs. Another carpeted hallway led to my left. A dark-haired man disappeared into another doorway at the far end.

Heart pounding, I rushed to where he had disappeared.

"Doctor Patrick Macaire" was etched in a bronze sign on the door at eye level.

I leaned toward the door and inhaled deeply, desperate—

Without my dragon's heightened senses, I never would have caught the slightest hint of dragonblood beyond the wooden barrier between us. The musk was similar to my beta's, but with the sharp scent of charred brimstone my dragon craved...and with a touch of sweetness that made my mouth water.

Alpha.

Her assured words flooded gratefulness through my

entire being, causing my eyes to well with tears and my throat to tighten.

I placed my palms on the office door, resting my forehead in between, attempting to calm my heart rate.

Unrelenting desire to rip open his door and throw myself at his feet coursed through me, and I bit my tongue to keep from crying out in my need.

CHAPTER 10

PATRICK

I stayed up all night packing Jessie's shit, and by morning, her belongings sat on my front porch. I shot off a last text to her sister telling her to have them gone by the time I got home from work, or they were getting put out with the trash next pickup day. Upon completing the task of ridding my life of Jessie, I focused on my future.

Jaxon sat in the forefront of my mind since meeting him the day before, and no matter how many cold showers I'd taken, my dick stiffened every other hour with the need to fuck the boy and threatened everything I'd accomplished in life.

I walked into Lockwood a few hours late by choice, as I had no wish to run into him and temptation before his release.

Doctor Holliday's notes suggested Jaxon suffered from dissociative identity disorder, also known as multiple personality disorder, but in his months of therapy with the young man, he hadn't come to the point where he felt confident in diagnosing him as such. Doctor Holliday's musings on various pieces of lined paper and sticky notes suggested something…more.

Perhaps supernatural.

My existence centered around science. I had dismissed his thoughts, focused more on Jaxon's family history. According to his parents, his paternal grandmother had heard voices others couldn't and often hallucinated, believing an inner being would allow her to fly. She'd thrown herself off a cliff on the canyon's southern rim and plummeted to her death before Jaxon had been born. They believed her to have been schizophrenic. That particular psychotic disorder was hereditary, which swayed me toward thinking Jaxon very well could be as well, regardless of my predecessor's musings.

My footfalls landed near-silently on the hallway carpet, and I filled my lungs deeply, ready to focus on moving forward in my temporary job, the new beginning I had with Jessie gone and now Jaxon having been discharged.

No more disturbances to my life, thank fuck—

The sweetest scent teased briefly at my nose, causing a rush of heat to flare in my chest.

Whispers attempted to escape.

Teeth gritted, I pushed against the darkness, denying it a voice. My body vibrated, causing my knees to weaken, but I strode forward, shutting myself into my office and leaving my past in the hallway.

Shaking, I set my briefcase aside and settled at the desk, determined to focus on the day. Seeing patients. Doing the job I'd been hired to fulfill.

And not getting hard over the memory of a boy who had made me question my sexuality.

His grin, the wildness of his youthful eyes, spoke of a mischievous soul, one who pushed limits, dared to explore beyond where he ought to—and had also suggested he'd wanted to drop to his knees to suck me off or bend over the desk, his ass on offer.

My dick swelled, and I tipped my head back against my office chair, powerless against the memory of him and the dreams that had haunted me throughout the sleepless night.

I'd seen him swallow around my cock, eyes tearing, nose running, the most gorgeous sounds leaking around his lips stretched to accommodate my girth. I'd shoved balls deep into the exquisite, tight heat of his ass, sinking my teeth into his neck. Marking him. Breeding him.

I'd also woken to the sheets tangled around me, soaked with cum from climaxing in my sleep for the first time since I was a teenager.

I cursed under my breath, pressing down against my aching length.

Choosing to avoid the possibility of running into the young man had been the right decision—

The hairs on my nape rose to attention, my skin prickling exactly as it had when our fingers had brushed.

The familiar hiss sounded in my ears, causing my entire body to tense, but I was frozen—*powerless*—to block and lock it back up.

My gaze flitted to the closed office door, nostrils flaring on instinct, my lungs expanding.

A rush of that same sweetness from earlier in the hallway coated the air like some goddamned fairy godmother waved her wand beneath my nose, worse than any cupid's arrow, piercing my chest.

My mouth watered at the cloying scent. It wasn't Jaxon's musky maleness tightening my balls but something so much softer. Richer.

Female.

The distinctive voice in my head was the same from thirty years ago.

Fear and adrenaline spiked in my blood, heightening my pulse and making it difficult to regulate my breathing. But every inhale filled me with the scent of her.

Female.

I swallowed hard at the rush of saliva coating my mouth, shivers rippling down my spine at the repeated word. Energy slid over me, and as though a leash attached me to the being in the hallway, it drew me out of my chair and across the office before I realized I had moved.

I threw the door open without conscious thought.

My breath expelled with force as though someone had punched me in the gut.

Golden hair spilled around the curves of a goddess' body that frumpy clothing couldn't hide. Her plump lips parted, high cheekbones tinging the most delicious shade of pink. Her light brown eyes, the color of whiskey, widened as our gazes locked.

"Alpha." She breathed the word, and darkness swirled through the walls I had erected in my chest, cackling glee sweeping up through my brain like a gale of wind.

Ours.

A sudden, dazzling smile lit her face with twice the rays of a morning's sunrise, causing my heart to seize and consume every part of me.

She leapt at me, and I caught her without thought, her generous curves filling my arms. Her lips landed against mine, and all sense of *self* vanished as the instinctive need to claim her took over my faculties.

One hand grasping her plump ass, the other tangling in her hair, I kicked the office door shut behind us and slammed her against it, licking across her lips in demand she open, share her essence with her owner.

A whimper passed between our mouths, oozing pre-cum from my straining dick as I ground against her core. The heat of her, the scent of her pussy aching to be stuffed full, sped through me, causing my ears to ring and tension to riddle my body.

I wrapped my arm beneath her leg, opening her thighs for my thrusts, and she gasped, her hands grasping at my shoulders as though I was the only thing keeping her grounded. I tore my lips off hers to taste the skin of her neck, down her collarbone…lifting her higher against the door to bite her straining nipple beneath her shirt.

"Oh!" She jerked in my hold, and I bit again, wanting in the worst way to sink my teeth into her soft skin and mark her for life.

Take—claim our female.

The stark words in my head returned my humanity's better sense.

"Please," the woman begged. "I am yours."

I hesitated in the instinctive drive to devour her whole, breath stuttering against the damp shirt my face pressed against. The fucking *insane* voice in my head, which I had hoped silenced forever, had taken over my body to the point I was desperate to tear through the young woman's leggings and fill her with one goddamned thrust.

A doctor in his office, ready to fuck a patient without even knowing her goddamn name—

Unacceptable.

A complete abuse of authority.

Shudders ripped through me, causing my spine to stiffen and hairs to rise on my nape.

"I am in control," I stated, focusing on slamming the walls back into place in my head and chest. The darkness inside me shrieked as I envisioned confining its presence in my consciousness, and I tore my hold from the woman, placing her on her feet. My hands clenched at my sides to keep from grabbing her again as I forced my steps backward, giving me some space even though every cell in my body vibrated, begging me to close the distance between us.

Regardless of the desperate need inside me, I stared temptation in the face, stoic professionalism barely standing between us.

She blinked pupil-blown eyes slowly into awareness, as though she, too, had been overwhelmed by animalistic desire. The sight of her swollen lips caused my dick to throb, pulses of pre-cum soaking my slacks. I clenched my teeth, once more cursing myself for going commando, my pounding heart matching the pulse thrumming in her neck.

I'd never felt such potent lust, a deep-seated yearning to strip a person bare and sate both of our cravings.

"Why did you stop?" she whispered, pain inflicting her words and furrowing her brow.

She was beyond beautiful, an alluring angel, a sure siren to destroy my mind—my heart.

"Who are you?" The words tore from my mouth with a raggedness I didn't recognize. "*What* are you?" The second question tumbled past my lips without thought.

"I'm yours." Tears filled her eyes. "And you're mine." Her voice caught on a sob. "My alpha…dragonblood."

An echoed hiss escaped past its prison, and I shook my head, retreating another step. "No."

"Please." Another sob, and she lifted her hand toward me, palm up. "*Please.*"

I doused the heat in my chest with a reality check of who and what *I* was—and where I stood, dick dripping for a female patient, for fuck's sake.

A muscle ticked in my jaw. "*No,*" I stated harshly through gritted teeth.

Her shoulders slumped, tears coursing down her cheeks, but I held steady even as the darker parts of me ached to hold her and soothe her suffering by taking what she offered.

She spun, yanked the door open, and sprinted from sight.

A muted roar erupted in my chest, buckling my knees, and I lunged for the open door, holding onto its edge to keep from falling. My gaze jerked side to side, up and down the hallway.

She'd disappeared.

CHAPTER II

PRIMROSE

I made it to the stairwell before collapsing in a heap, lower lip between my teeth to contain the sobs clawing at my chest. The coppery tang of blood slid across my tongue, but I didn't recognize that I'd injured myself. Eyes clenched, I fought to keep the pain inside me from causing my dragon to take over—help us escape the pain by burning down the hospital around us.

Even grief over losing Grandmother hadn't hurt us to the extent of our alpha's rejection.

He had pushed me away, and even though I could still feel the tether of energy connecting us, the darkness inside him lay quieter than it should. The human blood in him pumped with vigor, as strong as his will to hold his inner dragon contained. He feared—*hated*—that part of him he didn't understand.

Refusing to acknowledge what he was wouldn't ever make it go away.

The metal door behind me squeaked open, a rush of brimstone and musk trickling over me. The man's self-control was stronger than in anyone I'd ever met—and Grandpapa was the epitome of stubborn.

My alpha loomed above on the landing, longer hair slicked back, eyes dark and fathomless. Wide shoulders suggested he could carry the weight of my world, but the stoicism radiating from him was unparalleled. Hands clenched at his sides as he trembled, his inner beast imprisoned from my gift to hear Blood Born.

"How do you do that?" I whispered past the thickness in my throat. "Completely shut that part of you away from me? No dragonblood has been able to do so."

A deep groove lined his forehead. "Who are you?" he asked again, ignoring my question.

I decided to answer this time rather than flee, in the hope of making a connection he wouldn't be able to deny. "Primrose Cadet."

"You're a patient here?"

"No." I swallowed against the sudden dryness attacking my mouth at the realization his cock strained less than two feet from my face, the material trapping it darkened from evidence of his need to breed me. Heat rushed through me as I shifted closer, my hand rising to stroke his hard length.

He took a step back before I could touch what belonged to me and our beta.

"I want you to claim me against that door like you almost did moments ago because I belong to you," I whispered. "I *need* you."

He blinked, the energy linking us swelling with a blinding light that dimmed just as fast as whatever prison he locked his inner dragon within doubled its wall thickness.

"Your human has complete control." I mourned, my voice breaking, my hand dropping to my lap.

"I can help you," he said, his tone low, his voice sounding forced.

I climbed to my feet, holding his stare, and even though I couldn't hear his inner thoughts, I didn't need to in order to understand what he'd meant. My alpha was a doctor in a mental hospital. "I know what kind of *help* you refer to, but there's no cure for who I am. Even if there was, I would fight to the death to remain whole."

He stared at me, unblinking, and even though sexual energy rippled between us with potency, I struggled to resist his vocalized boundaries, his remained veiled.

Was it possible I had been wrong? My body and dragon knew Patrick was Blood Born, my alpha. Perhaps he didn't want *me*.

No.

Perhaps we're not enough, I suggested to the mourning dragon inside me. Perhaps I wasn't pretty enough. Too tall, too curved for his tastes, even though he had muscle enough to lift me in his arms as though I weighed no more than a sack of potatoes. My beast whimpered as the silence between me and the frowning man grew.

"Why did you come after me if you don't want me?" I asked, hoping for an answer that would soothe my tumbling emotions.

A muscle twitched the scruff lining his jaw. "Because you need *help*."

My shoulders sagged as I realized he would never give me what my body and soul craved, the bonding that would tie us together even after we rested among the stars.

I lifted my chin rather than crumple into my misery at his feet. Finding my mates wasn't supposed to have been difficult, but an easily traversed path toward my destiny. I had encountered nothing but road blocks at every turn.

A dozen or so curses flitted through my mind, but I kept my lips sealed. Dragonblood *and* my alpha, the man must smell the arousal smeared inside my leggings. How could he withstand the pull? I had read once that having caught the scent of his mates, an alpha would move mountains to claim what belonged to him.

No human side could resist their true form when faced with those fate had chosen for them.

Which meant…

He *didn't* want me. In his eyes, I was somehow tarnished, less than perfect. Too much or, perhaps, not enough.

My chest split open, causing a cry to erupt from my chest. I turned away and hurried down one level of stairs, cloaking myself from human sight. Uncaring about raising suspicion or alarm, I threw open door after door in my attempt to escape the tether wanting to pull me back to the one who had rejected what had been planned for us since the dawn of time.

The second the sun shone down on me, I shifted to my true form, shredding clothes, our wings lifting me in a rush of wind that blew two people approaching me onto their backsides, shrieking.

Tears poured from our eyes as we shot upward, yearning to escape the pain caused by our alpha, to somehow break the beginnings of the bond we had been created to fulfill. We wanted to roar our frustration, but couldn't afford to further raise human awareness of a beast in the sky after blasting wind over those poor ones below.

We banked toward the south, needing space. Time to find some semblance of peace we would be able to live with.

Our beta had wanted us, my human half didn't doubt, but he had disappeared as easily as we had from Lockwood.

South.

My humanity gave over to our dragon, and we flew onward, another town growing on the dusty horizon. Wings tucking, we dove, sweeping over buildings and houses around its perimeter, slowly moving inward, still grieving in silence, our heartache extending to the tips of our bones. While our dragon controlled our body, our other side licked emotional wounds that attempted to tear us apart limb from limb.

Perhaps I ought to return to Grandpapa and the mountains. At least some semblance of peace had been offered in our childhood home—even if it meant being alone for the centuries ahead of us.

A cool wind rippled over our wings, tinged with a hint of…

Beta.

Our heart leaped, the searing pain over our alpha momentarily quieted. I forced my human mind over my dragon's control, seeking out the energy rising from below. Same as the night before, the tether between us strengthened as we closed in on a cul-de-sac lined by homes. The one at the circle's end drew our focus.

We landed in front of the house and shifted into human form, naked and cloaked, my gaze roaming over the house as trembling took over my body. My attention moved toward the garage, to the set of stairs leading to a small balcony.

Yessss.

Would he turn me away as my alpha had? I bit my lip once more, refusing to spring forward as my dragon wished.

He wants us.

The energy between me and my beta swelled, and I found myself moving forward, hardly noting the wooden treads beneath my bare feet as I climbed the stairs to the balcony. The tether solidified into an almost tangible force, tightening around my soul. I could sense—physically *feel*—my beta's consuming desire for me.

The door flew open before I could grasp the handle, and my insides swooned at the beauty of him, the perfection of his dark hair, blue-green eyes, and freshly shaved jaw. His smooth, bare chest appeared chiseled from stone, lusciously bowed upper lip, and the one below full enough I wanted to sink my teeth into the soft flesh.

I could feel my beta's desire, see it beneath the jeans, clutching at his groin, scent it in the air swirling around us—but my alpha's true form had lusted for me in the same way.

And he'd denied us.

My eyes burned as I stood invisible on the edge of indecision over revealing myself and experiencing possible fulfillment or pain I didn't wish to endure twofold.

CHAPTER 12
JAXON

No one stood on my deck, but she was nearby. My heart pounded, sending blood pulsing straight to my dick.

Our female.

"I can't see you, but I *know* you're here." The words rasped past my lips, and I swallowed against the ache in my throat. "I can feel you. *Want* you more than my next breath."

The air around me crackled with an energy more potent than Patrick's. I tightened my grip on the door handle to keep myself grounded, rooted to the spot, when something inside me strained for release beyond a mere climax.

"Please show yourself," I begged. "Prove to me I'm not fucked in the head."

A feminine shuddered sigh whispered past my ears, and my beast moaned at the first proof I wasn't mad.

Golden light shimmered in front of me, swirling as a gentle breeze stirred fallen leaves. Like glitter glinting in the overhead sun, she slowly materialized.

Amber eyes full of painful hope met mine. My heart cried

out to soothe her more than my dick longed to fuck into her. The light of her fused fully together, bringing her entire body into focus.

Her very *naked* body—sun-kissed skin with more curves than a country road caused my blood to turn molten. Luscious, heavy breasts with tight, rosy tips made my teeth ache to bite. Her small waist led southward toward flared hips that my fingers itched to clutch. And the glistening, golden curls hiding heaven from my wandering gaze caused my mouth to water and dick to buck inside my jeans.

"You're my golden goddess," I stated with a rush, my pulse pounding in my ears as I stared where I wanted to bury my face to lap at her sweetness I could smell in the air.

Our female.

"Yes," she agreed, jerking my focus back to her face.

Need.

"Yes." Her breathless whisper and the beginnings of her smile tightened my balls against my body. She moved closer.

I held out my hand, and the first touch of her fingertips rippled that energy between us, up through my arm, piercing my heart sharply enough I grunted. Fighting to catch my breath, I stepped backward, pulling her in after me, our gazes latched firmly, something deep inside me connecting to her without hesitation or fear. Our fingers curled around each other's possessively, stronger than any magnet.

She wants us, to be beneath us. She'll willingly give what no man has yet claimed.

"You *shall* be my first." She spoke as though she heard my beast's rare, complete sentence, moving to close the distance between our vibrating bodies.

The scent of a fresh strawberry, juicy and ready to be devoured, flooded my nose, causing another rush of saliva to coat my mouth.

I reached out a hand to push the apartment door shut, closing us in complete privacy. The buzz of the TV registered in my ears, but the heavy breaths we shared held my focus. As though of the same mind, we erased the inches between us, coming together, her soft breasts against my bare chest.

She was tall enough I barely needed to lower my head to kiss her smiling mouth.

I'd fucked my way through my fair share of women, but with the first brush of our lips, I recognized that the golden goddess pressing herself against me and filling me with bone-deep aching want would be my last. Fate had destined us for each other. She was the one my heart and soul had longed for, the faithful lover who would accept me regardless of my shortcomings until I lay buried six feet under.

Where the assurance came from, I didn't understand— and I didn't give a fuck. I wanted to bury myself inside her body, piercing her as she'd done to my heart, filling her with everything I was, everything I longed for.

The fact she'd appeared like a ghost solidifying into flesh hadn't freaked me the fuck out as it should have, but I refused to pinch myself to see if I dreamed. The beast inside me recognized her, and as I cradled her cheeks in my hands, I experienced the truth my beast whispered.

Ours.

Fated.

Mate.

I groaned into her mouth, sliding my tongue along her silken lips, and she opened to me, the sweetness of her breath, the taste of her mouth beyond all fucking comprehension. Never...I would *never* get enough.

"Mine," I growled against her lips as I slid a palm down her back to cup one of her plump ass cheeks.

"Yes." She worked her hands between us, pulling at my

jeans, fumbling, her movements turning almost frantic as I trailed my lips along her jaw to nip beneath her ear.

I lusted for this woman—to fuck into her body, have her wet warmth welcome me home. "Need to be inside you. Be *one* with you."

Own our female.

"Oh, yes." She gulped as I squeezed her backside and lavished open-mouthed kisses down her throat, trying to draw her strawberry-like scent inside my lungs.

Her whimper of frustration with my jeans had me grinning like a goddamn fool. No woman had ever wanted me so badly, and the knowledge I would be her first, that I would be the man to fulfill her needs, caused my dick to jerk beneath her grasping fingers.

"Help me, please," she whispered, yanking on my zipper.

It hurt like fucking hell to release my hold on her softness, but I did—enough only to free my dick, shove my jeans to the floor, and kick them off. Our bodies came together, mouths crashing once more in desperation, the energy simmering between us enough I felt I would burst into flames if I didn't impale her on my dick right the fuck now.

She whimpered as I lifted her into my arms, her legs wrapping around my waist where they belonged. Her soaked folds rested along the back of my straining dick that leaked like a motherfucker. A few stumbling steps across the apartment as we continued to eat at the other's mouths, and the bed bumped against my thighs.

We fell onto the mattress in a tumbling heap until she lay beneath me, my dick sliding along the soaked mess between her thighs. I flexed my ass beneath her heels, sending my hard length up over her protruding clit, gyrating to stimulate her how she needed.

"Oh!"

I lifted onto my elbows and stilled, my gaze locked on her

face—widened eyes, the gold dominated by her swirling, black pupils. She was…otherworldly and perfect for me in every way. "You liked that?" I asked and moved my hips again, fucking up through her swollen labia, rubbing my shaft over her clit.

A moan rushed past her lips as she arched beneath me, exposing a throat I wanted to sink my teeth into.

While I wasn't usually one for violence in bed, something about my goddess called to deeper, darker desires in me.

Bury inside her heat, thrust and release against her womb—

Breeding. Kink. Unlocked.

She grabbed hold of my hair and lifted her head to capture my lips, swallowing the curses spilling from me.

I lowered myself wholly against her softness, angling my hips to notch my dick against her opening but hesitated at the thought I might cause her pain. She squeezed her legs around me, pulling me tighter against her with the strength of ten women.

I notched into her soaked pussy, my beast shuddering and hissing in my ears. "Fuck, you're tight," I stated through gritted teeth, fighting to keep from stabbing into her with one thrust.

She whimpered and licked into my mouth, as enticing as a siren hellbent on owning my soul.

Groaning, I pushed in a few inches before meeting resistance.

Take.

A fierce need to protect this woman I didn't even know, beyond the carnal lust that brought us together, hindered forward movement.

"Every part of me belongs to you, my beta," she murmured against my lips, her breath sweeter than any caramel.

Yessss.

I rocked in and out the slightest bit until my eyes rolled back into my head on a deep groan over how perfectly her body clutched at mine, enticing me to seek out the deepest reaches of her.

"Please," she whispered. "Fill me—"

I thrust through the barrier, her face in my hands, my mouth capturing her cry. Her wince, the slight sting of pain she experienced, somehow radiated down my spine, but the satisfaction, the joy of completeness following on its heels, spiraled the hurt away as I slid into her embrace.

Buried deep against her womb, I held still, allowing her to adjust to my dick stuffed in her tight pussy, our mouths fused as we attempted to catch our breath.

She was heaven.

Home.

Ours.

My beast no longer used the word to insist she belonged to us but relished in the truth of the unbreakable chains wrapping around us. I could almost feel a similar beast within her, whispering the same assurance to her mind, which caused contentment to settle inside me.

Batshit crazy for sure, but I couldn't find any fucks to give while her sheath clenched around me and made my balls firm up tight against my groin.

This woman was perfection.

I shifted my hips back the slightest bit, dragging my dick along her slick inner walls, and the whimper rising to her lips wasn't filled with pain.

Two animalistic moaned voices rose as one in my ears, and a gentle push into her pussy pulled a deeper, vocal groan from both of us.

Lifting onto my forearms, I cradled her face in my hands, and I held her gaze. "Tell me who you are so I have a name to cry out when I fill you with my cum."

She shuddered, her core pulsing around me. "P-Primrose."

I pulled out until my tip rested inside her body and slowly sank in until our groins pressed tightly together. "Prim," I groaned, fighting to keep my eyes from rolling into my head at how we seamlessly fit together. "My goddess."

I gyrated my hips while fucking in and out of her as gently as I could, my balls aching to erupt as the gold of her eyes shimmered, manipulating every goddamn string inside my body. She wrapped me up, tying me tight like she was a witch bent on binding my soul to hers.

"Yes," I heard myself groan, and her brilliant smile lit every last corner of my soul as I buried my dick against her womb.

Mine.

"You're mine." I gasped, fighting to keep my pulsing dick from releasing too soon while drowning in her golden eyes.

Mate.

"My mate."

She clutched at my shoulders and yanked me close until my chest rested against hers again. "Until we join the stars," she whispered against my ear, her legs clutching at my ass to keep me deep inside her body.

The stars...

They fucking exploded behind my eyelids without another thrust into her heat, and I buried my face in her neck as my balls erupted, the first jet of my cum inside her startling a gasp from her lips.

"Prim..." I moaned against her sweet flesh, and she cried out, arching in my hold, her pussy clamping down on my attempts to shoot my cum deeper, soaking into her body never to be expelled. The spasms of her walls around me drained the blood from my head—I went lightheaded, losing track of time, of myself, of all *fucking* consciousness as the most glorious euphoria swept me under like a tsunami wave.

One last shudder, and I lay atop her, heaving for breath, my blood racing, limbs tingling as she clutched at my shivering, dead weight.

"Fucking heaven," I groaned into her neck, and her sigh matched the emotion rolling over me.

CHAPTER 13

PATRICK

A massive tension headache splitting my skull in two, I logged into my computer and pulled up Lockwood's residence listing with their thumbnail pictures.

Jaxon had woken a raging beast of lust inside me, and I'd grabbed at the golden goddess as though I had a right to her body. Although Jaxon had been discharged, he was still in the system, the picture in his file too alluring to ignore. I stared at his rumpled dark hair, the fathomless ocean of his eyes, and the perfectly bowed upper lip I wanted to sink my teeth into.

Groaning, I pressed against my bulge, forcing myself to click out of his profile and scan the rest.

It took over half an hour of searching through Lockwood's patients, long enough for my blood to somewhat cool, but the young woman who had brought me to my knees wasn't listed in their files. There were no whiskey-colored eyes I wanted to stare into while sinking deep into her sweet warmth.

There had been no lanyard and ID around her neck, so

she wasn't staff. Upon further reflection, I realized she hadn't dressed as a patient either. The clothing she'd worn suggested she might have been a visitor—but no temporary pass sticker had stuck to the cotton covering her gorgeous breasts.

Had I imagined her?

Pulling in and slowly releasing a deep breath, I rubbed at the middle of my forehead, my eyes closing.

I replayed every second of the strange, passionate-as-hell encounter in my mind, causing my dick to stiffen again. The scent of her lingered in my nose, the feel of her softness causing my fingertips to tingle. Saliva flooded my mouth for another taste of her lips, and I growled at the darkness pressing against the void inside me, testing the tenuous walls containing it.

I would not give in to madness.

"I won't." I forced the words between my gritted teeth, my legs as restless as my conflicted mind.

I needed to get the hell out of here—

Sitting forward, I hit the phone's button for the main office's secretary. "Tell the director I'm leaving for the day," I barked when she answered, not giving two shits if my temporary boss appreciated me taking off or not. "I feel like shit," I explained before she could question why and hung up, grabbing my briefcase. I strode out, desperate to get some space between me and this hospital that had caused more mental and bodily strain than anything I had faced in my entire life.

Only my second day employed by Lockwood, and I'd been late showing up—and I was now taking off early. I'd be lucky to keep the temporary job, but couldn't bring myself to care with how turmoil ruled my better sense.

The darkness from my childhood had crept in along the edges of my mind that rainy afternoon in the attic, and the hospital's intensified pressure, what felt like an over-inflated balloon in my chest, threatened to explode and take my sanity along with it.

Fear and lust battled like bloodthirsty animals in my body, stringing me tight as I strode to my car, started the engine, and got the hell out of the compound. But the tension remained in my jaw as I lowered the windows, allowing the afternoon's warmth to swirl through my car's interior and whip my hair around my head. My heart pounded, the heavy thumps loud in my ears as I clutched the steering wheel with a white-knuckled grip.

I drove in a haze of desperation to put space between me and the place of temptation, allowing instincts to dictate my actions while *what-ifs* played in my head.

Giving in to lust for Jaxon, regardless of his being a legal adult, could have landed me in hot water professionally. No piece of ass was worth my livelihood, even if my body craved marking him with my fingerprints, my teeth, and my cum.

I could imagine the sated bliss of release, though, spine-tingling and satisfying in ways I'd never experienced with any woman. There would be no holding back, no gentleness needed, no coaxing his climax. He would have shot off the second I buried my dick in his tight ass.

A pulse of pre-cum oozed from my shaft, and I groaned, pressing against my bulge.

And her…

Regardless of who the young woman was, fucking someone in my office was beyond unprofessional, never mind reckless as all hell. I didn't carry condoms around, but had been ready to fuck into her bare, not knowing if it would have been safe to do so, let alone her name. I could have knocked her up—

An image of Jaxon and me stretching her pussy around both of our girths, releasing together inside her body, sent a jolt of pure electricity through my spine, zapping my balls with torturous, delicious pain.

"Fucking *hell*!" I barked, squeezing my junk to keep from nutting like a goddamned teen.

Buildings appeared in my peripheral vision, but I took no note of my location or how long I'd been driving aimlessly in an attempt to put distance between me and the temptation to go back and redo those moments with the two occupying my mind.

And losing everything I'd driven to accomplish in my life. A stainless reputation. A practice of my own.

Equal desire pushed and pulled, yanking my mind in separate directions, keeping me restless and on the edge of nutting.

A cul-de-sac appeared ahead of me, and awareness of where I'd driven in my clouded mind rose to the forefront.

I slammed on the brakes, noting the house directly ahead —especially its garage with the apartment above it.

Jaxon's place.

I'd driven close to an hour, buried deep in my thoughts.

"Goddamnit," I growled as my heartbeat kicked up to a worrisome rate and the full-body tension returned.

I needed to leave.

I wanted to stay.

I lusted to make him kneel before me, to fuck him until we both passed out from exhaustion. Tie him down and beat his ass for making me crazy with desire to the point I had grabbed at that luscious woman like a crazed animal, believing she would sate the madness he'd stirred up inside me.

A breeze teased at my hair that had been messed up from the open window, flooding my nose with the scent of musk and strawberries.

"No fucking way," I muttered. Closing my eyes, I inhaled

again, filling my lungs to bursting, the combined, delicious smells causing my body to curl inward with desperate yearning, the walls inside me threatening to crumble to dust.

Growling, I narrowed my focus on the deck at the top of the garage's exterior stairs and the door leading into Jaxon's apartment. Were they together, or was I so fucked-up in the head I imagined my senses heightened beyond even that of a dog?

"Jesus fucking Christ, what the *hell* is wrong with me?"

I breathed deeply, my eyes rolling into my head as I tasted their sated lust in the air. The scent of her virgin blood coated my tongue, causing my dick to strain and leak in my slacks. She'd given herself to Jaxon when it should have been me—

"Fuck." I fumbled to slide the windows up and swallowed hard once I sat enclosed in quietness. A flick of a button turned the air-conditioning on, but the noise couldn't drown out the thoughts in my head.

I had denied her, and she found the one man I'd ever been sexually attracted to, the kid who had consumed me since first meeting him. Jealousy should have burned in my guts, but longing for both of them overrode my senses.

His cocky grin. Her luminous eyes. Both of them, gorgeous to a fault, both so sensual that they made my bones ache with deep need to fulfill their every desire.

The darker visions of domination flooded my brain, and I groaned, grabbing hold of my dick through my slacks at the idea of inflicting the type of pain that promised satiated bliss I'd never considered partaking in before.

Beating two youngsters because of animalistic urges to sate my lust—

I needed to get the fuck out of there. Retain my goddamn sanity before I lost everything I had worked hard to attain in my still unfulfilled life.

Without a glance toward the garage, I pulled into the closest driveway, backed out, and headed north toward home and the solitude I needed to set my head straight.

An empty house awaited me. Sudden thoughts of Jessie sickened me, roiling my stomach, and I questioned why I had ever allowed her into my bed. She couldn't hold a candle to Jaxon or Primrose.

I wondered if anyone ever would.

CHAPTER 14

PRIMROSE

Awareness prickled my skin, but my beta nuzzled beneath my ear, trailing kisses along my jawline. He brushed his mouth over mine, retaining my full focus. Soft and unhurried, every caress of his tongue and swipe of his lips caused my heart to race and fulfilled me beyond what I had hoped for or imagined.

His cock remained buried inside me, and I kept my legs wrapped around his waist, holding him close. Our hearts beat in time through the skin and bone separating them, and I gloried in the total acceptance, the absolute joy radiating in the energy between us.

He has claimed us.

"Not every inch," he murmured, even though I hadn't spoken my dragon's declaration aloud, and pressed up onto his elbows to better meet my gaze. A twinkle lit his ocean eyes while he grinned a wickedly delicious smile. He shifted his hips, his length still hard even though cum trickled around where he was buried deep in my body.

Another burst of arousal rushed through my core,

offering him the slickness he would require for what I could hear his dragon whisper its need for.

Yessss.

I squeezed my inner walls around his shaft. "You can take it all."

Please.

He groaned and tipped his forehead against mine. "I can feel your thoughts, like whispers in the wind," he said, his sweet breath caressing my parted lips. "How is that possible?"

I ran my fingertips along his spine, his shiver causing goose bumps to rise along my arms. "Because of the dragonblood in us, the beginnings of the bond between fated mates who refuse any barriers between them."

Yessss, our inner beasts hissed as one.

"Fuck." He tangled his fingers in my hair and kissed me again with a ravaging hunger I felt within my soul.

Had I been fully human, soreness from his thrusts would have demanded we wait to mate again, but the dragonblood healed me faster, erasing all pain the second he'd torn through my maidenhead to claim me.

Lifting onto his hands, he held my gaze, dragging his length out, even though I tried to keep him close. The grin had faded from his lips, pure lust, instinctive, consuming need, replacing the bubbly feelings emanating between us as he stared down at me.

He pulled his rigid shaft from my body, releasing a flood of our combined cum from earlier, and slid along my sopping lower lips, rubbing the back of his length along the swollen bundle of nerves. "Tell me again." His rasped command caused me to shiver.

"You can take it all," I whispered what his dragon wanted to hear while clutching at his tensed biceps.

"Yeah?"

"Yes."

Holding my gaze with his gleaming eyes, he moved down over my body, pausing to lift my breasts together and lick across the sensitive buds, watching me closely for my reaction.

I grabbed hold of his head, moaning as zings raced from my hard nipples, through my stomach, and straight to my pussy, causing more arousal to well along my inner walls.

"I can smell how badly you want me." He grazed his teeth over my nipples, and I shuddered. "How the fuck is that even possible?" he mumbled and nipped one last time.

"Please," I croaked, shaking in my need.

He slid lower, his tongue flickering over my stomach, my navel—he nuzzled against the curls between my thighs, breathing in the scent of our cum and my want. He tongued over my labia and upward to flick the hardened nub at the top of my slit, causing me to jolt and whimper.

He swallowed and growled. "So fucking delicious."

Please...

"I—I need..." I whined, thighs pressing tight against the sides of his head.

Mouth latching onto the throbbing bundle of nerves, he slid two fingers deep into my soaked core, another rumble of satisfaction sounding in his chest.

His inner beast purred, enticing me to gift him more wetness for him to swallow down.

He coaxed continuous arousal from my human body with tongue and fingers, leading us and our true selves toward the satisfaction we craved.

I lifted my hips when he desired, cried out when he wanted me to come again. My body convulsed at his persistent onslaught, his fingers thrusting through drenching cum—the lubrication he needed and wanted to claim another first from me.

"Yes," I half-gasped the word as my climax robbed me of breath.

He knelt between my loosened thighs, rubbing his shaft through my juices. "If it's too much, tell me to stop."

"You'll know if it is," I replied, reaching for him, my gaze latching onto my release glistening on his lips.

Taste.

He groaned and leaned forward, his fingertips once more slipping into my soaked core when I yearned for him elsewhere.

"Need to get you ready first so I don't hurt you," he said, pulling his fingers from my body and trailing them downward.

I grabbed the backs of my thighs and lifted higher, desperate for him to claim my other hole and fill me there too.

Gentle, slickened circling around my puckered entrance heightened my yearning to be one with him again, and I bore down.

Want.

He pushed a finger into the first knuckle, and I groaned. "I know you do—I can fucking *feel* you in my head." He rotated his hand, exploring the inside of my ass before pressing in farther. "So smooth and warm—you're going to be silk around my dick."

I panted, licking over my dry lips, gaze ensnared by his. We were connected physically, but an invisible tether had latched us together. More radiant than the sun, more comforting than the moon lighting the night sky.

"More," I begged, my voice broken.

"Mmm," he agreed, sliding another finger along with the first, stretching me with a burn that raced fire up my spine. "You like the pain, don't you?"

"Oh, yes." I bit down on my lip as he worked his fingers

deeper, spreading them, opening my untried hole for his cock.

My dragon whimpered along with me, causing his to purr even deeper as he pulled his slick fingers from my back hole.

"Tell me what you want, Prim."

"You…"

Holding my gaze, he feathered the head of his cock against me, teasing with a coy smirk. "My name is Jaxon. And you better scream my name when you come on my cock again."

"Jaxon, my beta—"

He slid balls deep inside my pussy again, coating his shaft with my wetness before retreating once more. "Relax and let me in, baby."

He pushed my thighs wide, and my hands fell to clutch the sheets beside me as he flexed his ass, the burn of him breaching my puckered opening deliciously arousing.

Our inner beasts hissed their mutual desire, both voices loud in my ears.

"So tight," Jaxon stated through clenched teeth, shoving in a little more.

I moaned, my back arching, my body trying to draw him in deeper. "I can take it—you won't injure me."

"Fuck, Prim." Inch by inch, he worked himself deeper, owning what belonged to him. "Fucking right, your ass is mine," he growled, bottoming out so his tightened balls rested against my backside. "Mine. *Every* goddamn inch of your sweet body."

My dragon wept, tears sliding down my cheeks, and my beta's beast assured him they were ones of joy. Our bond radiated with overwhelming emotion, causing my heart to ache.

"How can I feel so much for you already?" he whispered, pulling out to the head and sinking back into my ass.

"We are fated," I managed to say before he fell over me to claim my mouth.

The overwhelming desire to love and be loved radiated between us in equal measure as he thrust in and out of me, the joy in finding a soul who understood, one who would follow the other to the ends of the earth and beyond.

"I need you to come on my dick, Prim." Jaxon groaned and snaked a hand between our sweaty bodies. "Before I blow my load and fill your ass." He rubbed two fingers along my clit, but I needed more.

"Harder. Deeper," I managed, raising my hips toward him.

Jaxon groaned again, his muscles bunching as he worked himself in and out of me.

"Yes." I moaned as he stabbed in again, giving me the slight pain I realized I needed. Without words, he fucked me harder—faster—taking me to the edge. One last violent plunge, a pinch to my clit, and I convulsed. "Jaxon!"

"Fuck." He thrust a few more times while I rode the high of my climax, his sexy groans, the growls deep in his chest, sending me barreling over again. "Goddamn." His cock pulsed, coating my insides with his release, and he squeezed me tight in his arms, shuddering as he emptied deep in my guts.

"What the fuck is this?" he murmured against my neck while trying to catch his breath. "Seriously. This is not... normal."

"Mmm." Smiling so broadly it hurt, I ran my hands down over the muscles rippling his back, the smooth skin heated and damp with sweat. "Dragonblood." I sighed the word, my smile fading a bit as confusion flickered through our tether.

"Dragonblood as in something more than human?"

"Yes."

Jaxon planked over me on shaky arms, his focus on my

face, tendrils of sweat-dampened dark hair sticking to his forehead. "You aren't shitting me."

I shook my head, even though he had to feel the truth—and hadn't asked a question.

"Holy fuck." He pulled out of my ass slowly, and I hissed my displeasure over the emptiness. "Gonna clean up—be right back," Jaxon promised, easing my mood.

I lay unmoving, my body relaxed, sated, every inch of me tingling in the aftereffects of our fucking.

Loving.

My smile returned, even though my beta was absent from my side, and I didn't argue with my inner dragon. What Jaxon and I had shared went far beyond the mere coming together of physical bodies and sexual release I'd read about. Our hearts and spirits had aligned more than I had expected outside of a real bond, one that required our alpha.

Pain arced through my chest, but Jaxon's reappearance in his bathroom doorway halted the hurt. Ripples of muscles covered his body, lean and defined from shoulders to calves, causing my mouth to flood with drool and my fingertips to itch with the need to touch. He had a beautiful dick and knew how to move to bring me pleasure.

His blue-green eyes twinkled as he drew near, grinning. "You think I'm sexy as fuck."

"Yes," I breathed my answer, my gaze on his flaccid length while wanting it to swell again.

"Give me a few, and you'll get your wish." Still grinning, he used a wet towel to clean between my thighs, wiping all traces of our cum from my skin. "You're not sore, are you?"

"Not a bit."

"*That's* not human either after the pounding I gave your little ass."

I snickered, my face warming. "My backside is far from little."

He flopped and sprawled on the bed beside me, eyes alight with mischief. "It's fucking perfection," he said, propping up on an elbow to lean over me, fingertips trailing over my breasts to rub my nipple.

I touched his smooth cheeks, caressed the square jaw that helped create his symmetrical face.

He pinched my bud gently before wrapping his arm around me and pulling me tight against his chest. "So are you going to drool over me until I fuck you again, or are you going to tell me what you are—what I am, because I sure as fuck know this is something out of a sci-fi or fantasy book."

I inhaled, filling my lungs, wondering where to begin, how to explain gently, tactfully, so he wouldn't think I was crazy, but I couldn't find the words.

"Blunt honesty will work best," he assured me, aware of my indecision.

A shuddering sigh rippled through my body at the continued proof of our bond. "Our ancestors were dragons."

He huffed a breath, but I sensed that his trust didn't waver.

"Real life, scaled and fire-breathing creatures." I continued with a bit of the history of beast and man interacting until they evolved into more than separate entities.

"Dragon shifters." He barked a laugh a few moments later when I paused, his beautiful smile causing my pussy to pulse with need. "Holy shit."

I smiled, staring at his expressive face that was sunshine on mine. "Born of ancient dragonblood."

"Holy shit," he murmured again, peering into my eyes. "And this strange vibe between us, this...lack of privacy in our minds?"

"Fated mates bond in such a way that we needn't speak a word."

"Fucking telepathy?"

"Something like that, yes," I said, rubbing a fingertip over his full lower lip as he squeezed me tight.

He nipped at my finger before kissing it. "I'd have to be fucking crazy to think you're telling the truth."

"But you do."

"Fuck." He heaved a sigh, his gaze seeing right into my soul. "I do," he confirmed, even though he experienced my belief.

His lack of hesitation or doubt in accepting what I had shared filled me with joy, and the tether between us radiated the same emotion back to me. I had found what I craved, and nothing would be able to tear my mind from his or the consuming need for his touch.

I rolled to my side to face him, our bodies pressed tight and tingling with growing arousal. I considered all I had, what fate had given us.

Alpha.

My dragon's whisper sent another pang through my heart.

Jaxon's brow furrowed, darkening his eyes. "What?"

An attempted smile twitched my lips but failed as I realized he could feel some of my thoughts, but not those of my inner beast. "It would seem my dragon can't yet communicate with you."

"Will it ever?" he asked, still frowning, soothing a hand down my back and pulling me tighter against him.

"Once we're properly bonded, yes."

"And how do we do that?"

I bit on the inside of my lip, the ache in my chest spreading.

The furrow in his brow deepened. "Tell me what the fuck is hurting you, sweetheart, 'cuz I can't fucking stand to feel your pain like this."

"Our alpha," I whispered, hating that tears hazed my vision and choked my voice.

"Alpha…" His brow eased as his mind worked over the word. "As in *our* mate."

"Yes."

"Is there something about dragonbloods you left out?"

"It takes three Blood Born to procreate," I whispered, my gaze dropping to his chin. "Three mates, fated by destiny, to be together until they rest with the stars."

Wonder replaced the hurt radiating through our tether. His inner dragon whispered in his head as the image of our alpha wavered in my mind.

"Patrick." He breathed the name.

"Doctor Macaire," I whispered, even though the stoic man didn't want anything to do with me.

CHAPTER 15

JAXON

The second Primrose had whispered the word *alpha,* a tingling woke inside me, a thirst deeper than she would ever be able to quench. I felt like a goddamn cheating bitch, unworthy of her perfection—

Primrose pressed her fingers against my lips even though I hadn't spoken the thought out loud. Seemed she could read my mind easier than I could hers. "Yes, I can, but only because it's my gift to hear the inner voices of Blood Born. And you're beyond worthy, so much more than I had hoped for in a beta."

Beta.

Yessss.

My inner *voice*—my goddamn *dragon* half—whispered then purred at having finally been recognized and named. Accepting that part of myself came as easy as his satisfaction since I'd been aware of his presence for as long as I could remember. He was my other inner half, and Prim...well, she was damned near perfect, but Patrick...

Want.

Yeah—I did. A whole fucking lot. I kissed Prim's fingertips, pulling her against me as guilt over burning for that sexy man crept into my head.

"It's not wrong to desire him." Prim's voice caught, and I frowned, studying her face.

Pain radiated from her, and my reaction was to feel like an asshole for being so greedy.

"*You've* done nothing wrong," she said, her emphasis assuring me.

"What did he do to you?"

"Turned me away," she whispered, tears once more coating her eyes. The ache in her heart mirrored mine. Or maybe our emotions fed off each other. Whatever it was, I hated that she hurt.

"We are meant to be one with him," I said, wishing the haze was gone from her golden gaze.

"Yes." Her pain-filled whisper tightened my chest like a vise.

"Then we'll go to him together. Tell him the truth—he'll listen."

"He won't." She shook her head, her eyes closing as though trying to escape the humiliation and pain his rejection had obviously caused. "His human side is strong, something I've never encountered before. It's like he's managed to cage the dragon within, smother its voice, its desires beneath his will."

I pressed my lips to her pouted mouth, wishing I could ease her emotional turmoil on my own while wanting to rip Doc a new asshole for hurting my woman. "Man's fucking crazy not to want you." I pulled back and smiled, hoping she could sense my determination to be content with her alone. "You're perfect, Prim. All woman, sexy as fuck, empathetic and caring—"

She snorted. "You don't even know me."

I pressed my palm against her chest and found her heart

beating in time with mine. "I can feel what's in here," I reminded her. "Not words, but a hint of your emotions. Wants." I studied her face, hoping she understood what I experienced through the energy linking us.

Her smile eventually returned, the sparkle in her light brown eyes making me so damn happy I wanted to leap off a cliff.

"Fuck." My brow furrowed again as memories flashed through my head at lightning speed. I huffed a laugh even while frowning and shaking my head. "Ever since I was a kid, I always thought I could fly."

"Really?"

"The voice in my head—I called him my beast—insisted I could take to the sky if only I allowed him the chance." I laughed again, my face relaxing. "That's why I ended up in Lockwood."

Her eyes widened. "Meaning you jumped off a building or something?"

"Twice."

Dragonblood—we do have wings.

A smirk curled my lips. I *knew* I wasn't crazy even though I'd told myself daily I wasn't right in the head.

Prim smoothed hair off my forehead. "He's spoken to you since childhood, and everyone thought you were mentally ill."

"Yep."

"I can show you how to shift—I think. We can fly the skies together."

"Holy fuck." I sat straight up, all trace of a smile gone from my lips as my pulse raced. "You're fucking with me."

"No." She clasped my hands, and the energy between us ebbed and strengthened, her emotions going from joyous to annoyance as she chewed on her lower lip, gaze latched on my eyes. "You can't hear my dragon, can you?"

I shook my head.

She exhaled a heavy sigh but perked up a second later, a gleam in her eyes I recognized.

I narrowed my gaze, even though the devil's glint in hers made my mischievous side giddy as fuck. "What are you thinking?"

A smile toyed with the corner of her lips as her focus roamed over me like she made a calculation in her pretty little head. "Where is the closest bridge?"

We lounged naked in my bed, sharing about our childhoods until full dark, when hardly a soul would be driving around to see us approach the one place high enough she thought she might be able to carry my weight. She'd never held something of my size and leapt from the ground into the sky.

But free-falling, where her wings would be unhindered in catching the air needed to soar us into the sky?

I told myself I *was* insane as we walked across the lone bridge in our town. Prim was decked out in my clothes that were slightly too large for her, feet swimming in a pair of my sneakers. She'd told me about her shift on Lockwood's front lawn earlier that morning that had left her naked, the reason for her showing up on my porch in nothing but her gorgeous, golden skin I couldn't keep my hands off.

Even though she and her perfect pussy enticed two more loads out of my balls and my dick still wasn't sated, worry ate at the back of my head.

Fly.

Yeah, my beast assured me we could, but would Prim's attempt to carry me end up with me floundering below in the river? Left a cripple from broken legs like I should have been when I'd done the same not that long ago?

She laughed lightly, shaking her head.

I'd forgotten already that she could hear my inner dragon even though I couldn't sense hers.

Strong.

"Indeed, I am," she murmured her agreement, eyeing the drop into the canyon below where we stood.

So goddamned beautiful—she made my entire body ache with unquenchable want.

"Let me guess," I said, my heart already in my throat. "You have X-ray vision."

"Hardly, but I can see in the dark and know your cock desires to be inside me again."

"Damn." Said cock bucked inside my jeans. "Not that I'm complaining over my sudden super-dick," I said with a laugh, "but why don't I have any of these special powers like you do?"

"Because you haven't shifted and become one with your inner dragon yet." She stripped down rather than shred my borrowed clothing while shifting, and I stared at her nakedness while she stuffed everything into a bag we'd brought along.

"You're gorgeous," I murmured, reaching out to run my fingertips down her neck and over the swell of her breast.

Her nipple hardened as shivers slid over her skin.

"So goddamned luscious." I dropped my hand to my bulge and squeezed as potent arousal coated the air around us, her sweet scent filling my nose. I worked my jaw, considering bending her over the guardrail—

"Come, my lover."

I groaned, head tipping back at Prim's command she hadn't meant in a sexual way, but my damned taint spasmed with need to obey. Grabbing hold of my base stifled my balls' attempt to make a mess in my jeans.

She laughed abruptly, lighting my soul on fire, and

climbed the barrier meant to keep people safe. She stood on the other side, one hand holding the railing, feet still planted firmly on concrete and steel.

The sight of her curves bathed in the moonlight made me itch to drag her back to safety and bury myself in her warmth.

"Jaxon—my beta." Her voice hinted at both admonition and arousal.

"Okay, okay." Flooding my lungs with oxygen, I released my hold on my junk and climbed over the rail to join her.

She wrapped an arm around my waist and leaned into me, brushing her lips over mine.

"The things you do to me, Prim," I whispered, shaking my head.

"Do you not like it?"

"You know I do," I growled, grabbing hold of her backside with a grip that would bruise a normal human, but I'd learned only lasted mere moments on hers. Fucking dragonblood.

"Trust me?" she asked, even though she was already aware of the answer to that question as well.

I offered her a verbal answer anyway. "Yes."

"Then let go, my beta, and we will fly."

My hold on the railing released, and we fell back into the air, a double shot of adrenaline crashing through my system. Breath caught, heart in my throat and unable to scream, I clenched my eyes shut as the ground rushed to meet us.

So much for my raging hard-on.

Death or Lockwood, here we come.

The energy linking Prim and me together rippled—muscles far beyond my Prim tightened around my waist—and a rush of flapping, like a thousand birds at once, shot us upward, leaving my heart in my toes.

I swallowed against rising bile as I forced my eyelids

open, gasping for oxygen as the wind abused my face. Shimmering gold scales covered the warm dragon leg I clutched at with a death grip. Dark talons, sharp as fuck, wrapped around my body in a gentle hold, keeping me from hurtling to my death to the earth far below.

"Goddamn!" I laughed, my heart throbbing inside my chest. "Fucking hell!"

I lifted my head to find the stars overhead blacked out—by a graceful neck. Every flap of Prim's wings took us higher beyond where I'd ever gone on foot. The lights of town twinkled far below, and overwhelming giddiness, fucking *delight*, had me whooping like a five-year-old on his first roller-coaster ride.

She banked, and I swallowed against the damn bile again.

Would I ever learn to shift and fly?

Did Patrick wonder about the same—did he even know what he was? Even more, would he ever accept what was destined for the three of us?

Forcing aside the sobering thoughts didn't come easily, but determination to enjoy my first flight, the talons of my fierce female dragon cradling me in safety, eventually lessened my unease.

Fate dictated a polyamorous relationship lay in my future, and even though I'd never been with a guy, the way Patrick turned me on assured me that I would enjoy whatever our physical relationship looked like.

I hoped he could be made to see the truth, or this sense of abandonment in my chest and the same emanating through the energy linking me to Prim would haunt us both until we rested with the stars like she'd promised we would one day do.

CHAPTER 16
PATRICK

With no clients demanding my presence at my office on Main Street this morning, I sat at my kitchen table, a second pot of coffee brewing. I'd been searching online for hours, scribbling down notes and crossing some out as other sources changed the way my mind sought to explain what I'd seen, felt, and *heard* from the golden goddess's hauntingly delicious mouth.

Dragonblood.

Even repeating the word in my head caused the darkness to swell inside me, pressing against the walls containing it.

Driven to find an answer beyond madness, which I refused to accept, I hardly got up from the chair the rest of the day. I ordered takeout so I wouldn't have to waste time cooking. I also ended up shutting off my cell, since Jessie texted and tried calling, begging me to answer, saying she had been wrong about the Dear John letter she'd left me.

I couldn't be bothered to care, and since she or her sister had retrieved Jessie's shit off my porch as I'd demanded, I finally blocked her number and all thoughts of her from my mind.

My search for the dragonblood nonsense the golden goddess had whispered didn't bring up any specifics, but digging deeper had taken me to an old blog, one no longer active, filled with Native American stories supposedly passed from generation to generation.

Were they a wannabe author obsessed with fantasy or a sincere old man trying to capture his past before their nation's lore faded into obscurity?

Whatever the truth, their words acted like a soothing balm to my unrest. A sense of rightness pushed me forward in finding the owner of the blog. I made a dozen calls, dug a little deeper, and finally reached the young woman responsible for uploading her grandfather's stories, where others could access them.

"He's been telling these tales to me since I can remember," she said a short time into our conversation, once I explained I was a doctor researching patients' inner voices.

"Do you know how much is based on fact?"

The young woman sighed. "I'm a dreamer, so I would love to tell you the stories of the dragons helping to see my ancestors through the bad winters are true. Imagine if they were?" She laughed lightly, and that sense of being on the right path took on more substance in my mind, even though she seemed to dismiss the supposed history of her people.

"There's never been any evidence of such beasts," I said, more for my own sanity than to refute her stories.

"No, but my grandfather told me when the dragons passed, their souls rose to reign in the stars, and that oval-shaped orbs covered in glowing scales remained behind as a reminder of what used to be."

I'd never heard of such an orb being found, no scientific proof of their existence.

"Is your grandfather available to speak with me?" I asked, thinking I might get more information from the source. "I would like to meet with him—sit and listen to those stories he's shared with you."

"I'm sure he would love that." Her voice betrayed her smile, and I found my heart rate kicking up, a peacefulness inside me like I'd traversed the proper path toward answers.

Only an hour away, she agreed to bring her grandfather to a coffee shop near the halfway point between us the next morning.

Lockwood expected me in the office tomorrow, but I left a message with the administrator's secretary, once more lying about not feeling well enough to come in.

While I didn't have any specific answers or the truth I sought, I at least had something to go on besides the darkness and its quietness over my searching for answers. The need to make sense of what I had experienced, of the puzzle the strange, beautiful woman had spread out in my mind, sat like fuel, ready to propel me forward in discovering the truth.

The old man's gray hair hung down his back in a long braid, his skin tanned and wrinkled from the sun, dark eyes and cheekbones evidence of his heritage. His granddaughter beside him had her ebony hair in a blunt, shoulder-length cut, a hint of hazel in her smiling eyes, her complexion a warm butternut.

"So, Dave." I pushed my half-eaten plate of waffles to the side and leaned onto the table, my stomach churning. "Your granddaughter's blog was very informative, but I would love to know more about your people's history with the dragons."

We had already briefly discussed what I'd read and how Dave's own grandfather had passed on the stories to him when he'd been a teenager. The tales, from what he'd said, went back to the first of his ancestors when mankind didn't yet rule the earth.

"The dragons owned the skies. Three families, three royal lines, all pure Blood Born." Dave, too, pushed his plate aside and wrapped his gnarled hands around the tan coffee mug our waitress had refilled. "They never bothered with man, and it has been joked in more recent generations that we were too tough to chew. They preferred the buffalo of the plains, the elk from the north."

"Your granddaughter blogged about how they had provided for your people in harsh winters."

"It was said they often did, and in return, mankind respected their need for privacy and the same right to live as all the beasts of this earth."

"Were you ever told how they communicated with mankind?"

Brow furrowed, he peered over my shoulder, his eyes hazing over as though searching his memory. "My ancestors could hear the dragon's voices in their minds—words of another language and yet understandable to my fathers' spirits."

I chewed on his explanation for a few seconds, hating that his words sounded right, *felt* right. The darkness in the void of my soul stirred, pressing against its prison with a strange gentleness, but I resisted its silent insistence to be set free.

A thought snaked its way into my mind, creating a tendril of fear to shiver down my spine. "Your fathers' spirits communicated with those of a dragon."

Dave nodded slowly, his dark gaze latching onto mine and holding steady. "It was said the first two dragons to become something *more* than mere animals claimed a female human, and they bore children together."

Beasts mating with humans…

"Your face has paled, Doctor Macaire."

I swallowed and cleared my throat, my body tensed tight, the hairs on my neck stirring as I fought to hold the darkness at bay. "Do you happen to know what the new species was called?"

"Those born by blood—of dragon and man were named dragonblood."

I clenched my eyes shut, willing the madness inside me to remain silent.

"My grandfather was the last to believe these beings still walked the earth."

I forced myself to meet Dave's steady stare, needing so much more than what he had offered me.

"I've never met such a person or beast, if the stories of them are true," he continued, his tone low, "but I have seen my share of people who hear voices."

"As have I," I murmured as hissing whispered around the edges of the prison in my chest. Adrenaline leaked into my blood, causing my heart rate to increase. Heat slid through my veins as my insides burned.

For more truth or to break free?

"Maybe it isn't insanity that troubles so many." His granddaughter spoke for the first time since we'd first sat down and introductions had been made.

I gave her my full focus, a sense of peaceful reassurance seeming to reach over the table and soothe me. I'd studied psychology and the human mind, known facts learned through science—but a part of me longed for the young woman's words to be true.

"Perhaps there is more to this world than is seen," she continued, staring into my eyes as though trying to root out the darkness inside me. "If they are real, it is for the beasts' safety that the dragonblood hide from humanity."

Or maybe their human halves fought for dominance out of their own fears of being seen as mentally unstable.

Unacceptable and unlovable to most.

My feet itched to move, my accelerated heartbeat needing to exercise the rush pumping through my blood as my greatest concerns flooded my brain. "I can't thank you both enough for meeting with me and sharing your family's history and stories."

Dave shook my offered hand. "I hope you find the answers you seek, Doctor Macaire."

I felt sure I *had* found them—and the possibility they went against all I had studied scared the shit out of me.

CHAPTER 17

PRIMROSE

I stared as Jaxon licked caramel sauce off a plastic spoon, every flick and stroke of his tongue lapping at the sweetness, reminding me of where his mouth had been an hour earlier, before we finally crawled from his bed.

A warm breeze scented by nearby flowering fauna drifted over us and the picnic table we sat at, but all I could think about was the heat growing between my thighs.

"Prim."

I jerked my focus upward to find his eyes shining with mirth—and lust.

"Eat your ice cream," he murmured, the twinkle in his eyes weakening my knees. It was a good thing I sat.

Focusing on the cold treat I'd never enjoyed before proved difficult. Even though the rich chocolate flavor pleased my taste buds, I couldn't keep from thinking about my beta, his touch, and the slickness of his tongue stroking along mine.

The small mound of ice cream atop my cone melted and dripped down my fingers, but I couldn't be bothered to lick the coolness from my skin.

"You have mapped out every inch of my body and claimed me countless times over the previous two days, and I have yet to taste you," I stated without tact since no one sat nearby.

He groaned and shifted on the wooden bench beneath him. "You can't talk about shit like that when we're in public, Prim. Jesus." He pressed against his groin discreetly beneath the table, and heat settled between my thighs as his desire reached through the tether between us.

"I will think of that and having your cock inside me again with an insatiable lust until we are finally bonded," I stated, ensnared by his bowed upper lip and the smear of caramel sauce he cleaned off with a flick of his tongue.

"We can't bond without Patrick."

My throat tightened, and I closed my eyes at his reminder, my chest caving in. Since taking to the sky with my beta, I'd been focused on the high of what I *had* found— rather than what was still missing. Jaxon's easy acceptance of the truth and his constant giving of himself to me couldn't fill the empty part of my soul that required an alpha's presence.

"I know your body desires him as much as mine, Jaxon, but he doesn't want me," I whispered, memory of Patrick denying the gift of my body and heart hurting almost as much as it had in the moment it happened. "He isn't interested in the consuming needs of his dragon. He is a doctor and won't be swayed into giving up control to what he believes is insanity."

"He *will*."

"Our shared kiss, the feel of my body in his arms—it wasn't enough." Tears clogged my throat, and I fought to keep the wetness welling in my eyes from coursing down my cheeks.

Jaxon reached over and grasped my free hand tightly in his own.

"He's a doctor trained to help people with mental issues, to 'right' those who hear voices in their heads," I continued. "He offered his services to me, but only in the way he thinks will ease my supposed madness."

"We'll knock him out, tie him up." Jaxon trusted his human side's abilities, leaning forward, his voice lowered and gaze piercing with its hint of mischief. "We'll show him what he's missing out on by denying what he is."

His insistence we use lust to prove a point didn't surprise me in the least, considering how much I'd gotten to know my beta in the last two days and how free he was with verbalizing his thoughts, especially when it came to mating.

"I won't force a bonding he has no wish for," I stated just as firmly as Jaxon had his suggestion.

He sat back, a slight furrow marring his brow. He glanced around the park, and I wondered at the slyness of his brain as his forehead smoothed out, the sparkle of ill intent once more filling his eyes as he turned his focus on me.

His desire flooded through me, causing my core to burn with need.

"I dream about him tying me up." Jaxon kept his voice low even though no one stood nearby. "Flogging me. Whipping me."

My pussy tingled, and I pressed my thighs together.

"I want him to mark me with a belt—a cane," he continued, "shove his dick so far up my virgin ass that I lose my breath." Lust darkened his eyes as his rumbled tone slid over my skin, causing it to pebble. "I want you to watch, Prim. For you to touch yourself, slide your fingers into your soaked pussy as our alpha claims me, drenching your fingers with cum as all three of us cry out our release—together as one body, one heart."

My muscles jumped beneath my skin, causing a deep restlessness in my bones.

"Don't do this, Jaxon," I begged, even though arousal overrode the pain of our alpha's rejection.

He tickled the back of my hand with his thumb with teasing strokes. "You're going to ride my dick when he takes your ass—both of us stuffing you full, shooting our cum deep inside your body where it belongs."

Yessss.

I clenched my eyes shut as my pussy pulsed with the need to be filled like he'd said. Ravaged until I had nothing left to give my mates.

"I want him fucking me while I'm balls deep in your sweet pussy," he continued. "I need to be the bridge between my alpha and female." We both groaned at the thought of finally bonding in the way I had explained to him last night. "I fucking *lust* for it so goddamn bad my body aches."

Jaxon hoped to heal my hurt with desire, to wash away doubt by creating erotic images in my brain that my dragon also longed for.

"I won't be manipulated," I said, stress leaking into my tone.

"Prim—"

"No." I shook my head, pain in the back of my throat making words difficult. "Our ancestors did this in the past." Swallowing, I met his gaze, holding steady, even though I longed for our alpha just as much as he did. "A forced or coerced mating means all three will suffer the emotions of the one wronged. Bitterness will overshadow any physical release among them. Such a bond would never be enjoyable or fulfilling, how we both desire."

In the way I had dreamed of my entire life.

Jaxon held my gaze, his jaw set.

"No matter how much my soul aches to be one with both

of you, Patrick must accept what he is in order to fulfill our destiny in a way that will please all three of us." The truth of my powerlessness flooded through me, causing my unease to intensify. My body vibrated with the need to do something other than sit and wallow in misery. I got to my feet and stepped away from the bench, ice cream cone falling from my hand to splat on the ground.

Cast aside.

Unwanted.

Exactly as I'd been by my alpha.

"All my life, I expected to be alone—feared it, even," I choked out. "Dreaded rejection from mankind, from any dragonblood I happened to hear whisper from another's mind. While you've accepted me, our alpha did not. He does not want me!" Tears coursed down my cheeks as the pain grew too much to bear. "I am not enough."

I shimmered from sight and gave my dragon her wings, leaving behind fluttering pieces of my ripped clothing.

"Prim!" Jaxon's wail faded as I shot into the sky, needing to escape not just my own pain but his as well.

CHAPTER 18
JAXON

The one thing I feared the most had come to fruition. She left me. Fucking *left* me. Abandoned me as though I'd been nothing more than a dick to ride.

"Goddamnit!" I swept my sundae off the table and slammed my fist onto the wooden plank before me. Pain radiated up through my wrist, but I smashed my hand down again, needing something to focus on other than the fact that the energy linking us dissipated with every breath, every aching heartbeat.

All traces of her in my mind faded, leaving me empty and cold.

Our female is gone.

As if I didn't *fucking* know that!

I hopped up and stormed off, fists clenched, my chest aching so goddamn badly I couldn't think straight as my dragon whimpered and raged over what I had attempted to do. She'd fucking ripped me apart by taking off, though, broken me in a way no person had done before, parents included.

Pain hazed my sight, my mind, and I found myself stumbling along aimlessly. A rumble of thunder sounded, and I lifted my head, hoping for a glimpse of golden scales. A droplet of rain landed on my cheek, and I closed my eyes as another splattered on my forehead.

Did she weep overhead, her tears falling from the sky to wash away my grief?

As though those heavens opened, rain poured down with a rare vengeance for this area, soaking me before I walked another block. I stumbled up the stairs to my apartment, palm pressed against my chest to keep from sobbing.

I didn't cry. Wouldn't fucking do it. My parents hadn't made me lose my shit in over eight years, and I wasn't about to let a mere woman I hardly knew claim a single tear. Even if she was my destiny, my fated mate, one of the two whom I belonged to.

The second the door clicked shut behind me, I sank to my knees, head in my hands, while rocking myself. The sweet scent of her lingered in the air, teasing my nose and body. My dick swelled with need, even though pain continued to lance through my chest. as though a piece of my heart had been cut away with a dull knife.

She'd ripped herself away from me, obliterating that strange energy linking us and leaving me more alone than I'd ever felt before.

"All your fault, you fucking asshole," I muttered, focusing on anger to keep me centered—to keep from crying. "Can't stop thinking about *him,* just had to bring him up and be all manipulative as usual. Fuck."

I sat on my haunches, head tipped back and eyes closed, trying to breathe through the pain.

Go to him.

I huffed a snort. "Yeah, right."

Go to our alpha.

I stopped fighting every goddamn emotion rolling in my

head and sat, listening to the voice inside me beg for what we wanted. Prim had jetted in her drive to escape the pain, causing agony to twist my stomach. And Patrick was to blame. Fucking stoic asshole was educated and probably stuck on science, refusing to believe the supernatural truth Prim had shared with him.

Well, I wouldn't be so easily dismissed. That man had hurt my female—

Gone.

"Fucking A!" I choked on a sob, gritting my teeth to will the tears from falling.

It took me fifteen minutes to find his card I'd shoved into a pair of jeans at the bottom of my dirty laundry pile. He'd jotted down his cell, but confronting him required I see him in the flesh, where he would be less apt to push me away.

I hoped, anyway.

According to his card, he lived on the opposite side of town from Lockwood.

The last thing I wanted was to be around a bunch of people, so I called an Uber rather than hop on a bus. Privacy would cost me a pretty penny in funds, but I didn't give a shit.

Silence settled over the car's interior as I stared at the rain still slashing at the earth like a scythe, sideways and danger-ous. Wind rocked the vehicle enough the driver cursed beneath his breath as he drove us northward, but I clamped my lips shut since I had ten times more shit to swear over than he could ever imagine.

The absence of Prim's energy in my chest continued to haunt me, and no matter how driven I was to face Patrick and light into him for causing my suffering, my mind wouldn't shut up.

What if he was married? What if a live-in girlfriend answered the door? What if he was celibate like a priest, determined to go without dick or pussy through what was left of his years?

Primrose had told me she would age slower due to the percentage of dragonblood pumping through her heart, but that the cum of our alpha would be needed to prolong my life to match her years—and mine, his. Just the idea of my dominant alpha submitting to *me*, dropping to his knees to swallow every white spurt I shot down his throat, tightened me to the point of pain.

And the thought of sucking *his* dick?

I shifted on the backseat, my mouth flooding with drool even while my eyes continued to burn.

The rain fell but with less intensity when the Uber driver finally entered town limits and pulled up in front of a smaller house with a covered porch. I paid in cash, muttered my thanks, and climbed out, my shirt and hair once more getting soaked from the rain. Muscles quivering and eyeing Patrick's front door, I approached by way of the cobbled pathway leading to the stairs.

Energy radiated from the left, licking over my skin and siphoning the air from my lungs.

I pulled up abruptly and turned my focus toward the left where Patrick sat on a wicker chair beneath the porch's roof, his gaze drinking me in.

Anger simmered in my guts, keeping them clenched, but desire flared bright, causing my pulse to race.

Ours—want.

Insides jittery, I strode closer and climbed the stairs, getting out of the rain. My heart thundered, causing my ears to ring. My dick throbbed—jutted against my jeans, leading me to the stoic alpha who lounged as though unaffected by my proximity.

"Jaxon." His voice slid over my skin like a silken caress, making goose bumps pebble my skin.

A muscle ticked in my jaw as droplets of water fell from my hair and chin, the war inside me one I didn't know how to resolve.

Patrick glanced down over my wet form without a hint of emotion on his face and stood. "Come on in."

He moved past me toward the front door with sure steps, and the scent of his cologne with a hint of brimstone swarmed my senses. The same draw between Prim and me acted like a magnet to my cells, making every inch of my body tingle with need for this stubborn man.

Hands fisted to keep from touching the asshole alpha who had denied both me and the woman I feared I would never see again, I stepped behind him into the entryway, taking a quick glance around as he shut the door behind us. Stairs on my left led to the second floor, and the living room lay on the right, gently illuminated by a lamp atop a small table just inside the entry.

"Stay here," Patrick ordered, climbing the stairs and giving me an eyeful of his flexing ass beneath thin sweats that hung low on his hips. "I'll grab you a towel."

I fisted my hands and locked my knees to keep from crawling after him. Drool flooded my mouth, and I swallowed harshly, attempting to smash down my desire. Closing my eyes rid me of the sight of him, but his alluring scent clung to the insides of my nostrils.

Want.

"No shit, Sherlock," I muttered, but I was pissed enough over what he'd done to Prim—and in return, me—that lust took a back seat.

A towel hit me in the face as Patrick's footfalls squeaked the treads of the stairs on his way back downstairs. "Dry yourself off."

I mopped my face and hair before rubbing at my shoulders and arms, my dick jolting at the cloying scent of the towel's owner embedded in its fabric.

Alpha.

Patrick's whiskers twitched as though he clenched his jaw —out of need to fuck me, the dripping of water on his pristine wooden floor, or annoyance I'd shown up at all, I couldn't tell—and he moved into the living room. I followed like a lost puppy when I wanted to pounce on his back, smash a fist into his temple, and knock some goddamned sense into him before impaling myself on his dick and riding him until we both shot like geysers.

"What's on your mind, Jaxon?" he asked while settling onto a recliner, left ankle propped onto the opposite knee, hands relaxed on the chair's arms. He didn't wear his glasses or that damned, sexy checkered vest, but the professional aura clung to him like a second skin.

Doc Macaire sat before me, in control and stolid as fuck.

Not Patrick or the alpha I desperately needed to pin me down and fuck me senseless so I could forget about Prim.

I stepped closer to him, enough he had to tip his head a bit to keep his gaze on my face. Still, he appeared unfazed. "A lot, actually." My focus slipped to his groin and the undeniable bulge begging for release.

I would manipulate the fuck out of him. Hurt his heart like he'd done to Prim's, and thus, mine.

He would pay for being a selfish asshole interested only in looking out for himself rather than the two fate had gifted to him.

I took the final step to close the distance between us.

Clothing separated his shin from my thighs, but the heat of him zapped through cloth, searing me clear to the bone.

He hissed but didn't move, the echo of not one but *two* inner beasts ringing in my ears.

Yessss.

Baring my teeth with a grin, I cupped my aching dick to keep from nutting way too damned early.

He swallowed hard and glanced away, the first evidence of unease I'd seen from him. "You're a patient of mine—we can't do this."

"*Was.*" I corrected him with a snip to my tone. "And yes, we fucking can." I glared down at him, waiting for his next excuse to deny the potent chemistry and draw between us.

His lips pressed into a thin line.

"The court let me out of Lockwood, so you can't send me back. That means I can tell you anything, right, Doc?" I lowered my tone, forcing some of my anger from my voice, while once more fisting my hands at my sides.

Eyes closed and lips in a thin line, he jerked his head in a nod.

"I met this girl, a woman so damn beautiful, so…golden. She's like a goddess, one I've dreamed about since I realized my dick got hard for a reason."

His gaze flitted toward my face, dark blue eyes pinned to mine and boring into me, demanding I give him more—everything I had.

If only.

Knowledge was what he lusted for, regardless of the want making his cock stir with interest.

"She opened my mind to a shit ton of truth I wouldn't have believed if not for the beast I've heard whispering in my head since I was a kid."

Patrick's knuckles whitened as he gripped the chair's armrests, the only tell I had hit a nerve. "Tell me," he demanded.

So, I obeyed—from that first night I'd felt her presence while in my old Lockwood room to that morning's fuck fest where I'd shown her how to ride my dick cowboy style before we'd lazed in bed for hours and finally dragged our asses out for some ice cream.

Patrick's unwavering gaze held me in place when my muscles jumped, my feet itched to move and ease the restlessness beneath my skin.

I shared what Primrose had told me about her ancestors —*our* ancestors—and the bond that is created when three destined mates become one. How all three would be driven to finish the process upon meeting one another—regardless of their hesitation.

Then, I told him about the rest of my afternoon. The discussion of our alpha and his stubbornness, his refusal to see beyond the strict reality he'd based his life around. How she'd shimmered from existence, the blast of wind clenching my eyes shut, evidence she had shifted to her true form and left me all alone.

"Because of you—Patrick *fucking* Macaire, our immovable alpha who has no clue what he's denying us."

Silence settled, my chest aching and forehead dented when he didn't offer an opinion or question the life-altering truth bomb I'd tossed on his lap. Energy continued to ripple between us, that damned tether of fated mates I'd explained to him.

Yessss.

"You *must* sense it," I insisted just as stubbornly as him, refusing to back down in swaying my alpha's mind toward the truth.

"What?" Patrick asked, his face deadpan even though a hint of insecurity flickered in his intense gaze.

Time to put the moves on. Seduce this fucker and bring out his darker side.

"The connection between us." I slid a fingertip along the thin sweats covering his propped-up leg that pressed against the front of my thighs.

Patrick's breath caught, and he stilled as though I was a viper curling up to strike.

"Tell me this doesn't feel right," I whispered, my heart thundering, voice shaking as my touch traveled to the bare skin at the cuff of his pants. "I know it does—I can hear your inner dragon purring."

At least, I thought I could.

A frown flitted over his dark brow as he gripped the chair tighter rather than stop my wandering fingertip. "My what?"

Lower lip between my teeth, I grasped his bare ankle. Electrical currents ripped through me at the contact, and I sighed, closing my eyes as the anger faded, giving way to pure lust. "Your *dragon*, Doc. My alpha. Need to put my mouth on you. Taste your spunk in the back of my throat. Feel the stinging stretch of your dick shoved up my ass, claiming me as your own."

"Jaxon…"

His condescending tone fucking said it all, but I wouldn't release my hold on his ankle. Couldn't back away and rip us apart.

He emitted a heavy sigh and stood brusquely, forcing me to stumble backward a few steps. "I want you to stay here tonight."

My shoulders slumped, throat tightening. "You believe I'm insane—that I made all this shit up and ought to be locked up again so I don't go leaping off a cliff because I think I can fly. Fucking good-for-nothing *coward*," I muttered, glaring, my entire body vibrating with the need to throw a few punches before hate-fucking the shit out of this man.

His gaze darkened, and I found myself shuffling backward as he prowled forward, my breath leaving in a rush as my body met the wall. The hairs on my arms stood, but he withheld from touching me, his lips thinned, brow furrowed as he peered into my eyes, the black overrunning the dark blue surrounding it.

"What do you truly want from me, Jaxon?" he asked, his tone on the verge of madness—exactly how I lusted for him to be. His eyes finally revealed a slew of emotion, but I couldn't begin to dissect a goddamned thing due to the jacked libido racing through my heated blood. "For me to give in to weakness like *he* did? You want me locked behind bars, too?"

Patrick grasped my neck in a firm grip, and I melted in his hold, whimpering at the rightness of the exchange between us, too lust-riddled to wonder who the fuck he was talking about. "Is *this* what you desire?" he growled, squeezing. "My dominance? My claiming of the beta you believe you are?"

"Fuck, yes." I slid my hand along the hard length tenting his sweats. "Need this down my throat just as much as you want to give it to me."

CHAPTER 19

PATRICK

Jaxon handled my throbbing cock with assured strokes that felt too damned good, and I stared at his parted lips, my breaths rushing out in perfect sync with his.

I stood on the edge of absolute ruin, my insides feverish, clothing restrictive as fuck. "You're a kid, for fuck's sake, a threat to everything I've built in my professional life." My voice sounded strangled to my ears, the words forced out in opposition to the darkness inside my chest shrieking for release.

"I'm legal," he argued, tightening his grip on my shaft to this side of painful.

"Too young to know what the fuck you want," I said through gritted teeth, the skin of his neck searing my palm.

"I know I want *you*." Jaxon swallowed, his Adam's apple bobbing beneath my hand, his pupils like a shot of pure lust to my groin. And the energy simmering, the flames rising between us…shit, I needed to fuck.

His tight, young body, all lean muscle, called out to me on a visceral level, tugging, enticing me closer. To just forget about reality and partake in the danger he promised to be.

The story he'd told hit me deeply, settling into a form of truth I didn't want to acknowledge, as though he'd sat with David and listened to the old man's tales as long as I had.

Telling myself I was too old for make-believe shit didn't lessen the rightness I experienced in holding Jaxon captive like this. I'd been just as drawn to Primrose as he was—everything about her turned me on with the same fierce need Jaxon did.

And here he was, shaking and smelling like a goddamned snack, his lust as potent in my nose as the chemistry lighting my insides on fire.

"Please," he whispered as though knowing I neared the edge of no return.

Take.

Fucking voice in my head—I closed the distance as though I was a puppet on a string, trapping Jaxon against the wall with my body. We touched from chest to thigh, his hand between our groins.

Jaxon squeezed my dick, and I groaned, my balls pulling up against my body. "Need to taste you—please."

Voice lost to consuming desire, I couldn't say no—couldn't find the goddamn word to stop him as he slid to his knees.

I loomed over him, a sense of power rushing through me, obliterating the goddamn wall I'd thought strong as he fumbled to pull my aching shaft from my sweats.

He gulped. "Commando. Fucking hot." At the first brush of his fingers against my leaking tip, the darkness inside me roared, overshadowing my humanity's better sense. My hands tangled in the damp, mussed hair atop Jaxon's head, and I pulled him close before he freed me completely.

I groaned as he closed his lips around me.

Hot. Wet. Yessss.

A low growl, unearthly yet familiar, rolled from my lips as Jaxon took me as deep as he could before gagging.

"Fuck. So good. Just like that." I pulled back and thrust in, needing to hear that toe-curling noise again.

An explosion brewed in my balls as I fucked his mouth, going farther with every slow glide over his tongue until his throat convulsed around the thick head.

"Yes—*fuuuuck*, you're taking me so good."

Pleasure coursed through my body, owning my heart and head.

Nothing but Jaxon, his tongue, and the cavern of his hot mouth existed.

Wet blue-green eyes peered up at me, raw and needy as they had in my dreams every goddamned night since first laying eyes on him.

"You want my cum?"

"Mmm," he moaned around my length, hands grasping at my thighs as though he couldn't decide if he should pull me closer or push away.

"Need me to fill up your belly with my seed?" I asked, gagging him with every forward jolt of my hips.

He whimpered, slobber dripping off his chin, eyes feral.

"Relax," I heard myself coo, easing my hold on his hair and caressing his hollowed cheeks with my thumbs. "Relax your throat, so I can fuck it deeper. Swallow around my shaft, and I'll give you what you hunger for."

Whatever instinctive fight had him tensed, drained at my command.

My chest swelled, and I hissed while slowly sinking in until his nose pressed against my groin.

"Jesus—fucking hell, your mouth is perfect."

Give.

My balls erupted, and I held Jaxon tight against me as spurt after spurt of my cum shot into his throat.

Jaxon swallowed, clenching against my pulsing dick, pulling more from my balls than humanly possible.

Heat rushed through me, burning like lava, seeming to sear away my skin. I gasped for breath, muscles bunching, twitching with otherworldly pulses ripping seed from my sac. Head tipped toward the ceiling, groaning, I gave him every drop, body convulsing long after I finished feeding him.

"Goddamn," I muttered, blinking my eyelids open as Jaxon fell back to rest against the wall, gasping for breath as harshly as I did. A wet spot covered the front of his jeans.

Satisfaction and a sense of completeness rolled over me, and I caressed his swollen lips while he peered up at me like a bright-eyed child who'd just tasted their first lollipop—

An audible intake of breath rushed oxygen to my lungs as I thought of the man I had hero-worshiped for many years.

My gut tightened.

"Fuck." I stumbled backward. Face hot and body trembling, I stared at the boy who was much too young for me, slumped on his knees, his face a mess of saliva and cum.

Wrecked.

Beautiful.

Mine.

I shoved my dick and balls in my sweats and turned away, shaking my head and fighting the voice slithering atop the walls Jaxon had brought tumbling to the ground. Teeth clenched, hands fisted at my sides, I closed my eyes and visualized rebuilding the fortress that had kept me safe.

Sane.

I was in control.

I am *in control,* I told myself on repeat.

The groan inside me grew to a roar as I fought against it, but it evaporated as the final block of the prison slammed into place, shutting whatever it was off entirely. Clutching my chest, I bent forward, desperate for oxygen against the knife-stabbing agony behind my breastbone.

"Doc."

I didn't turn. Couldn't. "I'm sorry, Jaxon, but you can't stay here tonight—you need to leave," I rasped, my tone nothing but pain and desperation. "Now." Without a backward glance, I staggered out of the living room and up the stairs, desperate to escape the energy attempting to lure me into weakness.

The connection between me and that boy remained, potent and tempting as hell.

My feet itched to run back downstairs, claim Jaxon's mouth—and the rest of his body as my own as the voice had suggested. Doctor Sorino had given in to his lust and paid the price, and it would be best to remember the outcome of his bowing to temptation.

"I am in control," I whispered what I needed to be true, leaning against my closed bedroom door, ears straining for the sounds of Jaxon letting himself out, giving me the distance I needed.

The door slammed shut seconds later.

Sagging onto the floor, head in hands, I warred with myself over being pleased he'd obeyed and pissed he hadn't fought to stay. The tether of whatever the fuck it was linking us together slowly faded, leaving behind an ache in my soul I didn't understand—and hated.

What had gone down between me and Jaxon wasn't a simple interaction between two horny men wanting relief for their aching balls. He'd weaseled into my head, into my goddamned blood.

Dragonblood.

"Jesus fucking Christ." I rubbed a hand over my face and stood, my thoughts an absolute mess.

At least the voice enclosed in my soul's void lay quiet,

properly closed off where it couldn't mess with my sanity and land me behind lock and key in either a psych ward or a prison.

Inner beast or not, this shit wasn't normal.

And the supernatural was nothing but myth and fairy tales for those who couldn't handle the pain of living in reality.

I'd risen above that years ago, and nothing—*no one*—would threaten my soundness of mind that focused on science, proven truths, and impeccable morals.

CHAPTER 20

PRIMROSE

I had hoped the agony in my chest would lessen with every mile speeding past beneath me faster than any commercial jet, but tears continued to spill from my eyes, whipped away by the wind as I shot northward in dragon form. Inept and untried with the opposite sex, I had no idea how to deal with relationships, how to traverse through the truth of Jaxon's words, his desires, and the pain we shared.

What should have bonded us closer only managed to intensify the pain of my alpha's rejection, making me want to flee as far from the hurt as possible.

Within a matter of hours, I could make out the jutting Tetons in the distance. Home for most of my life, the largest of the snow-capped mountains welcomed me, beckoned me closer as though wanting to offer comfort. I landed on the veranda of the cavern-like house my ancestors had carved with molten fire, the sinking sun leaving me in cold shadow on the mountain's eastern side.

Once shifted to my human form, a whisper of my fingers over the old, oaken door pushed it inward without sound. I stepped into the warm interior, the door swishing closed on its own behind me as my grandpapa, his alpha, and his female's scents swarmed my nose.

Chicken and…dog, I realized, breathing in.

"Tiggy!" I called as toenails clicking on stone hurried my way. I knelt to hug the bundle of fur that had kept me company until Grandpapa's return.

"She still hasn't learned to knock," a low voice said while chuckling—Vanni.

"Primrose?" Grandpapa lounged on a new couch to my left, his bare back resting against the equally unclothed chest of his alpha, who continued to smirk at me and my lack of manners he'd made note of when we'd first met.

Ashley, their female, lay sprawled over Grandpapa's front, naked as the day she'd been born, cum smeared between her thighs.

"Oh!" I averted my gaze, heat flooding my face, as I realized that I, too, didn't wear a stitch of clothing.

Announcing myself prior to entering would have been best.

Requesting clothes from them before entering, even better.

A low woof sounded, toenails clicking on stone.

"I'm sorry." I quickly stood and hurried across the open expanse of the main living area toward the hallway in front of me, taking the rough-hewn rock stairs two at a time, my dragon sight allowing me to see in the pitch black.

I had plenty of clothing and underthings in my dresser from when I'd left months earlier, and quickly pulled on an old frock that would hide what belonged to Jaxon. A sob caught in my throat as my fingers shook while attempting to button my nakedness away.

"Primrose?" Grandpapa stood in my bedroom's doorway, jeans now hiding his lower half. Although four hundred some years of age, Dolyn Kemmerly, my full-blooded drag-onblood grandfather, still appeared to be in his twenties, with the golden-brown eyes I'd inherited. "What's going on?"

A sob released from my heaving chest, and we moved toward each other at the same time. I sank into his strong arms, so brokenhearted that I didn't recoil from the scents of his mates' cum lingering on his skin. I could imagine he smelled the same on me—Jaxon's luscious evidence of loving me.

I cried harder, clinging to the only family I had left. Grandpapa's inner dragon made soothing noises in an attempt to ease my suffering. A long few minutes passed before I could catch my breath and quieted, Grandpapa's steady heartbeat beneath my ear comforting to my human half and inner beast who'd been quiet in her agony from having been ripped from our beta.

"You found one of your mates."

The pain in my chest pierced with the fierceness of a pissed-off dragon, but I stepped from Grandpapa's hold, trying to swallow the scratchiness from my throat.

"I—I thought this would be *easy*. My beta accepted me with open arms and mind, but our alpha..." My voice caught again, and I wiped my wet eyes on my sleeve, determined to be strong in the face of absolute misery. "He d-didn't want m-me."

Grandpop's brow furrowed, a murderous glint in golden glare. "You spoke with him—and he *denied* you?"

"I k-kissed him, even, but his human side is *strong*, Grand-papa. I've never come across a dragonblood who had the ability to lock their inner voice behind a stone fortress inside their soul."

"Did his dragon communicate with yours?"

"I heard it whispering to him—assuring I belonged to him, encouraging him to take me."

Grandpop's brow rose. "And he claimed not to desire you?"

I nodded, my shoulders drooping as I stared at my hands. "It was like Patrick slammed a lid atop his dragon, shutting him out. Sealing him off."

"I've never read of a human capable of controlling his inner dragon like that."

"No books in the library speak of such a gift," I said as a shiver—a *chill*—raced down my spine for the first time in my life.

"Come." Grandpapa reached for my hand. "Perhaps Vanni and Ashley can offer some insight on how you might sway your alpha into your arms."

I hated that word as much as I did manipulate, but I grew desperate to see my dreams come to fruition, the fulfillment I craved.

Both of Grandpapa's mates had covered their nakedness when we returned to the living space below, but Vanni continued to smirk, his bright green eyes alight with laughter. Ashley took one look at my face and hopped up to hug me tight, murmuring apologies for something she hadn't even caused, while Tiggy circled around us.

I hadn't been held by a woman since before Grandmother had passed, and I fought off another round of tears as Ashley smoothed her hand up and down my back. "What happened, Primrose?" she asked, stepping away to meet my gaze with empathy while holding my upper arms.

"It's a long story, but you need to listen so you can offer some advice," I stated abruptly, my fingers finding the top of Tiggy's head for a quick scratch.

"Still haven't learned any tact, either," Vanni said, smirking.

Ashley shot him a glare before turning toward me. "Come sit. Tell us everything." She settled between her mates, and the purr of all three inner dragons revealed what I had wondered.

Grandpapa and his two mates had bonded.

Jealousy curdled what was left of the ice cream still in my stomach.

I sat across from them in a single chair facing them, wishing desperately for the same as Tiggy settled against my bare feet, his tongue giving a quick wet kiss to my ankle. "Have you shifted?" I asked, my gaze flitting from Vanni to Ashley. "Flown?"

"Oh, we've taken to the skies, all right," Vanni said with a grin, stretching his arms along the back of the couch. "Strapped to Dolyn's body, experiencing the rush of wind, that euphoric feeling of soaring to the heavens."

Sexual tension sprang to life among the three of them, and I grimaced. "I don't want to know."

Vanni chuckled, Ashley's face flushed, and Grandpapa glanced at his alpha. "Vanni shifted long before our female—"

"Because I'm a direct descendant of the royal line," Vanni interrupted, pride lacing his tone. "It's why I was able to enter the vault where your ancestors' orbs rest."

I'd never been into the vault since I wasn't an alpha male, but I'd read about the room and how royal blood was required in an alpha in order to open the sealed door.

"Is that what made you finally submit?" I asked, turning my focus onto Grandpapa.

"No, but it certainly made me look at him in a different light."

"You're no longer a racist asshole," I stated what I read in his mind.

"Primrose." His lips stretched thin at the curse.

My face heated. "My beta is fond of swearing, and I fear I may have picked up his bad habit a bit over the last couple of days."

Grandpapa muttered under his breath about unworthiness as his mind thought it, but I glared. "He *is* worthy. He's mine, and you have no say about who I spend the rest of my life with."

"Well, that settles that," Vanni said with a chuckle.

"You would have accepted your alpha regardless of his lineage, wouldn't you, Grandpapa?" I asked, my head tilted to the side while peering into eyes framed by thick lashes like my own. I already knew the answer, but wanted to hear him confess the truth.

"Eventually, yes."

The happiness radiating from him returned the ache to my chest.

A whisper of…something other—not from the four of us met my ears.

I glanced around the room, my brow furrowed. "What is…"

New life.

I jerked my head toward Ashley, gaze settling on her lower abdomen where her hand rested. Swallowing hard, I fought to find my voice. "Are you…"

"Yes," she murmured as our dragons silently conversed the truth. "As of yesterday, actually." Her face flushed, and Vanni kissed her temple, tucking her against his side. Grandpapa settled his hand atop hers.

"It's a boy," I claimed as the whisper of dragonblood reached out to me from her womb.

"Told you!" Ashley declared with light laughter but quickly sobered. "Tell us why you're here, Primrose, and how we might help you."

I started at the beginning, sharing what I had encountered after leaving them months earlier, keeping the sexual encounters between me and my mates to myself. All three frowned upon learning my alpha didn't want me—had outright denied me and ordered me to stay away from his presence.

"Strip down, kneel at his feet, and offer the man a flogger," Vanni said, glancing over my simple frock.

Grandpapa leaned forward and, reaching around Ashley, backhanded his alpha's chest.

One of Vanni's eyebrows shot up as he glanced at my grandfather. "You'll pay for that."

"Good." Grandpapa's mutter curved my lips, but my mind went straight to seeing Jaxon tied up and taken by Patrick exactly as he'd painted the picture in my mind earlier while eating ice cream.

I shifted on my chair and glanced at Ashley.

She chewed on her lower lip, her gaze still on my face as though unaffected by the men on either side of her, the threat of violence, and the promise of sex. "Perhaps he just needs a little while to process everything you've told him. If I were you, I would continue to bump into him here and there, keep you fresh on his mind. A little flirting goes a long way—and if given the opportunity after he's a bit more familiar with you, perhaps trying to seduce him *might* work."

Vanni sat back, arms crossed. "If the man is a true dominant, one with a dragonblood's sex drive, I doubt he'll be able to resist. Keeping my hands to myself with Ashley was hard as fuck—pun intended—and the second she lifted her limit on physical touch, I dove in, half-crazed with lust."

"And that's when I slammed a fist into your face," Grandpapa growled the words.

Vanni's grin reminded me of Jaxon's. "There's been a hell of a lot of *slamming* ever since."

I bit back my smile as Vanni laughed, and Ashley's face turned red again. I'd seen evidence of Vanni's sex drive—and Ashley's response to him.

Because I hadn't knocked. At least they had finished this time before I barged in on them.

"In all seriousness," Grandpapa said, leaning forward, elbows on his knees, "what about Jaxon?"

"What about him?" I asked.

"You abandoned him without explanation, and you've come far enough away he'll have lost all connection to you. I can't begin to imagine what he must be thinking right now, how he must be feeling."

"You left us once upon a time, too, *beta*," Vanni stated, rubbing Ashley's shoulder as she leaned against his side. "It felt as though a part of me had been ripped away."

"Like a missing limb," Ashley murmured, the memory of hurt echoing through her inner dragon to mine.

Did Jaxon experience the same?

I stilled, barely breathing as I contemplated the results of actions I'd taken while not considering how my taking off like that would affect him.

"I learned the hard way that running—flying away—isn't the correct choice," Grandpapa said, his pained gaze flitting toward me once more, and his sense of continued guilt for doing so swept through my mind. "Staying and making things right, resolving issues, is what I should have done. I—I would have known your mother if I had. You wouldn't have been alone for all those years."

Although shame flooded through my soul for being so selfish, I had to focus on Grandpapa's emotions first since he sat a few feet from me. "I forgive you, Grandpapa, same as Grandmother did," I whispered, rubbing over the pain in my chest. "She never stopped loving you."

Neither Vanni nor Ashley's dragons growled, and I longed to be loved in the same way, without jealousy over the past, with assurance of the future.

Sudden yearning to return to my beta swept through me

like a firestorm, stealing my focus. "I need to go back." I hopped up, displacing Tiggy from where he'd rested so sweetly. I gave him a quick pat, but since he belonged to Grandpapa, I didn't feel bad leaving him behind for a second time.

"That's the best choice, even though I would love for you to stay longer," Grandpapa said, the pride in his heart radiating from his eyes.

All three followed me to the front door, and we quickly hugged before I rushed outside into the darkness. I threw myself off the veranda—ruining yet another set of clothes, Grandpapa's holler to be careful whipping away in the wind.

CHAPTER 21

JAXON

My apartment door opened and shut quietly, but I couldn't rouse myself from where I'd passed out naked after stripping to my skin and showering to rid my groin of the cum I'd released while swallowing Patrick's hours ago.

The sweet scent of my golden goddess flooded my nose, but even her return couldn't reel me back from the depressive funk Patrick's denial had put me in. I'd learned firsthand exactly how Prim had felt the day our alpha had hurt her, and I thoroughly understood the need to escape. But I hadn't been able to go any farther than my apartment—just in case she returned or he realized the wrongness of his stupid-assed decision to force me away.

"You smell like him. What did you do?" she whispered, her voice drawing nearer.

"Told him the truth. Everything," I muttered into my pillow, my chest aching. "Begged. Got down on my knees, sucked him off, and he *still* rejected me."

I could sense her empathy as she crawled onto my bed

and curled around me like a big spoon, all naked warmth and soft flesh. "I never should have left you like that."

I turned in her arms, expecting I looked like shit because I sure as fuck felt like it.

"I—I'm not very well versed in relationships," she whispered, her desperation to be understood traveling through the tether between us.

"Understandably so." I wrapped my arms around her, holding her tight to my chest. A shuddered sigh rippled through me at the sense of rightness and calm her bare skin against mine brought. "But it would seem I'm not so good at them either."

She buried her face in my neck, breathing deeply as her emotions quieted along with mine.

"Talk to me next time instead of taking off," I whispered, my voice breaking without permission. "Please. We can figure this out together."

"I will—promise."

Our breaths filled the silence, our heartbeats slowly pumping in sync. The warmth of her soft body seeped through the chill in mine, causing heat to kindle in my groin, pulling blood southward.

Tipping her head, she captured my gaze. A sense of guilt or perhaps remorse radiated from her. "I abandoned you, just like your parents did, as though you meant nothing to me, and yet you welcome me back with open arms and with acceptance I don't deserve. I'm sorry," she whispered.

"I forgive you," I stated, pressing my forehead against hers, breathing in the sweet scent of strawberries.

Arousal woke in her body, thickening the desire between us.

She brushed hesitant lips against mine, and I opened to the gentle probing of her tongue, groaning as she stroked into my mouth.

Arms tightening around her, I ground my hips against her thigh, needing to bury inside her wet warmth, become one with her in every possible way.

"You tasted him," she murmured, pulling back just enough to see my eyes.

My dick throbbed against her at the memory of gagging on his shaft buried in my throat. "Yes."

"What was it like?"

"Sweet. Tingly." I swallowed hard, drooling for more of his seed. "His cum is more addictive than any caramel sauce. So. Damn. Good."

"Mmm." She closed her eyes as I licked up her neck, needing a taste of her too.

"He'll have to suck me off in order to prolong his life, right?" I asked, shifting enough that my swollen cockhead rubbed over the coarse hair between her thighs.

"Yes."

"Fuck." I groaned, grinding our groins together.

"Take what you want, Jaxon. I—it's the least I can do for the pain I've caused you."

"Don't offer yourself out of guilt."

Pink flushed her cheeks. "I *want* you," she murmured, grasping my face with her soft palms. "Surely you sense that."

I could. Potently.

Taking her mouth, I rolled us, settling my weight atop her lush body.

She spread her thighs, clasping my ass with her heels.

Tip of my dick pressing against her slick entrance, I paused, capturing her gaze, soaking in the emotions and desire pouring off her. "I can feel that you want me, but say it. Tell me how much."

"So much that I'm going to die if you don't—"

I thrust, filling her with one deep stroke. She arched beneath me, grabbing at my back with sharp fingernails.

Yessss.

Our dragons hissed as one, and I licked into her mouth, fucking her tongue in time with my hips, gentle nudges to burrow deeper into the tight clasp of her silken pussy.

"Need you," she whispered against my lips what I could sense as strongly as my own desire for her.

I couldn't keep thoughts of Patrick from my mind as I moved inside her warmth, but I didn't want her to think she wasn't enough for me.

Buried deep, I stilled, lifting my head.

Emotions radiated between us as my dick shoved against her womb, causing both of our eyes to well with the overwhelming need for each other. "I love you, Primrose."

She clasped my scruffy jaw in her soft hands, a tear sliding down her flushed cheek. "I love you, too, Jaxon."

I licked the wetness from her face and nuzzled my nose beneath her ear. "Come around my dick, sweetheart," I whispered, nipping her skin. "Show me how much." I pulled out and thrust deep, grinding my pelvis against her clit.

She shattered beneath me, crying out my name and pulling me over the edge with her.

The emotions rolling through me were pure fucking euphoria, but that missing link hurt beneath the joy of being one with her.

"Don't feel guilty," she murmured into my neck as I collapsed on top of her. "He's our third. It's only right that we both long for him. Such desires don't make our connection any less powerful."

I kissed her soft lips, languid and gentle, tasting and imprinting her on my brain. "Thank you."

"For?"

I lifted onto my elbows, my fingers threading through her thick hair spread over my pillow. "For coming back to me. For not being jealous that I went to Patrick."

She smiled, the acceptance shining in her eyes, causing my throat to tighten.

"I've never told anyone other than my parents when I was a kid that I loved them. I've never wanted to. Never wanted to face the same rejection."

"I'll never leave you again, my beta," she whispered and lifted her head to kiss me.

I'd had plenty of rejection in my life, but Prim was the first to return and accept me as is. My fated mate, my female.

She slept pressed against my side, all soft sweetness I couldn't stop from petting, memorizing the feel of her skin against mine.

More.

I bit back my groan of agreement with my dragon. Prim was an addiction, same as Patrick, but she didn't deny me. Wanted me. Even while resting, her body responded to mine, causing her scent to thicken in my nose.

I palmed my dick, slowly jerking myself in the dark.

She stirred with a sigh, and I released my dick to run my pre-cum-covered fingers over her silky lower lips between her thighs. Dampness rose beneath my gentle caresses, and she moaned.

"I'm sorry, but I can't get enough of you," I whispered, rolling her to her back and settling between her spread legs again.

"Don't be sorry," she murmured. "The feeling is mutual."

"You're so fucking perfect."

She let out a soft snort of laughter. "Hardly, but you... you're an absolute delight." With a grasp on my arms, she flipped us, giving me a hint of the inner dragon's strength I'd had wrapped around my body as we'd flown. "All these *perfect* muscles," she teased, sliding down over my body. "This *perfect* cock."

"You haven't seen Patrick's," I said on a groan as she licked from the root of my straining dick to the tip, probing the slit and coaxing a pulse of pre-cum to slicken her tongue.

"What's it like?" She slid her fingertip back down the damp trail she'd left on my shaft.

I clenched my eyes shut as a deep rumble rolled through my chest at the memory of our alpha's taste. "Perfect."

Prim chuckled over my inability to find a better word and feathered her fingers over my drawn-up balls. She toyed briefly with my taint before gently running a fingertip around my puckered entrance.

"Fuck." I set my feet flat on the mattress, widening my legs to give her better access, so damn on board with having something shoved up my ass, my hole relaxed beneath her touch.

"You want him."

Eyes clenched shut, I swallowed hard, my pulse racing like mad. "So much it hurts."

She used the wetness on the tip of my cock to lube up my asshole. The heat of her mouth closed around my dick—and she sank a finger into my hole.

"Motherfucking mother of God!" My hips jerked, and I fisted my hands in her hair, jammed so far down her throat my climax rushed closer. "Don't stop. Fuck, don't stop."

Three glides of her finger in and out of my hole, three deep-throated thrusts, and I exploded, my nose filled with Prim's lust, her finger in my ass causing Patrick's face to flash through my mind.

Alpha.

Need.

I wanted his cock deep inside me, pulsing, filling me with his tingling cum. I yearned for his lax, sweaty body to drape over mine, our chests heaving, my spunk a slimy mess between our stomachs.

"Fuck." My dick gave over one last jerk in the back of Prim's throat, and I gasped, my legs falling to the sides.

She licked away every trace of my cum and kissed up over my abs, my chest, her teeth nipping at my nipples.

I wrapped my arms around her and squeezed her tight, her softness like the warmest blanket on a winter's night.

"I wish *I* could be enough," she murmured what I'd felt earlier.

I heaved a sigh, hating that we shared in that particular emotion. "We need to show him the truth, Primrose."

"Sooner than later," she agreed quietly.

"We'll find a way. Somehow." I squeezed her again while kissing the top of her head. "I promise."

CHAPTER 22

PATRICK

I drank like I was in college again, goddamn whiskey straight from the bottle, and I ended up retching and hugging the toilet long into the early morning hours. Half-sober, I lay on my bed, staring at the dark ceiling, wondering how the fuck Jessie could guzzle booze like that almost every night.

Grimacing, I focused on what needed figuring out in my head rather than my past.

The desire to be close to Jax was stronger than an hour earlier, refusing to lessen with drunkenness or time. Blowing my more-than-usual load down his throat was more fulfilling than anything I'd done. I wanted him on his knees again.

Yessss.

I closed my eyes, but rather than meditate to silence the voice that had weaseled its way out of prison while I'd been puking my guts up, I relaxed my hold on the void.

Nothing could go wrong in the privacy of my own home, I told myself, and I was strong enough to communicate with whatever it was without losing control.

Maybe answers could be found by not exactly embracing the madness but offering it a little freedom.

Like a sleek creature, shimmering in iridescent light, the voice, that inner *beast*, stretched. I allowed him to flow through my consciousness, and words I didn't understand filled my inner ear.

Images flashed in my mind—Jaxon chained in the center of a room, sweat-slickened skin, his dick dripping pre-cum to the floor, every lash of a flogger I wielded parting his lips on a groan.

My dick stiffened.

Primrose sprawled on my bed, my face between her thighs, my tongue buried in her pussy while Jaxon watched, panting and dripping with the release I denied him.

Mine.

Ours.

The hypnotic hiss reached through my mind, and I considered the truth it spoke. Two youngsters—one male, one female—belonged to me. Fated mates according to Jaxon, half animal shifters, destined to bond regardless of what the humans' consciousness might wish.

Too much of an age gap; they're mere children, I told myself as unease over a complete lack of scientific truth crept in. Inappropriate as well. A previous patient of mine, even if only for a day, so he was completely off-limits for that reason alone.

Shame over my desires filled that conscious wish to remain aloof, closed off to the mystical world Jaxon had painted in my head with his enticing words. My body, my heart, however, warred with what would be considered wrong in most humans' eyes.

"You're a professional with an ethical path set before you," I muttered to myself, clenching my eyes shut and rolling to punch my pillow. I breathed deeply, meditating and envisioning the prison inside me as I should have done the previous hour, shutting out the existence of that damn *thing* inside my soul that wished to lead me into darkness.

He slowly disappeared in sparkling, black light, screaming at my strength—his weakness. The walls slammed shut around him, and I breathed a sigh of relief as my muscles finally grew lax atop my mattress.

Sanity saved.

For the time being.

A coffee mug sat before me at the kitchen table, but I hadn't touched it. My insides twisted, and not from alcohol's lingering effects. The darkness I'd allowed to sneak out the previous evening fought for freedom, begged to be heard, its purr and murmured pleas like a tickling whisper between my ears the second I'd woken up from a feverish, dream-filled night.

My pounding head, weakened by my hangover, was an affliction I wouldn't wish on anyone.

I stood and strode back upstairs, needing to rid myself of the madness lingering along the edges of my mind. A cold shower didn't ease my aching balls or dick, and I shot another ridiculous amount of cum down the drain to fantasies of Jaxon and Primrose bowing before me.

Jaw aching from clenching since I'd turned off my alarm, I arrived at Lockwood Monday morning, determined to go about my day, same as every other—work, professional empathy, and a desire to help those in need. That was what had driven me for most of my life, but I found as the hours trickled by that I couldn't keep my focus as I used to.

The need to fuck, to own, to *claim*, brewed in my balls, but I withheld from jerking off in the office bathroom like a horny teenager who didn't know the meaning of the word self-control.

Jaxon began his job bagging groceries today at the store a few blocks away from the apartment Doc Holliday had helped him acquire. I wondered, while leafing through and not paying attention to my next patient's file, if Jaxon enjoyed smiling and chatting with all the ladies—and jealousy burned my gut.

I tossed my pen onto my desk and pinched the bridge of my nose beneath my glasses.

"Doctor Macaire?"

The timid voice lifted my head. A petite blonde girl, perhaps thirteen or so and matching the image in the open folder's picture, stood in the open doorway of my office.

"Are you Emelia?" I asked, forcing a smile and standing.

"Yes." She stared at me with uncanny seriousness, her face void of emotion as I rounded my desk.

"I'm sorry I didn't hear your knock. Please," I motioned toward the chair facing mine. "Won't you sit?"

She shut the door behind her and shuffled forward in her slippers, a tattered Hello Kitty robe cinched tight around her narrow waist. Perching on the chair's edge, she held my stare until I turned my back on her to round my desk.

I sat, unease prickling the hairs on my nape. My smile forced, I glanced quickly at the file I should have thoroughly studied before she'd arrived, the whispering thing inside me trying the walls containing him. "So, Emelia—"

"I can hear him."

The soft murmur jerked my head up. "I beg your pardon?"

"Your beast. He speaks to me."

I cleared my throat while curses flooded my thoughts. Even though cameras weren't mounted inside my office for those above me to keep tabs on what went down in private sessions, I still knew better than to be reckless with my words and hint at belief of anything outside reality. I needed to ask my questions about what she thought to be the truth with care and withhold from agreeing with this young woman in any way.

"What exactly can you hear, Emelia?"

"The voice inside you." She tipped her head to the side, her dark as coal eyes peering into mine as though she listened to the cackling laughter escaping the box inside my soul. "I have one of my own, you know." Emelia finally tore her intense stare off me to glance at the folder on my desk. "But you *do* already know that."

"Mmm." I nodded absently, horrified at my lack of focus, the disaster that was supposed to be Doctor Macaire. "I, ah, do. Yes." I tried for another smile and closed the folder, wondering how the fuck to rectify the situation my distraction had put me in without admitting to anything that would tarnish my reputation.

"You need to listen to him."

Perhaps going with the flow would bring some clarity for a change. "And why should I listen to this supposed voice?"

"Because *he* is what you've been driven to find in your search for fulfillment, and you won't experience true contentment until you become one with him."

I swallowed the million questions rising in my mind and focused on the young woman and the mental instability that had landed her at Lockwood. "I'm assuming listening to the voice in your head is what brought you to this facility."

"Yes."

"I can't imagine doing so has made *you* happy."

A soft smile lit her face. "But it did. I've met you—the man I was destined to help along on his journey."

I stared, my heart stuttering as I gasped, "Wh—what?"

"You, Doctor Macaire." She smiled again, hands clasped

lightly in her lap. "You're one of the reasons I'm here. The orb I found told me to show you the way to your mates."

Orb...

I frowned as the memory of David's granddaughter stating something about orbs being what was left of a dragon when their souls rose to reign over the stars.

I scrubbed a hand down over my mouth and whiskered chin, cursing in my mind. Emelia had found a fucking orb— and it spoke to her about my mates. "My mates?" Rasped to hell, my tone barely audible.

"Yes. Your beta and your female."

I hopped up, hands fisting and releasing. "I—I'll be right back. Don't go anywhere."

A quick trip to the bathroom and a splash of cold-as-fuck water on my face didn't clear my head. The measured breaths on a counted intake and exhale didn't either.

Orb.

Voices.

Goddamned fated mates.

Emelia's declaration that I wouldn't be happy until I submitted myself to this thing inside me echoed in my ears.

No lightbulb flicked on in my mind on how to get out of this mess, and I had no choice but to return to my office and face the unsettling girl who seemed intent on filling my head with more shit.

Or perhaps, answers to what was really going on in my head.

I found her where I'd left her, a hint of her smile still curving her lips as her gaze followed me as I settled behind my desk once more.

While I could simply quit the temporary job at Lock-wood, sell my father's house, and hightail it back east once more, I refused to let this puzzle haunt me for the rest of my life. "Tell me about this orb, Emelia. What does it look like?"

"An egg, but much larger, almost the size of a football." Her head tipped to the side again. "It spoke to the voice inside me in a language I didn't understand, but my inner beast shared what I was to do."

"Find me."

Her smile dazzled again, like sunshine to the darkness of my soul, as though my vocalizing her statement from earlier meant I'd accepted her words as truth. "Yes."

"And help me in my journey," I added, sure that pushing for the ridiculousness of her mind wouldn't suggest I traveled a path toward madness along with her.

"Yes."

We sat in silence for a few seconds. "Did the, ah, orb tell you anything else?"

"Not directly, no." A frown flitted over her brow. "But my beast whispered about the history of the souls in the stars, of ancient beings, my ancestors—and yours—watching us from the night sky."

She shared too familiar a story to discount, unfortunately.

I muttered a curse beneath my breath while slumping back in my chair. "So, how were you supposed to help me?"

"By simply sharing truth."

"The truth of what you believe you heard," I asked for clarity.

"What I *did* hear."

I glanced around my office, my brain even more of a scattered mess than before Emelia had arrived for our scheduled session. "Why come to Lockwood? Why not approach me on the street?" I suggested, thinking I might be able to make her stumble in this story she wove in order to trip me up.

"Because I, too, am meant to be here." She laid her hand over her flat chest. "My mates would not locate me otherwise."

"But you're only what? Thirteen?" I asked, my voice low, brow furrowed, remembering I hadn't read her file.

"Sixteen, going on seventeen." She shrugged and smiled again. "I'm a ward of the state, considered mentally inadequate, so this is where I'll stay until it's time for my alpha to whisk me away."

The clock on the wall ticked as I processed—or tried to, rather—what she'd said, every damn word aligning not just with David and his granddaughter's blog but also with what Primrose had told Jaxon, my supposed beta.

Changing the subject wasn't ideal, considering I now had more questions about myself than before, but I had a job to do at Lockwood, and Emelia was a patient entrusted to my care.

Long after she left my office, I sat and stared unseeing at the beige wall of the stifling office, wondering what the fuck I should do, what I should believe, even though the evidence stacked toward the insanity of dragonblood and shifters.

An idea flitted through my head, and I grabbed my cell, pulling up a number I hadn't called since we'd gone our separate ways not long after college.

Steven Hasslet had always been a nerd who loved sci-fi and the possibility of supernatural shit. We'd studied countless hours together while working toward our bachelor's. We'd also shared a handful of women but had kept our hands off each other by unspoken agreement.

"Patty?" Hasslet's voice betrayed a wide grin. "That you?"

I found my lips responding. "How are you, Steven?"

"Well, and yourself?"

"Not so well—which is why I called."

He chuckled. "The emotionally untouchable Patrick Macaire needs a sex therapist?"

I settled in my chair and closed my eyes, his teasing sliding off my back like it always did. "Not exactly, but I have a case that is eating away at me, and I would really love your opinion since your brain has always been a little out in…well, left field."

"Whatcha got?" He got down to business, unbothered by my statement as I'd been with his. His pursuing his doctorate in New York while I'd stayed in Boston for mine had separated us from getting together and eventually as close confidants, but one truth about real friendships—they stood the test of time.

I exhaled a long breath before telling him about Jaxon—without naming him—and how the voice in his head made him believe he could fly.

"I've seen a handful of similar cases that don't fit into the science we both studied," he said once I finished my brief recap of what had been in Jaxon's file opened atop my desk.

"Did any of them ever mention dragons—or dream of dragons? Alphas, betas, and females? Fated mates?"

He hesitated long enough that I checked my cell to make sure Steven and I hadn't been disconnected.

"You were never one to beat around the bush, Patty."

I heaved another heavy breath and frowned at the half-lie about to leave my mouth. "There are two men, actually, who have dreamed of dragons and flying. I've done research." I went on to fill him in on the bit about the stories the Natives in the area passed down from generation to generation, even tossing in the word "dragonblood" in hopes Steven might know something about the mess I found myself in.

"Well?" I pushed when he went silent yet again.

"I think it's arrogant of man to believe we're the only beings in this universe," he said slowly as though choosing his words carefully. "I studied the same textbooks you did, though. What does your gut tell you?"

I pinched the bridge of my nose, knowing I had to admit

to questioning my sanity out loud—but I trusted this man's ability to remain professional. "I'm not sure."

"Are these two men hospitalized?"

"No."

"Should they be?"

I still managed to contain my weakness for the most part, but I considered Jaxon, the wildness that had gotten him into trouble, and the mischievous glint in his eyes. I also imagined taking my belt to his backside to teach him a thing or two about not making stupid choices.

Clearing my throat, I shifted on my office chair, and it squeaked beneath me. "I think they've both accepted reality."

A snort drifted through the walls imprisoning the beast inside me, and I frowned, pulling oxygen deeply into my lungs.

"Are you happy, Patty?" Steven asked as though seeming to know I needed a topic change.

"I'm not sure how to answer that, to be honest."

"Have you found that fulfillment you've been driven to snag for yourself since the day I met you?"

"No." At least, that answer was easy to answer with honesty.

"In a relationship?"

I stared unseeing across the office, all too happy I had rid myself of Jessie even though I'd always longed for companionship and acceptance of what I hated about myself. "No."

"Still sharing lovers?"

"Fuck," I muttered and closed my eyes against the sudden images flashing in my head of Jaxon and Primrose that filled my dreams every goddamned night.

"You know..." Steven paused, and I imagined him tapping his chin like he'd done while deep in thought when we were younger. "I might have a lead for you."

I waited, breath held.

"A close friend of mine owns a sex club downtown, and I've referred countless patients to him."

"He's a dominant?"

"Yes—Giovanni DiLoreto. He disappeared toward the end of last year, and I finally just heard from him a few days ago. He moved to Wyoming to live with what he called his beta and female. I always knew he was a kinky fucker, but he spoke about them like he was bonded to them or some such shit. He didn't use the words 'fated mates,' but that's the gist I got from the brief conversation."

I stilled, unmoving except for the beating of my heart. Beta and female—bonding.

Yessss, truth.

I swallowed, slamming every ounce of self-control I had into solidifying the vault containing that damn voice.

Emelia had said there were other dragonbloods. Perhaps this DiLoreto guy and his two partners would have the scientific answers my brain required to make sense of what owned my thoughts.

"Do you happen to have his number?" I asked, my voice ragged.

"I do." Muffled noises sounded. "I'll forward Vanni's contact card to you," he said, "but he doesn't have service where he lives off-grid. I'm sure he'll get back to you if you leave a message, though. Just tell him that I gave you his number."

I glanced up at the clock to note the time and made my goodbyes.

Steven's text came through seconds later, but before I had a chance to make a call to his friend, my next patient arrived.

CHAPTER 23
PRIMROSE

Jaxon made love to me twice before rushing out the door for his first day at work. I'd told him that between the two of us, we had more than enough funds to see us through—for years—but he insisted on working. My sweet beta was driven to support his female, and I bid him goodbye with a lingering kiss that had heated our blood.

After he'd left, I'd retrieved my bag from the motel and checked out—on Jaxon's insistence, I moved in with him. I returned to the apartment, breathing a sigh over being able to strip naked again, waiting impatiently for his six-hour shift to end. I'd spent almost four of my twenty-two years alone in the cavern beneath the Grand Teton and hadn't once experienced loneliness like I did with every passing minute now.

The need for Jaxon's closeness, to bask in his nearness and the warmth and scent of his body, filled me to distraction, and I turned off the TV I had been attempting to pass the time watching. While some shows proved to be interesting, the constant noise screaming from the box atop a small table drove me half-mad. Especially the commercials that tried every trick to capture and hold a watcher's attention, prompting them with brilliant wording to buy now or miss out.

Regardless of the TV's attempt to take my thoughts off my inner turmoil, my bare skin continued to crave Jaxon's touch. My feet itched to move, my wings to burst free and carry us to his side where we belonged.

His lingering heartache earlier this morning over Patrick hurt me more than that of my own rejection from our alpha. I longed to be the healing bond between the two, the one who would link them for a long lifetime together.

Go.

I blinked, wondering if my inner dragon knew something I didn't. Both Ashley and Vanni had suggested approaching my alpha, but the thought he might push me away again twisted my stomach into a knot.

Regardless of my misgivings, I gave in to my beast's instincts. We would make things right, gift my beta with what he longed for.

Cloaked and chest fluttering, I stepped out onto the deck, not a stitch of clothing restricting my movements. Warm spring air wafted over me, the scent of warm soil and flowers filling my nose. Knowing I didn't have room to leap and shift, I made my way down the stairs and into the cul-de-sac, my gait slow but steady. Determined to put Jaxon's desires above my own fear of further rejection, I closed my eyes and gave my inner beast her wings.

Ripples of energy converted human skin and bone to that of a dragon, and we purred a heated breath at the freedom my beast half experienced. Three running steps down the road, one flap of wings, and we shot into the sky. The rush of fresh air, cleansed by the storms on the previous day, expanded our lungs.

A bank to the left took us northward for Lockwood.

Alpha.

The dragonblood in him called to us from below, our desire to bond speeding us toward the earth. The second we landed inside the compound's fence and shifted to human form, I realized I'd forgotten to bring a bag with clothing to change into.

Perhaps naked *would* be better once I made myself visible. Patrick had been able to withstand the desire between us before, but maybe with his female's body on full display, he would be more apt to cave to his beast's drive to breed and claim as Jaxon had done when I'd stood upon his stoop in nothing but my skin.

Warmth flared to life between my thighs. Having been sexually awakened, I desired my alpha with a breath-stealing want that only he could satisfy. I loved Jaxon with a fierceness of one already bonded, but we would never be complete without our alpha.

Sure of my decision to approach Patrick, I strode toward the hospital on feet unaffected by the bite of pebbles and cement. I snuck through the front doors by following visitors up the main path and directly into the lobby, where his brimstone scent teased my nostrils.

Shoulders back and heartbeat thrumming, I made my way toward his office down the western wing, then the connected second building, sidestepping more than one person, the carpet hushing our footfalls. A lack of energy passing through the door bearing his name pulled me up short.

He wasn't inside, even though a slight awareness of him being nearby made the hairs on my nape rise.

I glanced left and right, but no one traversed the hallway. The unlocked door pushed in with a quick turn of the nob, and I slipped over the threshold, shutting it quietly behind me. Lingering traces of Patrick's cologne filled my lungs as I inhaled deeply.

My inner dragon purred, and arousal swelled the lips of my pussy, wetness growing to ready myself for my alpha. I swallowed down a moan and forced my mind on learning more about him, to find possible ways to entice him, without his presence distracting me.

Jaxon had told me how Patrick had recently taken over for the previous doctor, but my alpha had yet to unpack or make the office his own, other than the nameplate on the door. No framed photographs, certificates, or awards hung on the walls like the other doctors' offices I'd snuck through on my first visit to the hospital.

Files were stacked on his desk along with a blue-ink pen and a small clock. The attached bathroom held no personal items and smelled of bleach.

My skin pebbled a second before I felt him draw near. I chewed the inside of my lip as my heart thudded, and I glanced around, wondering where to stand—to uncloak or remain hidden or flee to protect my emotions.

No—stay.

We would succeed, I told myself, ears straining to hear his approach, muscles tightening in readiness to seduce the strongest human male I'd ever met.

The door snicked open, and my knees weakened as Patrick stepped into the office.

Dark-framed glasses hid his eyes as his head jerked side to side, lips thinning, brow furrowing. His nostrils flared as he audibly filled his lungs, pushing the door shut behind him.

"Fuck." His head jerked my way—and stared directly at me as though I stood visible across the room, same as that night, concrete and fencing had separated me from Jaxon. Holding my gaze, Patrick moved around his office, tossed his cell phone on his desk, and sank into his chair. "You're here, aren't you, Primrose?"

"Yes," I stated, unable to keep from answering my alpha.

The short whiskers of the trimmed beard along his jawline twitched. "Show yourself."

I shimmered the cloaking ability off my body.

A strangled moan escaped his parted lips, his gaze sliding slowly over my nakedness. "Why do you do this to me?" The roughness of his voice sent a trickle of wetness down my inner thigh.

I whimpered but lifted my chin, meeting his gaze when it returned to my face. "Because you belong to me—to us. You are our fated alpha, the one meant to dominate, give pleasure, and accept our worship in return."

Patrick's inner dragon groaned, causing his frown to deepen.

Want.

Need.

Take.

Warmth flooded through me at the distinctive voice of my alpha's beast whispering in my head. "I can hear him," I said, stepping toward Patrick as his dragon continued to purr words of enticement to both of us. "I can feel that your desire aligns with his."

And I would not be denied this time.

I grasped the arm of Patrick's chair above where his fingers clenched in a white-knuckle grip and swiveled him toward me, our gazes locked. Darkness swirled in his eyes, the blue overrun by his pupils.

Pain, his dragon whispered.

Pleasure, mine responded, attempting to dismiss the negative thoughts.

I draped my body over my alpha's knees, legs on one side, arms and head dangling on the other. "Put your hands on me like you want to," I murmured, knowing he must smell my arousal. "Use me to ease your frustration and set us both free."

CHAPTER 24

PATRICK

This half of my temptation wasn't forbidden in the same way as Jaxon being a former patient of mine, but she coaxed the darkness inside me to a strength I struggled to contain.

I needed to tell Primrose to leave—and never return. I wanted to fuck so deep into her body she forgot everything but the feel of me claiming what belonged to me. But her plump ass all up in my face…

"Fuck." My hand released its grip on the chair's arm, and the satiny skin across the back of her thighs warmed my palm, causing my throbbing dick to jerk inside my slacks.

I had hoped to get hold of Steven's friend before meeting up with either Jaxon or Primrose again, but no such fucking luck.

I'd sensed Primrose as I had approached my office, had known she waited for me inside, but fuck if I could make my feet turn and take me away from a deep, instinctive urge to bow to insanity. Her sweet scent, like summer flowers, the delicious, juicy strawberry-like aroma of her arousal had flooded my nose, coated my mouth, and stiffened my dick so damn fast I'd gone lightheaded while stepping through the door.

Give.

Without fully intending to, my hand landed on her gorgeous ass cheek like she desired, the smack and jiggle of her flesh more fulfilling than a full symphony—her gasp an aphrodisiac, an instant addiction. Hissing in annoyance with myself and driven to sate my lust, I swatted her other cheek, jolting her forward with the force of frustration in my swing.

Pre-cum welled at the tip of my cockhead, smearing the inside of my slacks.

"More," she whispered, wiggling her hips against my leg.

A fresh, mouthwatering scent rose from between her thighs, and I clenched my jaw, smacking beneath the first blooming handprint, punishing this gorgeous siren for what she did to me.

Ours.

I groaned, losing myself to the slithering beast pressing against the bonds I'd fought so hard to keep him behind.

Yessss.

Twice more, instinct demanded I smacked her pink flesh, her hips rising to meet my hand on the last.

"Feel good?" I asked through gritted teeth, winding my fist in her hair and tipping her head enough she arched her back.

Please our female.

"Yes," she whispered, widening her legs as goose bumps broke over her body.

Owned by the darkness swirling inside my soul, I slid my touch between her thighs. Slick wetness coated her puffed lower lips, and even though I longed to have her insides clutch with desperate need around my fingers, I slid downward, her hips rising to accommodate me. A single slow circle around the swollen hood over her clit sent a shudder through Primrose, causing her to shiver in my hold.

Yessss.

She whimpered as I backed off, once more trailing my fingertips across her slippery labia.

"So wet." I hissed, tightening my grip in her hair and lifting her head even farther. She whimpered, grinding her pelvis against me.

I swatted hard and fast, and she cried out, fucking music to my ears.

Cupping her entire pussy, I leaned down to brush my lips across the shell of her ear. "You lust for me to claim this."

"Yes," she gasped an answer even though I hadn't asked her a question.

"You need my dick to stretch you. Fill you."

"Oh, yes. Please." She lifted her hips in invitation, arching her back to the point of what had to be pain.

The beast inside cackled and growled demands, gnashing teeth and flashing erotic scenes behind my eyes.

"You want my cum to flood your womb." I spoke what the inner voice screamed for. "Claim you. *Breed* you."

"Yes!"

I pushed Primrose's head down and swatted her hand-printed ass rapidly, grunts ripping from my chest as I attempted to cling to my sanity, easing my annoyance exactly as she'd offered. Her cries fueled me on, and I didn't hold back, the sting of flesh meeting flesh searing across my palm.

Wetness dribbled from her pussy, soaking my thigh, and I finally dipped into her tight sheath, her pussy walls clamping around my two fingers as I stroked inside her.

"Oh…" She shuddered and pressed back against my hand, spine arching even deeper.

"So fucking needy for me," I growled the words, dragging

my fingers out and shoving back in. My dick leaked and jerked, my balls so tight they ached. "Fuck."

Take.

Own.

Claim.

Powerless against the onslaught of commanding desire, I pulled her upright, her long hair cascading around us as I stood, intent on locking the goddamn door like I should have done before touching her in any way. Her legs circled around my waist, but I grasped her nape to keep from devouring her mouth as I strode across the office, my focus riveted by her golden-brown eyes, glazed by her need to come.

I pushed her back against the door, trapping her with my body. Sharing heavy breaths, we stilled—hovered on the edge of a cliff I had no power to stop us from tumbling over together. My heart thrummed in harmony with hers beneath the soft breasts pressed against my chest.

The sweetness and heat of her panted exhales caressed my lips, my aching dick throbbing against the damn confines of my slacks and the pussy they kept me from plundering.

She owned *me*. I could feel the absolute truth inside my soul, and there would be no denying that truth or the desperate desire to claim her in return.

Take what has been meant for us since the beginning of time.

Eloquent fucker—

She squeezed her legs around me. "Please," she whimpered, fingers clutching at my shoulders with an ungodly strength that would mark my skin.

I relished in the touch, hissed over how her arousal dictated my need to ease the ache as I'd taken out my frustration on her lush ass that I gripped with equally bruising force.

Bury us inside her warmth.

"Yes," she whispered as though my inner voice had spoken

aloud, snaking a hand between us to grasp my straining dick in her strong grip.

I hissed.

"Take what you crave, my alpha." She squeezed my length.

My eyes rolled back into my head as I bucked into her grasp, fighting to hold onto my sanity. But her touch, the rightness of having this woman in my arms—

"Fuck."

"Mmm." Her murmured agreement caused more pre-cum to leak from my slit, and I shuddered as the beast inside me pushed for more—freedom and pleasure, the right to exist and claim as fate intended.

Control slid from my grasp.

The thing roared, darkness sweeping through my limbs, numbing my mind to all but claiming.

Taking.

Breeding.

I ripped my slacks, freeing my dick one-handed, the other palming one of her ass cheeks and lifting her higher.

A single thrust buried me inside her welcoming, slick clutches, and we gasped, eyes locked.

A sense of coming home warmed my chest, and we stilled, sharing breath and heartbeat, deeper parts of us seeming to weave around each other far beyond how we physically connected.

Yessss.

Satisfaction coursed through me twofold, a heady yearning to give and fulfill the beautiful creature in my arms who stared at me as though I'd hung the moon in her night sky. She owned me, my vocal cords lost in the wave of longing flooding through the otherworldly tether bonding us together.

Move. Two voices echoed as one between my ears, and powerless against the onslaught of raw desire, I obeyed.

I slid out to my swollen head, her clutching walls sending a rush of adrenaline through me so strong my entire body shook. Lost to lust, I thrust deep. "Goddamn—" I captured her mouth, lips bruising, insatiable hunger driving my hips up and into her, over and over, desperate to mate with this young woman I knew nothing about.

The sweet scent of her flooded my lungs, the taste of her soft tongue igniting a craving deep inside me that would never be satisfied.

Delicious.

Indeed, she was the embodiment of a goddess, perfect in every way.

Please our female.

Growling against her lips, I thrust, fingertips digging into the flesh of her ass to keep her impaled on my shaft.

She whimpered and writhed in my hold, hands clutching at my shirt, my hair. Pain from her raking fingernails over my neck broke through the bloodlust to own, but wasn't enough to stop my dick from the mission before us.

I bit her lower lip, the tang of copper coating my tongue.

She cried out, inner walls tightening around my plundering shaft. "Please!"

"Need you to come on my cock, sweet goddess of mine." I gasped between words, sweat breaking out over my back and forehead from the exertion of fucking into her. "Soak me with your release. Goddamn." I buried my face in her neck, eyes clenched shut while chasing mutual release. "Give it to me—now."

Her shriek filled my ears, inner walls clamping around me, coaxing me to gift her what she needed.

Grunting, I buried the tip of my shaft against her womb.

Ours.

My balls erupted in a fountain of cum, her clenching core milking my dick with steady pulls on my shaft.

Groaning, I feasted on her mouth as copious amounts of spunk flooded her with every pulse of my taint, seeming to drain my soul dry.

Golden light shimmered behind my closed eyelids, and a flood of adoration rained down over me like a summer storm, drenching me with force enough that I lost my breath.

Tearing my mouth away from hers, I lifted my head, panting, one last spasm of my balls giving Primrose everything I had. Euphoria filled me from the inside out, and Primrose's smile lanced my chest with a joyous ache so damn intense my knees almost buckled.

I clutched at her backside, our combined cum leaking around where I impaled her, making a mess over my thighs and soaking my slacks.

The beast inside me purred his pleasure, and Primrose sagged in my arms, a glorious smile lighting up my soul and filling me with her peace.

"I can feel your emotions," she whispered, and another rush of happiness swarmed over me, her fingertip brushing over my lips. "The bonding has begun."

Bonding.

Fated mates.

Dragonblood.

I blinked at the strength of the words echoing in my head —and reality crashed over me, ripping me from the pleasure-hazed euphoria I'd lost myself to.

I lifted Primrose off me and stepped away, stumbling, my dick wet and hanging from my torn slacks as I pushed— fucking *heaved* against the slithering beast inside my soul who had gained control over our faculties.

"No," I stated through gritted teeth, hands fisting at my sides, slowly taking back what that thing had stolen from me. My eyes lost sight of the beautiful vision before me as deep, meditative pulls of oxygen expanded my lungs, allowing me clarity, offering me strength to contain the sickness inside me.

I was in control, and no instinct or lust would dictate my actions.

The walls slid shut as I envisioned them doing so, cutting off my weakness.

The joy blinked out.

Pain ripped through my chest, and I staggered back a step.

"What did you do?" Primrose said with a gasp, both hands clutching against her heaving breasts, eyes wild with fear I could taste in the air.

"Get. Out." I clipped my words short even as my voice shook, betraying my tenuous grip on every truth I had built my life upon.

Hurt and regret flooded through me but didn't originate in my mind or heart. I could sense Primrose inside me as distinctly as my stubborn determination to remain sound of mind.

One sob, and her body disappeared—fucking *vanished* from sight—as quickly as she'd arrived, further proof I was losing my goddamned mind. My office door tore open, slammed against the wall, and the sense of her inside me slowly leaked away with every tick of the clock on the wall behind me.

Relief tinged by shame settled in my head, and I stood like a goddamn fool, flaccid dick hanging out, the gaping doorway in front of me a silent, mocking laughter of my so-called self-control, my professionalism—my goddamn *weakness*.

I kicked the door shut and shoved my dick away, but I'd managed to mangle my cum-drenched slacks enough I couldn't properly tuck myself behind the zipper and clasp.

"Fuck!" I punched the doorjamb, the pain radiating up my

arm remaining long after the emotional tether between me and Primrose faded to the point I no longer sensed her crushing agony.

I'd never felt so empty, so *alone,* in my life.

Silence sat behind the wall containing the voice of the beast inside me.

"Not real. Not *fucking* real," I muttered over and over, trying and failing to force the need for Primrose from my head and wishing like fuck Steven's friend would call me back to tell me I wasn't insane.

CHAPTER 25

JAXON

Work sucked ass worse than I'd expected. Bagging fucking groceries. Sure, Prim and I had a nice stash of money between the two of us, but I didn't want to blow through it like a couple of irresponsible kids. I needed to prove myself a working *man* she could rely on, a nest egg tucked away for our future together, one I feared would only ever see us as a couple rather than the threesome fate dictated.

I'd promised to figure out how to convince Patrick he belonged in our lives, but my brain couldn't figure shit out. Without my usual manipulation tactics, I was powerless. Fucking useless. And that shit messed with my mind toward Prim, too.

I longed to be her everything. Take care of her needs, not just sexually and emotionally, but physically as well. That meant a good job that would provide better than a handful of dollars per hour.

Never mind, I wouldn't even be able to fulfill those first two without the one man we craved.

After a quick lesson in making sure I didn't pack bananas

on top of bread in the store's brown paper bag, I stood behind a cashier as she beeped item after item across the scanner, the lame-ass music and murmur of voices only aggravating me more than the clothing causing every inch of my skin to itch.

I wanted Primrose, missed her enough I kept rubbing my chest like a cavern had split open inside me due to her absence.

The twenty-something cashier to my right kept checking me out—I swore I could feel her calculating stare. Glancing her way twice earned me smiles, but I ignored the gesture, uninterested in a transactional hookup like I used to seek out. If she'd been looking at me like that before Prim had stormed into my life, I'd have been buried between her thighs before night's end.

The girl brushed past me while heading to break, but rather than causing my dick to twitch with interest in her big breasts, the appendage shriveled even more with disgust.

At least cheating would never be in the cards thanks to my body's recognition of who I belonged to.

Five minutes later, I went to the break room to grab something to eat—and found her there by herself.

"Hey," she said, her voice all *come and get me, hot thing.*

Not wanting to be more of an asshole than I'd already been, I mumbled a greeting and pulled open the fridge for my bottle of water I'd left on the bottom shelf earlier.

My backside tingled.

"You new in town?" she asked as I straightened.

"Yeah."

"Got a girlfriend?"

My dragon purred. I smiled as the bottle lip rested against mine. "Something like that." Long pulls filled my mouth with cold water, and I swallowed, the chill reaching to my empty stomach.

She stood and rounded the table, pressing against my side while straining up onto her tiptoes. Her hot breath brushed over my neck, and I stepped away, capping my water as my dragon growled a warning for her to back the fuck off.

"Not interested," I said before she could do whatever she'd planned in her attempted seduction.

"What, are you gay or something?" she asked, hands on hips and scowling at me as though she thought she was God's gift to men and hadn't ever been turned down.

Which, considering the size of this measly town as compared to Phoenix, she probably hadn't.

Kinda…reminded me of myself pre-Primrose, goddess of my life.

What a punk-assed little bitch I'd been, cocky and arrogant.

"You're not my female." I glanced down over her generous curves, unmoved and hardly enticed to take a taste. A smirk pulled my lips upward. "And you're definitely not the *alpha* I belong to."

"Fucking weirdo." She shoved past me, the door slamming shut behind her.

I slouched in the chair she'd vacated, blowing out a breath, shoulders slumping.

College. That was what I needed to do. Get my GED and a higher education, one like Patrick had. Stable and sure, with a much better promise than minimum wage. I could afford a community college for a couple of years with what my grandfather had left me, but not much else.

"Shit." I propped my elbows on the table and ran my hands through my hair.

I wouldn't *ever* be enough.

Jaw tight, I hopped up and strode from the breakroom, determined to at least finish my shift so I wouldn't add "quitter" alongside the "failure" label I was sure attached to my forehead.

I sensed her gut-wrenching pain long before I opened the apartment door. She threw herself into my arms, sobs and tears—and the scent of our alpha and his cum—sending me staggering back onto the porch.

What the fuck had he done?

What had *she* done?

Holding her tight, I strode inside and kicked the door shut, my face buried in her hair as her tears soaked my shirt. The ache in her chest filled mine, the feelings of failure intensifying to the point I needed something—a shot of alcohol being the top of my list, even though I didn't drink.

"What the fuck happened, Prim?" I asked, sitting on the couch and snuggling her tighter against my chest.

"I t-tried again." Another sob cut off her trembling voice. "I—I hoped to change his m-mind." She sniffed and whimpered. "I wanted to give you the thing you long for the m-most."

Fuck. I heaved a sigh and kissed her head a few times, unable to contain my absolute adoration for the naked woman shivering and shaking in my arms. How could that love not be enough? Why the fuck did she have to experience the pain I did because of it?

"I *want* your emotions, Jax," she whispered, pulling back to give me the stunning view of her wet, golden-brown eyes. "Your happiness, your desires, your hurt. I *need* it." She cupped my cheek and kissed me lightly on the lips, the taste of salty tears lingering as she pulled away. "As sick as that sounds, I don't feel…right…without you being near or inside me."

Of course, my mind went straight to dick and pussy, but I knew what she meant. "Same, sweetheart."

We stared at each other for a few seconds, sharing our grief and the underlying happiness over having found one another that bordered on contentment—except for the loss of him.

"Tell me, Prim."

And fuck, did she ever, my dick springing to attention imagining her slammed against Patrick's office door as he ripped at his pants to get inside her warmth that was like coming home every damned time.

"Fuck." I scrubbed a hand over my face, my asshole clenching at the thought of him releasing deep inside *me* after a few animalistic thrusts that brought just as much pain as they did pleasure.

"He shut me out, Jax." Prim's voice wavered again. "With ten times the force as before. It hurt."

I kissed her, swept my tongue into her mouth, wanting nothing more than to ease her pain, that feeling of rejection I knew too well. "Let me care for you, sweetheart."

"Yes." She lay back on the couch, and I yanked my clothes off, desperate to get inside her and make her forget about our asshole alpha for a while.

Knowing Patrick's cum probably still coated her pussy, I shook with instinctive need to add mine, fill her as he had.

But first…

I buried my face between her thighs and feasted. Tasting the sweetness of Patrick's tingly cum with every shove of my tongue into her pussy roused my inner dragon into a growling, prowling beast who wanted to break free from my human body.

Breed.

"Fuck, yeah," I mumbled against her swollen labia before suckling one lip into my mouth.

Prim yanked on my hair. "Jaxon."

I obeyed what her desire swirling through me dictated, sliding up and *into* her body while claiming her mouth. Frantic hands, deep, needy thrusts, gnashing teeth and lashing tongues…we fucked hard and fast. Cum brewed in my drawn-up balls, and I reached between our bodies, my fingers finding her clit swollen for me.

"Come around me, Prim." I thrust deep and flicked back and forth over her slickened nub. "Fucking take me with you so I can shoot my spunk against your womb with our alpha's."

"Jax!" Wetness gushed around my dick, and I wrapped my arms around her, fucking deep, her inner walls pulling, pulsing with enough force I fucking exploded, shots of light behind my clenched eyelids.

Yessss.

My balls erupted, jerking my dick inside her, spurting insane amounts of spunk—fucking badass dragonblood.

One final groan, and I relaxed against her softness, my nose in her hair, every quick breath tickling strands over my lips. Her pleasure and peace radiated through me, appreciation and adoration ten times more than I had dreamed about and secretly hoped to find. "Fuck, do I love you."

She squeezed her thighs around me and sighed a quiet repeat of my sentiment, the release rolling between us almost enough to erase the discontent lingering in the deepest parts of us.

As cheesy as the thought was, I would die without Prim. I would literally *die* without her nearness, her touch, the sense of energy linking us—

I planked over her as an idea jolted through my head.

"What?" Eyes widened, she grasped my shoulders, peering from one of my eyes to the other. "What?" she repeated.

"He needs a swift kick in the ass," I said with a grin,

gyrating my hips around, grinding my pelvis against her clit. She squeezed her pussy around my semi with coaxing tugs that made my eyes roll back into my head. "And I think I know just the way to do it."

"How?" she asked, her voice breathy as a goddamn siren.

I pulled out a few inches and slowly fucked through the soaked mess between her thighs, my dick thickening again, filling her perfectly. "Show him what he's missing."

Her brow furrowed. "That's exactly what I tried to do."

"Mmm." I groaned at the feel of her tight slickness as I dragged my length out and pushed in, my hips moving in a seductive dance that sent rippling pleasure through both of us.

She arched beneath me, her fingernails digging into my straining shoulder muscles. "I'm not talking about your sweet-as-fuck pussy, Prim."

One more withdraw and slow, teasing sink into her body, and I stilled.

"He needs to see you in your true form, all golden scales and spines. Claws and glowing eyes."

She lifted an eyebrow, probably knowing I wasn't done laying out my plan. "And?"

"He also needs to feel fear." I nudged toward her cervix, coaxing a gasp from her lips as I flexed my ass, burrowing deeper. "Sometimes, the only way to realize you need some-thing is to believe it's lost. For fucking good."

"The bridge," she whispered as my plan blossomed in her own mind.

"Mmm." I undulated above her, fucking in and out of her with my rolling hips, our gazes locked. Emotion and arousal simmered, heating the connection between us. "Same as the first time you took me soaring."

"But how do we get him there?"

My mind went straight to where it always did when I

wanted to get my way, but at this point, what choice did we have? "Forget the bridge. We'll use the canyon. He's a doctor. He'll come if I call and tell him I'm going to jump off the same ledge my grandmother did."

"Jaxon." Her tone said it all, even though I could feel the unease reaching through our tether.

I clasped her face in my hands, imploring her to understand with my eyes and the emotions in my heart. "Manipulating him in this way wouldn't be forcing a *bond* but a reality check. It's not anything like what some of our ancestors did in the past. We just need to get him to the place where he realizes what he's missing. The choice will be his, but I think in the face of losing his fated mates, his dragon will take control and protect us."

Her brow furrowed. "Wouldn't he reach out to the authorities rather than run to the rescue?"

What a goddamn conversation to have while making love to my female. I chuckled and ground my pelvis against her slippery clit again since the serious convo hadn't done jack shit to soften my dick. "He could—but I don't think he will. There's too much of a connection between us. He can deny it all he wants, but he won't allow someone else to talk me down. I guaran-fucking-tee it."

Another slow drag out and slide into her warmth caused us both to groan.

"Do you believe it will work?" she whispered, wrapping her arms around me with possessive vibes that made my balls draw up tight.

"Yes," I whispered against her lips and turned my focus on making her come undone beneath me again.

CHAPTER 26

PATRICK

I was losing my shit. Fucking thirty-eight years of age, hard-fought for stability built inside my head, and it was all being ripped to shreds by two kids.

Old enough.

"Shut the fuck up!" I slammed my fist on my desk, jostling the pen close by. I'd managed to quiet the voice in my head almost the entire previous day—even with Primrose's scent lingering in my nose and on my fingers long after I had showered and fallen into bed.

I'd passed Emelia in the hallway not long after losing control with Primrose, her gaze pinning me, weakening my defenses against the darkness that immediately began whispering its need to be free, to seek out, to taste, and take what belonged to us.

Couldn't fucking stand it.

I held my head in my hands to keep from jerking off or grabbing my keys, sprinting from my three-room, struggling practice on Main Street, and tearing off to the next town. To stop myself from striding into Jax's apartment and owning them both in the way I lusted for. On their knees. Worshiping. Begging for pain and pleasure. Easing the ache in my chest and my goddamn balls in their willing holes.

"Fuck."

Whiskey would be the better option.

Safer, at least, I thought while glancing around the sparsely decorated space I could finally call my own practice. Blue tones meant to soothe covered the walls, a beige couch and chair, soft enough to offer comfort but not lull people to sleep. I had managed to pay the bills accrued over the previous month, and my only patient for the available evening hours had left not long ago.

Caught up in my head and the driving need attempting to own my body, I locked up my office, not meaning to head southward when I backed out of my allotted parking spot. I held the steering wheel steady, my gaze straight ahead, while my humanity, my better half, told me to turn around.

Give in. Fuck them both, find the release we desire, and I promise to be silent afterward.

"Manipulative little fuck," I said through clenched teeth and gripped the steering wheel even tighter over the eloquence of the thing in my soul who had escaped its prison without my noticing.

Take what we desire. Fulfill our lust.

Visions flooded my head of satiated bliss…blessed quietness in my head, allowing me control.

"Fuck them out of my goddamn system in privacy where no one would know," I said as the plan unfolded in my head, "then walk away."

I would rid myself of this need to own their bodies and return to building my business and creating a life without drama.

One set in science and truth.

The slithering beast chuckled even though my dick jerked in my pants.

If I gave in to my lust behind the door of Jaxon's apartment—no cameras, no phones recording the act of wrecking the two youngsters—I could finish this unfazed, my profession intact, even if my self-pride shattered for giving in to my baser instincts.

That, I could fucking live with. What I couldn't continue handling was the desperate need, the consuming craving dominating my thoughts and hindering my ability to focus on responsibilities.

The sunset smeared purple across the sky as I turned into the cul-de-sac. Tires crunching on the road, I rolled to a stop and peered back at the driveway to the apartment above the garage.

Same as the first time I'd approached Jaxon's place, no awareness of his presence tingled over my skin as it had when occupying the same room. I rolled the window down and breathed in the cool evening air. No scent of either Jaxon or Primrose filled my lungs as it had a few days prior.

Scowling, I reached for the door handle, but my cell's buzzing stopped me.

Was Steven's friend finally returning my call?

I grabbed my phone off the passenger seat. A number I didn't recognize showed up, and scowling, I tapped the ignore button and tossed the cell onto the seat.

I climbed out of the car, intent on Jaxon's apartment, my skin buzzing and pulse thrumming. No one answered my knock, and other than the bathroom, I could easily scan the empty interior through the window to the left.

Rather than feel relief at having temptation removed from my path, I scowled, hands on hips as I peered around the neighborhood from my vantage point on his deck, wondering where the fuck a young couple went on a Tuesday night.

Movies? Out for pizza?

How they managed to stop fucking each other to go out into public, I had no clue. Cursing some more over the images now flashing in my head, I climbed into my car and started the engine. A glance at my cell showed a voicemail had been left from the number I hadn't recognized.

Reminding myself of my profession, I grabbed it and keyed in the code to access the message.

"Doc."

My cock swelled at the sound of Jaxon's voice.

"I…uh…I'm really struggling."

I pinched the bridge of my nose beneath my glasses, my eyelids sliding shut as concern and longing swamped my mind.

"I've been so confused, so messed up in the head—I can't do this anymore."

His voice broke.

"Shit." I held my breath, the hairs on my nape rising.

The message cut off without another word.

Hand shaking, I hit the recall button, my stomach churning.

"Doc?"

"Jaxon. Thank fuck." I clutched at my chest, fisting my shirt. "Where are you?"

"The canyon." His whisper made shivers slide down my spine and my brow furrow. "Where my grandma ended her suffering."

My inner *whatever* the fuck it was, went still—a predator paused, muscles tensed and ready to spring.

Go.

"What are you doing, Jaxon?" My voice barely escaped past the tightening of my throat.

"I can't stand it anymore." The line muffled as though he fumbled with the cell.

"Jaxon!"

"I gotta let go. Need to fly, Patrick."

"No!" I turned the key and tore out of the cul-de-sac. "Jaxon!" A glance down at the cell showed he'd hung up—or fucking jumped. "Goddamnit!"

I sped northward, a cold sweat breaking out on my upper body, clammy hands clutching the steering wheel. I knew the exact southern rim viewpoint he spoke of, which lay well over an hour away. The overlook mentioned in his file, the image in black and white his parents had provided. I'd wondered what had led his grandmother to leap to her death.

Voices, they had claimed, similar to the one enticing Jaxon to leap, to *fly*—even though he couldn't.

I hoped, fucking prayed to whatever deity reigned over the universe, that everything I'd learned since Sunday morning with David, every goddamn tale of dragons and dragonblood was true.

We are real.

"Shut the fuck up!" I hollered with a shrill voice, my insides shaking.

True. All true.

If Jaxon threw himself off that ledge and didn't sprout those fucking wings he swore he had beneath his skin…

I tried to call, but he didn't answer.

My foot already lay like lead against the gas pedal, but I couldn't get there fast enough. The sun sank in my driver's side window, the sky darkening along with my thoughts as another call sent me to an automated voicemail.

"Fuck!" I tossed the cell onto the passenger seat, swearing at every slow-moving asshole in my way and the stretch of road still needing traveling before I reached him.

If that boy jumped, it would be my fault. I should have invested more time with him to assure my own mind of his stability before agreeing with Doctor Holliday's conclusions that he was fine and ought to be released. I should have kept my damn hormones and dick in check when he'd shown up at my house, and I sure as fuck shouldn't have been so harsh when telling him to leave, dismissing him as though I didn't give a fuck he'd spilled his guts to me.

How would he feel anything other than rejected? Used and discarded like a piece of trash—the same as he felt over his parents' treatment of him, according to Doctor Holliday's notes in Jaxon's file.

"Goddamnit!" Again, the boy didn't answer, and I found my hands shaking and eyesight hazing over the fact I might be too late.

When I approached my destination, darkness coated the land. Even with my cell phone's light, I wouldn't be able to peer into the canyon to see if he'd survived. I swung into the overlook, my headlights illuminating a figure on the other side of the fence.

My breath left in a rush, the relief of finding him alive after talking to me nearly an hour and a half ago, weakening me to the point of passing out. "Jaxon." I slammed the car into park and hopped out, my legs shaky as hell, sweat on my forehead, guts tight even though he stood right *there*. Alive. Whole.

Mine.

Teeth gritting, I approached with hesitant steps, hands clenching and releasing at my sides, adrenaline crashing through me.

Back to me, Jaxon leaned over the rim, hands closed around the top railing, and holding himself at an angle out over the cliff.

"Jaxon," I called, hating that my voice shook and betrayed my fear—my longing for him to hear me. To stay.

He finally glanced over his shoulder, his face pale in the blinding headlights. "You came," he murmured and turned, still gripping the railing.

"Don't do this," I said, stopping a good twenty or so feet away—close enough I caught his scent on the cool breeze. Swallowing hard, I shook my head, concern for his well-being stronger than any arousal that energy between us dictated overtake my body.

"You have to see for yourself that I'm not crazy," he said, his eyes wide, hair mussed as though he'd been running his hands through it.

"I know you're not," I assured him with a quiet voice.

"I need you to understand." He let go of his hold with one hand.

"Please, Jaxon." I reached toward him, palm up, even though he wouldn't see my face from the headlights at my back. "Please don't do this."

"You'll never believe me if I don't." A soft smile tilted his lips—froze my fucking insides.

He let go.

Arms spread wide, he tipped back.

Disappeared into the abyss.

"No!" I hollered and leapt forward, the inner beast in me roaring.

Too late—I'd been too fucking late!

CHAPTER 27
JAXON

Patrick's scream was nothing less than perfect as wind rushed against my back. I seemed to float on air, the blackness of night swallowing me whole.

But I didn't fear smashing against the rocks like Gramma did.

A harsh flap of wings sounded, and talons grabbed hold of me, yanking me from my free fall, shooting me up toward the sky.

My grin widened even as my heart sped to my toes at the abrupt change of trajectory.

We shot upward, car lights blinding me for a brief second as another flap of Prim's wings damn near blew Patrick off his feet.

He stumbled backward—but I couldn't see his face to tell if he had his eyes open and finally saw the fucking truth of what Prim and I had been trying to explain to him.

Prim's heartbeat thrummed in time with mine, adrenaline coursing through my system, making my entire body shake in her hold. I patted her leg with a trembling hand. "Land, Prim," I hollered, even though she had to feel my readiness to land as clearly as I did her hope we had accomplished what we'd planned to do.

She circled and set me onto my feet gently outside of the reach of the car's lights before touching down beside me in a clattering of pebbles.

Patrick had turned toward the car's headlights to keep his focus on us, his face finally coming into view. He stood unmoving, shoulders hitched, his lips parted—and face deathly pale as though he was ready to pass out.

"Holy fuck," he whispered, his audible gulp immediately afterward making my smirk return.

I stepped forward, Prim moving to my left with heavy steps that betrayed her bulk even if Patrick couldn't yet see her clearly.

As one, we stepped into the light.

Brilliance glimmered off her golden scales, and I slid my hand along her side, needing the connection of shared hesitancy and hopefulness between us. Her warmth soothed me clear through to my inner beast, who purred as our energies weaved with one another.

"Holy *fuck*," Patrick swore again, his hands clenching and relaxing at his sides as his gaze slid over the beauty of our female.

We stopped ten feet away from him, and although fear widened his eyes, his pupils swelled, revealing his desire.

The scent of brimstone flooded my nose, and my inner beast groaned with want, dick twitching to life inside my jeans. Sweetness wafted atop Patrick's earthier smell, all strawberries and deliciousness.

"Prim," I said, encouraging her to do as we'd discussed. She hesitated but finally leaned down, stretching her neck toward Patrick.

He blinked.

Slowly blew out a breath.

His hand shook as he reached for her lower jaw.

Prim shivered at the stroke of his fingertips, her arousal in response to his touch making mine intensify.

"My God." Patrick breathed the words, settling his palm against her scales.

Primrose purred, her eyes closing like a cat's, head tilting as though begging him to pet her.

Contentment rolled off her like billowing smoke, her sense of completeness causing my soul to ache.

Desperate for connection, I laid my hand on her flank again. Electrical currents shot through my body as the three of us linked physically for the first time.

A sense of wonder slid through my conscience.

Strength.

Stoic authority that made my inner beast weep and my knees weak with the need to drop and worship my alpha.

I belonged to him—and he was mine.

Mates.

Swallowing hard, I recognized that everything my life had been lacking before, everything I had always wanted, stood before me.

Belonging.

Acceptance.

And the emotions and thoughts weren't mine alone.

"You see?" I half-choked on the words, the sight of wonder on his gorgeous face growing hazy as my eyes welled.

His head jerked up and down, and he finally tore his focus off Prim's face to meet my gaze. A rush of annoyance slid through the energy linking us, his eyes narrowing even as lust flooded through us both. "The fuck, Jaxon?" he growled, shoulders tensing even as he continued to stroke over Prim's neck.

"I'm sorry, but I didn't know what else to do." I blew out a breath, attempting to ease the crazy rush of emotions causing my body to shake. "How to get through to you."

"Fucking nearly gave me a goddamn heart attack!"

Prim wound her tail around us, and her rising distress and need to shelter and hold us close rolled over my mind.

My inner beast purred his delight at her desire to nurture, something else my humanity had never truly felt from anyone who should have loved me.

Patrick turned his focus back on our female, shoulders relaxing along with the displeasure my manipulation had caused him. "Change back—please."

The light shimmered around Prim in golden waves, almost like flame, and both Patrick and my touch fell away from her as she shrank into her human form.

"Holy fuck," he murmured for a third time, his gaze flitting over her nakedness and back up, swallowing as his gaze rested on her face. "This is real—all of this…everything I imagined and dreamed about…shit." He rubbed a hand over his face, the sound of his palm brushing over his short beard loud in the stillness surrounding us. "Jesus." Swallowing hard, he held out a shaking hand toward Prim.

She slipped hers into his grasp, both gasping as though struck by lightning.

My feet itched, fingertips tingled.

Please.

As though sensing my need, Patrick tore his attention off the perfection of our female. "Jaxon." He offered me his free hand, and I stumbled forward with a choked cry, desperate for his touch.

Our fingers brushed first before palms clasped tightly together.

Yessss.

Fulfillment flooded through me, causing a tear to slide down my cheek. "Prim," I choked out, reaching for her.

Her fingers wound through mine, the completed circle bringing the three of us together, the tether linking as it was always meant to be.

Currents of emotion rose and ebbed, up one arm and down the other in a continuous flow like a gentle tide. Giving and taking in, sharing as the water did with earth, quenching its thirst over and over again.

Whispers tickled my ears, the beginning of what would come to fruition, Primrose had promised, once we consummated our bond.

My balls throbbed, but I pushed against rising desire for physical fulfillment, longing to feel the complete acknowledgment of truth from Patrick before we shared in our lust to mate.

He stared at Prim's face, her smile more glorious than anything I had ever laid eyes on in my life.

Her gift allowed her to hear our alpha's inner dragon, and the fact she smiled rather than overwhelm my senses with heartache told me all I needed to know.

Relief flooded through my soul, weakening my knees again. Wetness filled my eyes, and I bit my tongue to keep from whimpering like a needy kid. Fuck knew Patrick's mind would demand he stick to stubbornness over the age gap between us if I behaved like the youngster he'd seen me as from day one.

I clasped and held on tight to his hand, refusing to be denied *again*.

Fate had given me everything I had always longed for.

And nothing, no one, alpha included, would rip this gift away from me.

CHAPTER 28
PRIMROSE

My heart lay on the verge of exploding, my dragon desirous of taking flight once more and roaring her delight in feeling both of our mates' touch at once.

Patrick's inner dragon offered him words he wouldn't understand but needed to speak out loud as fate dictated. He stared at me, his mouth clamped shut, lips pale, his acceptance of the truth real, but stubbornness clung as though he still questioned his sanity.

"It is your responsibility to speak what you hear, even though it's a language you don't yet understand." I begged with my eyes for him to release what was needed to begin the bonding among the three of us. "Please, my alpha," I whispered, my throat swelling.

His Adam's apple bobbed, and he glanced at Jaxon.

"Do it, Patrick." Tears slid down Jaxon's cheeks, the fullness in his heart overwhelming my own.

Patrick's inner dragon pushed for freedom, expanding and taking up place inside our alpha's soul. The ancient words that would bind us together sounded loud in my conscience, but it wasn't my place to vocalize them.

Perhaps Patrick understood the importance of the beast's urging—but his humanity still didn't want us.

Found us lacking.

Tears slid down my face. "We are destined for each other, Patrick," I managed to whisper past the tightness in my chest and throat as my dragon cowered inside me. "Drawn together in ways I know you don't yet understand, but we *do* belong to one another. Alpha, beta, and female." I swallowed to withhold the keening readying to pour past my lips.

Anger lit like a flare in the night, rippling through Jaxon's grip on my hand.

He clasped my fingers tighter, cursing beneath his breath, the beginning of agonizing heartache rippling through the energy linking us together.

"Please," I pleaded, shaking my head, unable to bear Jaxon's rising pain atop my own.

Patrick's whiskers twitched as though he clenched his jaw, and his eyes closed. A heavy exhale lowered his shoulders and bowed his head. "I have questions."

"Ask them," I urged, trying to sift through rising anger and fear to reach our alpha's worries.

"What you *need* to do," Jaxon said, his voice firm—pissed as hell, "is speak the goddamn words like you're supposed to! I promise everything, and I mean absolutely *everything*, will fall into place. This will feel right—you'll understand. There won't be any more of this concern over our ages or the fact you're a professional who should have the self-control of a goddamn monk!"

Patrick's head lifted, his eyes narrowing as he lasered in on his beta. "What do you know of my thoughts, *boy*?" he asked, his voice low and shaky.

A cocky grin split Jaxon's face, even though it carried no

joy through the tether. "They're all over your face, *Doc.* You ooze insecurity like a gaping wound."

Yessss.

"Let us help to heal you," I said, slipping to my knees and tugging on Jaxon's hand to make him do what my dragon had placed in my mind. "The emptiness inside you will be fulfilled."

My beta dropped beside me, and we stared up at Patrick, both of our physical bodies aroused by kneeling before the one who owned us, heart and soul.

The dragon inside him growled—groaned—with a longing so intense, I couldn't understand how he had managed to withstand its power for so many years. His physical desire for us radiated through the circle, but still he hesitated, his anxiety palatable and sour in my mind.

"Fucking us out of your system isn't an option," Jaxon said as though he really could read Patrick's mind. Perhaps it had something to do with them both being men, but I couldn't pinpoint what made my beta's claim rational. "It'll only make you want us more."

Deeper need lay beyond the longing for release, but I couldn't yet make sense of what was causing our alpha to stand firm.

A brisk wind blew my hair across my face, but I clutched at my mates' hands, refusing to ease the tickle of strands over my cheeks. "Allow us to love you, Patrick."

Jaxon's brow furrowed at Patrick's continued silence. "You *are* whole of mind," he stated as though, again, he understood something within Patrick's psyche that I didn't, "but allow fate to have her way in gifting you everything else you desire."

Patrick swallowed. "You're asking me to end the career I've fought to build, halt the forward momentum toward what I have been driven to accomplish my entire life. You expect me to give up my dreams for what...to get my dick wet?" He shuddered as arousal rushed through all three of us, inner beasts moaning their desire for that very thing.

"This is only the beginning," I argued softly, my chest aching and core pulsing with the need to be filled. "And nothing about your current existence needs to end. You aren't losing *anything*, Patrick. You'll be gaining so much more than you could ever have imagined."

Another shiver caused his body to twitch, and he exhaled heavily, tipping his head back. "Jesus fucking Christ," he muttered, shoulders slumping—but his hold on our hands remained strong and unwavering.

The failing of his human stubbornness fell over us like a spring rain, gentle and cleansing. Still, a part of him wished to hold firm, but the darkness within him wound about his soul, coaxing quietly, pushing. Enticing. Snaking its way through his walls.

Patrick exhaled with a grunt, delicious darkness swirling through our linked arms.

A deeper voice, one full of wisdom, spilled ancient words from our alpha's lips, their meaning and intention sweeping through us.

My dragon, along with Jaxon's, wept.

CHAPTER 29
PATRICK

Exhaustion from trying to keep the truth—the *beast*—imprisoned inside me gave way to the voice needing to utilize my vocal cords. I didn't submit. The beast took over the second I *considered* doing so.

I'd never been anything but driven to excel, to prove myself sane, whole, someone who took pride in their control, and as I lost the battle to madness, I hated my weakness. Yes, I had seen things that would sway any scientist, but stubbornness clung to the deepest parts of me.

Humanity lost to a supernatural being that could very well ruin me.

I held no control as words poured from my mouth in a language I didn't understand, but zero trace of fear resided where panic should have laced my blood.

Dark blue fire ignited around my legs without an ounce of pain as it licked up my legs to consume my body.

Still, the unnatural words spilled from my lips without my permission.

Tears slid off Primrose's chin as her eyes glowed golden, similar colored flames licking at her body. Jaxon—fuck did the boy make me crave darker desires—stared at me, lust radiating from his brilliant blue-green gaze. The whorls of fire around him glinted aqua where the two colors of his eyes intermingled.

The voice in me quieted to a purr, and the world around us appeared brighter.

I wanted to believe I dreamed, that this was a figment of my imagination, but I felt *alive* for the first time in my life.

"You haven't felt anything yet," Primrose promised as tears continued to leak down her cheeks.

Images flashed in my head, the beast whispering them into existence of all the ways I would have my mates, how I would bring them pain and pleasure.

"Yes," Primrose whispered as Jaxon groaned a cursed agreement.

Their arousal intensified, rousing the burn in my groin and heightening my craving to dominate and conquer.

I wanted to release my grip on their hands and tear off my pants, command them to worship me as they seemed so eager to do—as the weird energy linking us *begged* for.

My cock swelled so quickly I grunted again, hunching in on myself as the beast fixated on finishing what he'd started. "Fuck."

"Yes," they both said as one.

A muscle in my jaw ticked as I fought to control the drive inside me, demanding I claim them both. Own them with my hands and mouth. Flood them with my seed until they both lie spent, completely wrecked.

Fulfilled.

A muscle ticked in my jaw as the voice inside me groaned, causing pre-cum to spill from my slit. I would give us all what instinct demanded of me, but in the privacy of my home, where there would be no chance of damage to my reputation.

"In my car," I bit out the command, refusing to be ignored. "Now."

They scrambled to their feet and spun from me as though their asses were on fire, our hands slipping free from one another, leaving me...bereft.

Hissing like water to flames sounded in my ears, and I could fucking feel that damned beast inside me slithering around through my soul in annoyed dissatisfaction from having something stolen from him.

Inwardly, I told the damned thing to calm the fuck down. He had taken advantage of his freedom and gained control over my mouth, but I was the one in charge now.

Not him.

He continued to hiss at me as I stalked behind Primrose with her gorgeous, naked ass and Jaxon's flexing backside cradled in tight-as-fuck jeans.

Curses rang in my head, and I pressed down on my aching bulge, wetness from copious amounts of pre-cum leaking through my slacks.

Un-fucking-natural.

It was time to fuck these two out of my system and set my head on straight again.

Jaxon reached the car and glanced over his shoulder at me, an eyebrow raised, a coy smirk on his lips. I could sense his need to fuck, so he must feel mine.

"In," I demanded, my voice more of a growl than words.

His amusement floated over me as though we still held hands. "Balls deep," he said with a chuckle.

Little shit.

"Jaxon, up front," I ordered, ignoring his taunt even though I wanted to thrust into his body as far as I could go, hopefully ripping the air from his lungs in the process. "Primrose, on his lap."

Needed to keep them close.

They obeyed without a word, and I climbed in the driver's side, slamming the door shut behind me. Their scents filled the small interior, making breathing—and withstanding my lust—damned near impossible.

Without glancing at either of them, I turned on the car and tore out of the pull-off, suddenly realizing that we *could* have been seen by anyone—dragon, naked woman, otherworldly flames licking at the three of us.

But there had been no hint of headlights or a car of any manner in the dark wilderness surrounding us.

"How did you get out here?"

"We took an Uber," Primrose replied.

That...*fuckery* had been unseen by anyone but the three of us.

My shoulders relaxed, and I glanced over at them.

Jaxon's hand lay on her thigh, her knees pulled up, hiding the golden curls at the apex of her thighs.

Our sweet mates.

As though in response to the whisper inside me, Primrose's strawberry-like scent that had imprinted on my brain the day before flooded my senses.

I pressed hard on my bulge, needing to strangle the hell out of my shaft. "You can hear the voice inside me, can't you?" I asked, my voice shaky.

"Yes."

Taste.

Primrose whimpered as the sweetness of her arousal thickened in the air, causing my balls to tighten against my body.

Jaxon groaned, and I clutched at the steering wheel, focus glued to the road.

An image flashed in my mind, and needing *something* to tide me over until we could seek our release behind closed doors, I gave in. "Face forward, Primrose."

She scrambled to do as told.

"Good girl."

A whimper on her lips caused my cock to buck inside its prison.

"Shit," Jaxon muttered as though our senses fed off each other.

"Spread her legs, boy. Tell me how wet she is."

"*Fuuuuck.*" Jaxon groaned, shifting Primrose on his lap in obedience, but she didn't put up a fight, widening her thighs over his before he even settled her back against his chest.

I glanced over as she tipped her head on his shoulder and grasped his hand, pulling it between her thighs as though he wasn't moving fast enough to please her.

I tore my gaze off them to check the empty road—and promptly glanced over again.

Jaxon worked his hand against her pussy, and I cursed the lack of light. "Is she wet?"

"Fucking *soaked*," he replied, his voice low and full of lust. "Hot and so damned *slick*. Jesus, you need our dicks, don't you, sweetheart?"

"Yes!" She gasped, gyrating on his lap, her sweetness cloying. Mouthwatering.

"Do you like his fingers inside you, Primrose?" I rasped, uncaring my lust for them laced every word.

"Yes," she repeated and arched, and I gripped the steering wheel tighter to keep from reaching out to feel how needy she really was.

"Make her come, Jaxon."

Primrose writhed on his lap, her shifting hips and whimpers causing my dick to leak like a faucet.

The wet sounds of his fingers fucking her pussy fueled the prowling, growling beast inside me. Heat raced through my body, tightened every muscle to the point of exploding.

"Oh!" Primrose cried out, her back bowed, hands clasped around Jaxon's forearm as he worked her over.

"That's it, Prim," he murmured in her ear with a crooning tone that pulsed need through my groin as she found her release. "She's pulsing around my fingers—coming all over my hand, Doc. Fuck, do I want to be buried in you, sweetheart. So damned hard for you. Need to bust a nut deep inside your warmth. Jesus, you're perfect."

She quieted and went limp against Jaxon, who groaned a few more curses before releasing a slow, steady breath as though in an attempt to get a hold of himself so he didn't nut in his jeans.

"Put your fingers in my mouth," I told him, not taking my eyes off the road.

Primrose moaned but didn't move a muscle.

Jaxon shifted, and the sweet, musky scent of her cum hit me like a wave as he held his hand in front of my mouth.

Eyes on the road, I flicked my tongue out, licking up his middle finger.

The beast inside me roared his need for satisfaction as I grunted, abs contracting in attempts to keep myself from coming untouched like a goddamned pubescent kid.

She was perfection, just like Jaxon had claimed. Pure fucking heaven—I couldn't begin to imagine what Jaxon would be like on my tongue.

"Fuck," he murmured what seemed to be his favorite word as I sucked his finger into my mouth to swallow every trace of her essence off him.

I pulled back once finished, needing to adjust my aching shaft behind its soaked prison. Christ, I was a mess—and I hadn't even climaxed.

More.

I wanted the same as the voice—but a hell of a lot more than a mere taste.

CHAPTER 30

PRIMROSE

While our alpha may have experienced euphoria while beginning the bonding process among the three of us by speaking the ancient words, an underlying discomfort radiated off Patrick, making similar feelings trickle down my spine.

I still floated from my orgasm, my body lax and pressed against Jaxon's warmth, but a sense of Patrick refusing to give in completely caused my stomach to clench. His inner dragon had spoken, but I had a feeling our alpha wasn't pleased he'd lost his humanity briefly to his beast.

Tilting my head to the side, I watched him suck my cum off Jaxon's fingers, and a spasm clenched my pussy with renewed desire. The hard length pressing against my ass and the lust-filled energy ripping between us let me know Jaxon felt the same, regardless of the unease I sensed swirling beneath Patrick's need.

He stared straight ahead, hands clasped on the steering wheel, and I struggled to vocalize what he needed to hear, what would settle his mind over the bonding he'd begun among us. Perhaps fucking it out of his system, as Jaxon had said, *would* work. Once more feeling inept at relationships and choosing to trust my beta, I closed my eyes, basking in the scents of my mates and the warmth cradling my body that grew heavier with every passing mile.

Jaxon soothed his hands down my thighs, drawing my legs closed as he nuzzled in my neck, attentive and aware of my spiraling emotions as always. "This is only the beginning of our dreams coming true," he whispered into my ear as if to assure me Patrick would eventually give in without holding back. "Ask your questions, Doc," he stated after a quick nibble on my lobe.

Patrick readjusted his hold on the wheel but still didn't glance our way at Jaxon's suggestion. "I can't process all of this right now."

I pressed my lips tight, wishing with an ache in my chest for our alpha to work through the emotions battling in his head.

"I didn't speak those words—whatever they were—willingly," he finally said what I'd been sure about, his voice low. "It's only fair that you both know."

Jaxon's disappointment slammed into me like a brutal winter wind, stealing my breath.

A feeling of dread beneath the desire for fulfillment overshadowed us all.

"It can't be taken back," I whispered, hating that I needed to give my alpha the truth when I'd been desperate for him to understand everything for days on end.

He nodded as though accepting my words, but his discomfort grew. "How long will this…this driving desire for you two continue to own my thoughts?"

I swallowed as Jaxon tensed beneath me. He knew the answer—we'd discussed everything about three fated dragonblood mates. "It will lessen over time," I finally answered, "but only after we've bonded fully."

"Meaning?" he pressed, his tone tight.

"You began the process, and unless we complete it, desire for each other will heighten until our human bodies submit to our dragon halves into performing the act—whether your human half wants it or not."

"Fuck." Patrick rubbed a palm down over his mouth. "What the fuck did that damn *thing* set into motion?"

Both Jaxon and I held our silence, the wind buffeting Patrick's car as he sped southward.

I curled against my beta, needing comfort and our alpha to ease the emotional pain both of us experienced, and yet fearing he wouldn't.

Once we arrived at Patrick's house, tears clogged my throat from an array of emotions I hadn't expected after the beginning of our bonding. Nothing in the histories of our people mentioned or even suggested this kind of heartache accompanied a connection destined by fate. The difficulty hurt, terribly.

Jaxon's arms offered what I longed for, but he wasn't enough, just as I wasn't enough for him. We required our alpha to complete us, to fill the gaping hole that suddenly seemed larger than before. But we also needed for him to do so *willingly,* out of desire to be one with us, or our entire existence would be riddled with misery from his human half having been manipulated.

Without a word, Patrick pulled into the garage attached to his house and hit a button to close the door behind the car. He climbed out, and Jaxon followed suit, keeping me in his arms as he followed our alpha to the door leading into the house.

Patrick clicked on a light, tossed his keys on the kitchen counter, and turned, hands fisted at his sides. His dark blue eyes, troubled and hurting, reflected the emotions simmering in the energy linking us. I almost feared the true bond snapping into place, revealing every last bit that our alpha felt and thought.

The rejection would be unbearable, and his human side's desire for freedom would sink like a knife into my chest. Knowing how Jaxon would react would only heighten my misery.

A pained noise escaped my throat as Jaxon slowly set me on my feet, and I grasped his hand, desperate for something solid to hold onto.

Patrick glanced from him to me, over my body and back up, heating me through with a need that overshadowed my fear and disappointment over how my childhood dream was turning out. "You scared the fuck out of me tonight," he said, shifting his focus to Jaxon.

"Can't say I'm sorry, so don't bother asking for an apology."

Patrick's eyes narrowed as his shoulders seemed to broaden, his height increased. His chin tipped upward, and he peered down his nose at our beta. "Strip."

In his haste to obey, Jaxon stumbled sideways into the island, and I bit the inside of my lip to keep from laughing regardless of the hurt still lancing through me.

"I'm going to take what I want," Patrick stated, slowly unbuckled his belt, drawing it from the loops. I swore he thought to say more, but he held his silence.

Regardless of unsaid words, a rush of wetness slickened my core, and Jaxon groaned, his cock thick and dripping.

"Upstairs, boy," Patrick ordered, his tone firm. Unyielding.

Jaxon started toward a set of stairs, and I glanced at Patrick, wondering what he wished from me. Our alpha tipped his head after Jaxon, and I scurried along, my backside tingling from his stare, my pussy pulsing from the arousal-filled energy behind me.

Jaxon hesitated at the landing but turned toward the door on the left. I followed on his heels, the scent of Patrick's cologne and brimstone coming strongest from that room.

Through the dimness, I could make out a bed against the wall, four corner posts jutting upright toward the ceiling.

Jaxon moved forward and grasped the two at the foot, his back toward me, arms stretched out wide.

Patrick's presence behind me sent a rush of tingles over my skin.

"Mmm." His low growl of approval of our beta's actions slickened my thighs. "On the bed, girl."

I scurried to obey, sliding against the headboard as Patrick closed first one blind then the other before turning on dimmed lights overhead.

My gaze flitted from Jaxon's parted lips to Patrick's glare as he took in our beta, who had offered himself up in a delicious pose of submission.

I wondered at Jaxon's ability to expect what Patrick wanted, but he seemed to have gotten our alpha's desire correct.

Patrick unbuttoned his shirt, revealing tanned skin over prominent pectorals that were bare from hair. A silver chain graced his neck, and tattoos snaked around his side from his back, ending before inking the ridges of muscle lining his core. Gaze locked on Jaxon's ass, he stalked close, looped belt gripped in his right hand. He pressed against Jaxon, and our beta sagged, closing his eyes and groaning at the contact, knuckles white where he grasped the bedposts.

"You know what I'm going to do," Patrick whispered in his ear, sending a shudder through Jaxon.

"Yes."

"Do I have to tie you in place?"

"No—Sir."

"Mmm," Patrick hummed his approval, reaching around to cup Jaxon's groin.

Our beta grunted but held still.

"If you take your punishment for scaring the shit out of me like a good boy," Patrick growled against his ear, "I'll reward you."

Jaxon swallowed and nodded, his eyelids sliding open. Our gazes latched, and the desire simmering between us caused my breath to catch.

"Give him something to focus on, girl," Patrick said to me while stepping back. "But no coming."

Patrick hadn't entirely submitted to his dragon side, but his instincts still led him to fulfill his role in gifting his mates pleasure—this time, through pain.

A heavy sigh left me as I widened my legs and ran my fingers down over my pubis. Ignoring my throbbing nub to keep from coming like my alpha had stated, I stroked through the soaked mess between my legs.

Jaxon groaned, his gaze glued to my pussy as I slid two fingers deep inside my aching core.

Patrick drew his arm back and let loose with the belt.

CHAPTER 31
JAXON

ire flared to life across the back of my thighs, and I jolted forward, my grip on the bedposts keeping me on my feet.

Yessss.

My inner beast purred his delight in the lash of our alpha's belt, but I bit my tongue to stop myself from cursing aloud. My eyelids slammed shut against the pain radiating over my body—and in my chest from Patrick wanting to deny the truth of us.

I'd expected a sting from the first strike, not the full force of Patrick's arm that stalled out my lungs and made fire race over my skin. Determined to get to the place where euphoria would overshadow everything else, I clutched at those damned bedposts, keeping myself upright—determined to be a good boy for the darkness owning Patrick's soul.

Another stroke of his belt hit the underside of my ass cheeks, and I winced, jaw clenched at the anger coming off him like deadly waves of radiation. Twice more he hit, slowly making his way upward, and my erection flagged at the sting that refused to fade regardless of my dragon's delight over Patrick's sadistic side coming out to play.

Where was the goddamn promised pleasure? The morphing of pain into something so intense I would weep with need to blow my cum all over his goddamn bedspread?

Relax—submit.

I shook my head, my human body unwilling to obey the voice I'd come to trust as deeply as I did Prim.

"Jaxon." Her ragged whisper pulled my eyelids up, and I caught her gaze as another hit landed across my upper back. She felt the sting—shared in the agony I wanted to transcend beyond. And I experienced her desire for me to give in, seek out the release I could find beneath our alpha's dominance.

"Look how wet you're making me," she whispered, her voice husky, like a siren calling to my soul.

I glanced down at her hand, breathing deeply as she pulled her fingers from her pussy. Wetness glistened in the overhead lights, her slit dripping onto the bed beneath her. My mouth flooded with drool as the sweet, strawberry tang of her filled my nose.

Patrick groaned behind me, the noise escaping him turning into a grunt as he let loose with another blow. The leather belt landed with more force, but my body didn't jolt forward to escape as I focused on our female's need.

Prim rubbed her clit, her hips lifting before sliding her fingers into her sopping, pink core. "You're so hot, Jaxon," she whispered on a moan, her hips rising again as she fucked herself. "So beautiful offering your body to our alpha."

My dick twitched as I thought of sinking deep into her juicy pussy, its wet heat clamping down on me, drawing me in deeper until my cockhead nestled against her womb where it belonged.

Submit.

Another lash against my shoulders barely registered as I

imagined pumping in and out of her—and Patrick pressing against my back while sliding his cock deep into my ass.

"Fuck." I groaned the word as blood rushed to swell my dick.

Another grunt from Patrick, another hit landed, and my body tingled, the desire to fuck soothing the stinging pain he dished out.

My dick dripped as my skin broke out into a sweat, the sweet surrender of my body to the promised pleasure like diving into a cool lake on a hot summer's day.

I whimpered and pressed toward Patrick's belt, my ears ringing, senses overrun with the scent of arousal. The taste of Primrose coated the air, the musk of Patrick's pre-cum oozing in his slacks flooded my nose.

He heaved behind me with another slap of leather while I stared at the pink heaven between Prim's thighs she toyed with, needing to bury myself deep in our female, giving her what fate demanded of me.

Patrick heaved for breath, moving in close to press against my back, the heat of his body like a furnace, a chain of metal around his neck cool against my nape. "You've earned your reward," Patrick rasped, his dick hard, the material between us chafing the raw lashes on my skin. "Take her, boy, but your climax belongs to me."

I released my finger-aching grip on the posts and rushed to fall between Prim's spread thighs, her arms lifting in welcome. One rushed thrust buried me into her pussy and flooded me with her love, her complete acceptance, making me feel almost whole again.

Our inner beasts groaned their pleasure, swirling around each other, a gorgeous blending of gold and greenish-blue in our souls.

Patrick had ripped me to shreds—fucking broke my heart with his confession he hadn't started our bonding willingly

—but I pushed the hurt away as Primrose embraced me wholly.

I wanted to fuck her hard and fast, blow my goddamn load, but our alpha hadn't yet granted me that right. Through the fire beginning our bond, I'd slipped past his defenses, saw into his darker half, his need to vent frustration. He'd had the same desires of my inner beast, of bondage and pain.

Thank fuck I'd been able to find the pleasure in submitting to his heavy hand by simply focusing on our female, or I would have feared for our future that would demand I give myself up to him again and again.

Primrose had told me dragonblood alphas enjoyed dominating their mates, and having found the lightheaded, floaty feeling from the pain Patrick had dished out, I knew I would never get enough of him.

I captured her mouth, offering her all my love, every ounce of my goddamn heart meant for her. She clutched at me with her thighs, heels, and hands against my welts, but the lust spurring me on kept me focused on bringing her to completion as our alpha had commanded me to do. With every slow thrust burying me against her womb, Prim held me close, whimpering into my mouth, both of us longing for our alpha with an intensity that caused goose bumps to break along our skin.

Awareness of Patrick stripping at the foot of the bed, the knowledge of his instinctive drive to fuck, and the scent of his pre-cum swirling past my nose caused my cock to buck inside Primrose.

Need.

"Soon," she murmured, nipping at my lower lip.

I planked on my knees, hands pressed into the mattress beside her head. Gazes locked, we continued to make love, our hearts already bonding beyond what I had felt with her before.

The bed dipped behind me, and my asshole clenched and relaxed at the thought of our alpha finally joining us. He kicked my knees wider, and Prim glanced beyond my shoulder, her pupils wide, lips parted as arousal, hot and heavy, wept around my thrusting dick.

I imagined how Patrick must look looming over us—hard body, straining cock.

Groaning, I burrowed into her welcoming warmth, wishing I could drink him in as she'd gotten to do.

As I pulled out of Prim's pussy, Patrick settled behind me, grabbing hold of my dick and squeezing to keep me from thrusting back into heaven.

"Aw, fuck." My eyelids slammed shut as he coaxed me from her inner wall's clutches, sliding his palm down over my length, milking pre-cum from my slit.

"Horny fucker aren't you?" he mumbled, positioning me at Prim's pussy.

I groaned my agreement while sinking back into her.

"Good, because this and my own pre-cum are all the lube you're going to get."

Yessss.

My dragon needed the pain even though my human half wasn't super thrilled about having a thick cock shoved up my backside without real lubricant.

"It will be enough," Primrose whispered against my mouth, and my muscles relaxed, my trust in her unquestionable.

Patrick rubbed soaked fingers over my asshole, and I bore down to let him in. Compared to the lingering sting on my backside from his belt, his finger sinking into my ass didn't burn one bit.

More.

"Goddamn." I swallowed as he easily worked a second

finger into my ass as though having heard my inner beast's begging.

"You like that, boy?" Patrick growled, leaning over me as I pressed my chest to Prim's, my face in her neck.

"Fuck, *yes*. So damned good I'm dying for more. Need your cock inside me, Patrick. *Fuck*."

Prim's pussy contracted around me, her heart thrumming along with mine. "Let him in, beta. Be the bridge between us."

Her whispered words, laced with love, reminded me beyond the lust clogging my brain of what would happen when he did.

I shifted out of her body, pressing against Patrick's hand. "More," I groaned as he moved his fingers inside me with a scissor action. "Please."

His touch disappeared as I sank into our female, but he grasped my ass cheeks, pulling them apart, trapping me against her body with his powerful thighs.

Patrick pressed the slick, blunt head of his dick against my asshole.

"Breathe," Prim whispered.

"Yes, oh fuck, yes." I gulped as he slowly stretched my rim.

My dick jerked inside her as he gently pushed against the muscle keeping him out when I'd expected a fast, brutal claiming like the darkness inside both of us craved.

"Shove your dick inside me, Patrick," I demanded through clenched teeth, fear of his humanity causing him to pull away again, denying us fulfillment, leaking into my thoughts.

He didn't hesitate in his slow press forward, but he also didn't give me what I needed to be assured of our future.

I thrust backward, yanking my dick from Prim's pussy while stuffing my ass full with his thick length. My breath ripped from my lungs at the feeling of being split in two. "Jesus fucking Christ!" I bit out, my asshole throbbing around his shaft as I struggled to accommodate what I had forced deep into my guts.

"Stupid boy," he stated through gritted teeth, hands in a vise grip on my hips, holding me still.

My hole fucking burned like hell, but he'd buried to the hilt. I would have grinned if not for the stinging fullness of finally having our alpha's dick where it belonged.

Ours.

Goddamned right, he was.

And there would be no going back, no matter how much it hurt having him inside me.

CHAPTER 32
PATRICK

Fuck.

Fuck.

Fuck.

The darkness swirled freely around in the void of my soul while I was buried inside Jaxon's body.

Glee inflected in the beast's tone, and I couldn't keep the sick grin off my face even though I hated how my beta had hurt himself out of lust.

Desire—rightness.

Mates.

Give.

Hissing, I reached around our interlocked bodies to grasp Jaxon's dick. He was still hard and dripping even though a sense of his pain flickered through my mind, same as every lash of my belt had done.

Jaxon grunted when I tugged him forward, my groin tight against his ass cheeks while notching the head of his cock against Primrose's slickened lower lips.

She met my gaze over Jaxon's shoulders, golden eyes glowing like fire, pink flushing her face. "Yes."

I slammed us forward at her consent, Jaxon's cock sinking deep into Primrose.

Alpha.

Beta.

Female.

The whispered words resonated inside me. Light flooded through me, filling up the darkness I'd been attempting to escape from my entire life.

I'd planned to simply fuck the desire for these two from my body, but there would be no single time of satiated bliss to see me through until I breathed my last and was buried six feet under. I wouldn't exist without them by my side throughout every day I had left on this earth.

All those years I had been driven by *dragonblood* when I'd thought my humanity simply needed accomplishments stacked atop each other in order to find the fulfillment I had craved.

Jaxon and Primrose completed me, made me feel whole for the first time in my life. *This* was what I had been longing for, exactly as Emelia had claimed.

Yessss—now give.

Fulfill.

Hands in a bruising grip on Jaxon's waist, I pulled out and slammed into his ass, pushing him deep into Primrose. All three of us groaned regardless of Jaxon's pain of my girth stretching him, but a satisfied swell of emotion in that tether among us, sucking me into an ocean my humanity feared to trust but couldn't help dive into deeper.

I backed off, pulling Jaxon with me, and Primrose whimpered, releasing her hold on Jaxon's shoulder to lift her hand toward me. Her need for me was like a living energy, and I held her golden stare while lacing my fingers with hers and fucking into Jaxon, forcing him into her body again.

He lay lax between us, allowing me to do as I wished,

using his body to find release even though he hadn't yet grown accustomed to my dick stabbing into his guts.

Such a good boy.

My jaw clenched at the thought of his age as it always did when I thought of or spoke that word that described him in my mind, but nothing would stop me from finishing what we'd started. I lusted to stuff his ass full of my cum as he filled Prim. I wanted her writhing beneath us, her cries coating our ears—

The taste of her blood on our tongue.

"Yes," she gasped, and Jaxon groaned as though we'd all shared my inner beast's thought, his back arching, pain subsiding.

The darkness spurred me on, the goddamn *dragon* inside me fighting for free rein. I thrust harder—deeper—both of their cries sending a glorious ache through my chest. My balls tightened, and I planked over Jaxon's back, his body tensing beneath mine.

"Fuck," I growled, slamming balls-deep into his ass. "Can't…"

"Please," Primrose whispered, wetness coating her eyes.

"Need to come," Jaxon gasped, eyes clenched shut, his lips against her neck. "Fucking *need—*"

My balls erupted. The beast roared.

And I sank my teeth into Jaxon's neck as he did the same to Primrose.

With every violent spurt of cum into Jaxon, I felt the pump of blood through both their arteries—tasted the coppery tang of him—and her.

Light erupted around our writhing bodies, bringing fire and pleasure that seemed to know no end. I continued to thrust in mindless abandon, emptying myself into my beta as he did in our female.

Like a fucking sledgehammer to the brain, emotions—

fucking insane whispers similar to my own darkness—rushed through my head. I gasped, tearing my mouth off the base of Jaxon's neck, one last jerk of my dick in his ass releasing the final drop of cum that marked his insides as mine.

Yessss.

Three voices echoed as one in my head.

"What the fuck—"

"Don't," Primrose said, grabbing hold of my shoulder blades with inhuman strength as I began to back out of Jaxon.

I shuddered, eyes clenched shut as though reality would disappear along with my sight. The woman beneath us was strong as fuck—there would be no escaping her clutches.

"You have completed the bonding."

I swore in my head, fighting off the emotions that weren't just mine assaulting my mind with vivid clarity.

Jaxon's hurt tasted of ash and cinder.

Primrose's fear beneath lingering pleasure was sour on my tongue.

There was no science to back what had happened—couldn't fucking wrap my head around this damned...unity among us—but I had given over willingly, unlike what had happened at the canyon when the beast had stolen my vocal cords.

"You *did* choose this time," Jaxon stated, the tension leaving his body, making it obvious he could hear my thoughts as clearly as I did his.

With both of them somehow in my mind, a lie wouldn't allow me to avoid this mess my lust had gotten me into. Desire that would never be sated then escaped.

"I did," I admitted what I hadn't been able to help longing for and driving forward toward completion, my muscles going lax.

Primrose released her hold, soothing her soft palms down my back.

I tipped my forehead against Jaxon's shoulder. Relief poured through me at my decision to stay put, but that emotion was not my own.

How would I explain having two lovers, barely legal, living in my home? Because they sure as fuck weren't going anywhere. Just the thought of being without them felt like someone dug claws into my chest, attempting to rip my heart out. They had been ingrained into the cells of my body. There would be no eradicating them without unimaginable agony.

Lockwood would send me packing for sure once they learned *who* was in my bed. A goddamn patient I had agreed to let go and a young woman any sane therapist, social worker, or doctor would keep under lock and key.

If Jaxon didn't press charges, would I escape the law? Would my choice to fuck a past patient form a stain on my reputation rather than my ruination?

"Fuck." I backed off, and Primrose let me go. Half-stumbling, I walked to the ensuite bathroom, shutting the door firmly behind me. A million thoughts filled my head, and I hated that my mates responded in kind.

Fuck whoever can't handle the truth. Jaxon's inner dragon spoke, the one that had sent him leaping off roofs and bridges. Or was it his humanity? Couldn't fucking tell.

We can go far from here, start over. Primrose's voice in my mind held a soothing note, her desire to ease all our apprehension was the type of nurturing I expected, which fulfilled a part of Jaxon I wouldn't be able to touch.

I clutched my crowded head, brow furrowed. I had two others, beasts and humans alike, their emotions and thoughts threatening to turn me toward madness.

I turned the faucet on full blast, gripping the sink until

the water heated. Still fighting to find privacy in my goddamn head, I grabbed two washcloths and wet them.

My steps were a bit slower in returning to the bedroom, but I refused to be a coward. I'd used them both in hopes of ridding myself of lust that had consumed me since meeting them—and it seemed my dick wasn't nearly satisfied.

The creature inside me stirred upon seeing Jaxon still atop Primrose and buried inside her pussy, my cum dripping from his abused asshole.

Dick swelling and teeth clenched, I wiped him clean with clinical thoroughness when my shaft ached to sink past his puffy, red pucker into his tight heat.

"Doc."

"No," I stated firmly, even though the three beasts were in agreement in wanting what Jaxon asked for without voicing his ache to be filled again.

I nudged him with my knee to get him to roll off Primrose. He did so with a groan, grabbing hold of his cumcovered, still hard cock, but I refused to meet his gaze. Using the other towel, I focused on cleaning Primrose of his seed, trying like fuck to get the idea of licking his spunk from between her swollen labia from my mind.

Fucking animals.

He huffed a laugh. "It's not a problem, trust me."

I finally gave him my eyes.

A smirk lifted his lips, although disappointment in my thoughts over the whole mess continued to knife his chest.

"Your balls will always have plenty to spare, and there's enough pre-cum to keep from growing chafed."

"Fuck." I scrubbed a hand down over my face while glancing at Primrose.

She, too, smiled, although a bit more hesitant, as she studied my face as though trying to reach deeper beyond the inhabiting of my head I had unknowingly allowed them by bonding us together.

I tossed the rags aside and sat back on my haunches. "Care to tell me what the fuck this is?" I said, holding her gaze and motioning between the three of us. "Because having the *four* of you inside my goddamn mind atop this purring fucker in my chest makes me believe I should be committed."

Her smile melted my heart, and I found myself pulling her into my arms. Instinct settled her onto my lap, her softness and scent soothing some of the unrest inside my soul.

Our female.

I couldn't argue that fact. Didn't want to. Everything inside me wished just to give in and accept the unnatural feelings that were insanity to my educated brain.

But I fucking couldn't.

Stubborn to a fault, I didn't know how to see beyond truth I'd set in front of me since the day I'd been locked inside a white room that stank of bleach and madness.

CHAPTER 33
PRIMROSE

Being bonded to my mates was nothing like I had dreamed about.

I had imagined pure joy, zero doubt, and a total lack of all hesitancy or wariness. Unconditional love and acceptance. Unfathomable happiness, a sense of completeness at having fulfilled the beginning of my destiny.

Unfortunately for my own scattered thoughts, both Patrick's and Jaxon's accosted my mind, and I fought an upheaval of emotions I didn't know how to deal with.

I wouldn't fly off, though. I would stay and make things right, resolve the issue as Grandpapa had told me to do, as Jaxon had asked of me if I was ever again desperate to flee what I couldn't make sense of or didn't have answers for.

My alpha had asked for clarity on what had happened, but beyond explaining the facts about the dragonblood bonding process, I wasn't sure what he needed to hear in order to ease his mind and make him accept what had occurred—and appreciate what fate had gifted him.

Two adoring mates who would lay down their lives for him. Worship the ground he walked on. Lavish love and affection to fill the void in his life I could now feel as though it had become my own.

I rubbed at my chest, swallowing hard, and forced myself to remain on my alpha's lap where he'd settled me, regardless of his unrest. My inner beast prowled beneath my skin, her own flight instincts kicked into high gear.

We traversed a difficult path I never expected to walk upon once bonded with my mates, but I would *not* flee and inflict even more hurt on my beta, like I'd done the first time I'd selfishly abandoned him in my pain.

Lack of movement on my part allowed my beta to relax on the bed beside us—he trusted me with his heart, and I vowed silently, as I'd done before, never to leave him again.

My voice shook as I laid out the details I had learned in the books of my grandpapa's library to our alpha. Three destined mates, once bonded by blood, would be linked emotionally until their deaths. The sharing of thoughts, feelings, hopes, and dreams couldn't be erased as normal humans did once they fell out of love with or turned their backs on their partners.

"It's an unbreakable bond," he murmured once I finished, and I held out my hand to Jaxon, who lay a short distance away.

"Yes," I whispered as our beta laced his fingers through mine and eased my emotional torment the slightest bit.

"For the duration of our lives," Patrick murmured again as though speaking to himself.

I sat silent since he hadn't asked a question, his heartbeat in tune with mine beneath my ear as he processed what I had shared, and the reality of how his existence had changed. His rambling thoughts over sanity versus madness slowed.

Accept, his beast urged him, and although a wave of relief poured through me at knowing a part of him gave into what fate had set before us as bonded mates, unrest festered in a section of Patrick's soul that had been wounded subconsciously.

Jaxon squeezed my hand, a hint of coyness informing he was about to open his mouth— "Tell him about the whole dragon years versus human."

I bit back my smile as our beta's true intent came through loud and clear—along with the lustful path his thoughts took whenever it did with manipulation of a sexual sort.

But my sharing what he suggested wouldn't be laced with ill intent upon my tongue. There would be no coercion, simply truth.

"Those with a higher percentage of dragonblood will live longer than others," I said.

"Meaning?" Patrick asked, his hold still tender as his exhale stirred the hair atop my head.

"*Meaning*," I continued slowly, while toying with the chain around his neck, my body responding to Jaxon's heightening arousal, "in the natural, with my being more Blood Born than human, I would outlive both of you. But the substance of your seed will prolong our beta's years and vice versa, so that we might have more time together."

"Our cum is the elixir of life for each other." Jaxon's eyes twinkled up at our alpha from where he sprawled beside us, his lips curled in a flirtatious smirk that made my core pulse with need.

Patrick groaned and shifted me against his thickening length. "I thought I knew what you were going to say before you did...this whole feeling your desires and hearing your thoughts shit is fucking crazy," he muttered, shaking his head.

"Crazy *good*," Jaxon said, and I moved off Patrick's lap as desire and a resulting vision of what I longed to experience filled my mind.

Wetness grew between my thighs.

Both my mates stared at me as I sat against the headboard, biting the inside of my lower lip.

"Fucking irresistible," Patrick muttered while glancing at Jaxon as our beta pushed up to sit on his knees. "You know what she wants, right?"

"Fuck yeah, and I also can feel how badly you lust for the same," Jaxon said, but withheld from reaching for our alpha, hands resting on his thighs, his cock throbbing against his lower abs.

One of Patrick's eyebrows shot up. "Same as you, it would seem. Fuck it." Gaze locked on our beta, he crawled the distance between them, powerful muscles held in check, same as my breath. He claimed Jaxon's mouth in a bruising kiss, and our beta sank beneath the onslaught until he sprawled on his back, hands grasping at Patrick, who settled his weight atop him.

They groaned as their bodies came together, and the burst of lust emanating through the bond caused my nipples to tighten. I pressed my thighs together to keep my arousal from trickling onto the bed.

Patrick growled, grinding his hips against Jaxon's, their level of lust beyond what I had ever experienced before. Skin slickened, and I swore I could feel both of their shafts as though they were a physical part of me, sensually gliding against each other's in a mess of pre-cum.

"Gonna blow if you keep that up," Jaxon said the second Patrick allowed him breath.

"Not until I say so." Patrick pushed up slightly and turned his body, facing Jaxon's feet. "Let's fulfill that fantasy our female cooked up." His focus flitted toward me from where he knelt over our beta, dark blue eyes overrun by the black of his swollen pupils. "Touch yourself, but no coming until we do."

I jerked my head up and down and spread my thighs wide, shaking fingers sliding down through my slick labia.

"Suck me, *beta*," Patrick ordered, his voice haggard as he lowered his body.

Jaxon held the base of his cock, pushing it up toward Patrick's waiting mouth. They closed over each other, and my moan mingled in the air with their deep groans. Through our bond, I could taste the musky flavor of Patrick and Jaxon's earthiness, both sweet and salty at the same time. My mouth watered as I slid two fingers deep into my pussy, but it was the sight of my mates sucking each other, their lashing tongues and hollowed cheeks that heightened my need for release.

Jaxon teetered on the edge of climax, his whimpers and writhing beneath our alpha just as riveting as Patrick's flexing ass shoving his cock down our beta's welcoming throat. Patrick's hair fell forward, hiding most of his face, but his groans, his dragon's simmering lust rose with its need to finish.

Patrick fought for control, wished to make us wait longer, but our need overrode him. He thrust into Jaxon, his dragon roared, and cum erupted into both of their throats. I cried out, a spasm ripping through my body as both my mates did the same, wetness soaking my hand, the taste of the men's seed flooding my senses.

Euphoric tremors raced through our bond, their climaxes intensifying mine, yet leaving me unsatisfied as I gasped for breath. Still pulsing and wanting, I moved forward when Patrick lifted off Jaxon.

"Ride him," he ordered, and I hurried to obey, needing Jaxon's cock deep inside me.

I settled my thighs on either side of Jaxon's, and he pulled me down, taking my mouth and filling my pussy with one slow glide as the lingering flavor of Patrick's cum swept over my tongue.

More.

Patrick's dragon growled his agreement with my desire, and he settled behind me, his hands on my ass cheeks as Jaxon continued to slowly fuck in and out of me. Our alpha spread me wide, his thumbs rubbing over my puckered hole.

I tore my mouth from Jaxon's swollen lips. "Take what your dragon wants."

With a groan, Patrick moved closer and rubbed his cock along Jaxon's as our beta pulled out of my core. "You're so wet," Patrick murmured, and Jaxon clenched his jaw, his passion-hazed eyes holding my gaze. "*So* wet," he repeated, his fingers sliding along either side of Jaxon's cock where it disappeared into my body. "And how the fuck am I still hard? Christ."

"Mmm." Our alpha removed his touch, and Jaxon pushed in deeper.

Wetness smeared over my puckered hole, and I dropped my head, eyes closed as Patrick pressed two fingers into my body to stroke along the thin skin inside me, separating him from Jaxon's shaft.

"Fuck," Jaxon said through clenched teeth, his voice strangled. His dick pulsed against my inner walls as Patrick's fingers slid along his length through a mere membrane a second time. "Sadist," he breathed, and Patrick chuckled.

"You seem to bring out that side of me," our alpha stated.

"Please," I whimpered, trying to fuck myself on his fingers.

"Have to stretch you first," Patrick said through clenched teeth while scissoring me open, and I shook my head.

"Dragonblood heals quickly—I won't be in pain for more than a single inhale. I need you—*please*, my alpha."

"Irresistible," he muttered.

Patrick's fingers slipped from my ass, but the much larger head of his cock moved against me, smearing a mess of pre-cum over my hole as my beta fucked up into me with a groan. "Stop moving, Jaxon."

Jaxon stilled immediately, concern filling his chest, clear through to mine.

Patrick pushed forward slowly. "Breathe," he murmured as Jaxon's thought to do the same flitted through my head.

As though they controlled my body, my muscles relaxed, and my lungs flooded with oxygen when I hadn't realized I held my breath.

Yessss.

Patrick notched the flared head of his cock in my ass and hissed as I tried to press back to stuff myself as my dragon desired. "Hold *still,*" he repeated, swatting my ass without force, and Jaxon groaned, his cock twitching inside me at the sting on my backside from our alpha's palm.

"Hurry the fuck up," our beta ordered, and Patrick's dragon snickered.

His thought of punishment for Jaxon's bossiness sent a rush of shared arousal through us, and our alpha sank deeper, stretching my hole to accommodate his girth. "Move, Jaxon," he said, his voice ragged, revealing the tight hold he had on himself.

Jaxon pulled from my warmth, and Patrick sank in, his balls resting against my body. As he dragged backward, Jaxon thrust in.

Dizzy on our shared lust, I couldn't voice my need. Knowing they felt what I did, I gave over to their use of my body, the weight of Patrick against my back, Jaxon's hard muscle beneath me. This was what I had dreamed of and hoped for.

A feeling of *home* radiating among us as we shared heated

breaths, unrest quieted in our moment of gifting one another pleasure.

My mates rocked in and out of me in opposing movements, exquisite friction sweeping me up until I panted and whimpered, begging my need to come between their sweat-slickened bodies.

"P—please." I licked my dry lips, tasting the salt on Jaxon's neck from where my face burrowed.

More.

Harder.

Faster.

My mates gave me what my beast requested, fucking into me with abandon, their grunts and groans heightening my readiness to come.

The slapping of flesh, the musky scent of our fucking, the shared passion among us…

Their desire to protect and care for me poured into me from both sides, my heart and mind linking alpha to beta.

Come as one, Patrick's inner beast demanded, and all three of us gave him what he required of us.

The noises of release flooding my ears weren't human, the force of pulsing cum filling my body, shuddering me in their tight hold. I rode the wave of my climax, my eyes clenched shut as Patrick took Jaxon's mouth over my shoulder, swallowing his cries, their shared orgasms prolonged by the dragonblood coursing through their arteries.

We stilled, in what felt like hours later, a heap of sweaty, exhausted bodies, physically connected, but emotionally bound together as well.

Exactly as we were meant to be.

I smiled as my mates' dragons whispered their agreement with mine.

CHAPTER 34

PATRICK

Two gorgeous-as-fuck youngsters lay tangled in my sheets, exhausted from a long night filled with sucking, fingering, and fucking. My balls ached from overuse, but I wouldn't complain about the other-worldly ability to get up and off like I was still Jaxon's age.

A boy I'd met one week ago.

What the fuck alternate reality had I dropped into?

A muscle ticked in my jaw, and I sipped my second cup of coffee while standing at the foot of my bed, staring at the two of them. I was showered, dressed, and ready for work, some-what more at ease with the reality of my life than I had been ten hours earlier. Both Jaxon and Primrose's minds rested, the purrs of their dragons mimicking the one within me, allowing me a moment of respite from the constant noise in my head while they were awake.

That shit was going to take some time to get used to, and while I could appreciate nothing but honesty lay among the three of us, zero chance of misunderstandings or outright lies, the connection was…concerning even now.

Acceptance over truth hadn't yet settled inside my soul,

even though a part of me longed to give in completely to what I truly wondered had been fated for me. A few days prior, Jaxon and Primrose had rocked my foundation, and I'd exchanged one bitch of a girlfriend for two new lovers, both years younger and much more pliable than she had been.

Best decision you ever made besides giving me my freedom.

My better sense questioned my inner beast's voice, who had gained power by being with the two, but I pushed the unease aside lest the negative emotion stirring in my chest awoke my mates. Another sip of hot, black coffee coated my tongue, but I could still taste the tingling sweetness of Jaxon's cum, the life-giving elixir he'd joked about prolonging my years even though Primrose claimed his statement to be truth, and thoroughly believed the fact. I'd never considered sucking another man's dick until her thought the night before filled me with the need to tangle in the hottest sixty-nine of my goddamn existence.

Again.

More.

I adjusted my thickening cock in my slacks and found myself smirking at all the other ways I planned on having my mates. Tied to my bed posts. Chained up from the ceiling. Flogged and teased until they sobbed for relief—once I ordered some toys.

Sadist.

"It would seem so," I murmured, powerless after the bonding to silence the voice I'd fought to contain since childhood. The darkness swirled inside me, inky black and lustful in ways most humans weren't, and I could admit to not exactly hating its desires and the sense of fulfillment I'd been longing for my entire life.

I found myself stroking my hard length through my slacks before I realized my hand had moved.

Yessss, my inner beast hissed even as I mentally cursed this new virility that didn't allow me to focus on work and the responsibility of completing the plan I'd set into place to expand my own practice here in town.

Primrose stirred, her blonde lashes fluttering. Her golden-brown gaze landed on me as her mind woke, instant happiness upon seeing me floating through the bond between us, winking out my concerns about reality. Her smile made my groin tighten, and I swallowed a groan as she acted on the first thought to flit through her mind.

She crawled toward me across rumpled sheets, her breasts swaying, hair a golden wave along her back and framing her face as she peered up at me. I moved closer to the bed's edge, unable to help the instinctive need to offer what her mouth watered for.

I sipped my coffee as though unfazed as her fingers worked to free my straining dick, but she felt my want, the longing to fill her belly with my cum. Wrapping one hand in her hair, I guided her open mouth to my throbbing shaft, groaning as her lips closed around my leaking head.

"Goddamn...deeper. Just like that. Yes, Prim—you're such a good girl taking all of me like that." A low groan rumbled from my chest, beast and human in agreement. "Jesus." My hand fisted her hair, lust to shove past her gag reflex and fuck her throat swirling through the darkness in me.

Awareness that Jaxon woke shivered through me, but I focused on the golden irises peering up at me through thick lashes as Primrose licked and sucked me deeper with each gentle thrust of my hips as I fought for control over the beast inside growling at me for not gifting our spunk to our needy female.

"What a sight to wake up to," Jaxon said on a moan. He moved behind Prim and buried his face in her ass.

My dick jerked inside Primrose's mouth as she whimpered around my girth, arching so our beta could reach every inch of her asshole and pussy with his searching tongue.

The sweetness of her arousal coated my taste buds as it did Jaxon's, but without actual substance to swallow down and keep forever.

"Take her, Jaxon," I stated through gritted teeth, the warmth of Prim's mouth, my beta's sac tight against his body acting like fuel to the flame inside me, begging to please all three of us.

He obeyed, lifting onto his knees, grasping her hips, and sensually sliding into her body. Head tipped up, veins popping in his neck, he groaned, and his elation at being inside her wet warmth swelled my length. I could feel him more intensely through where Primrose suckled on my shaft, like she'd become a conduit, the necessary link joining us.

To our beta.

"Yes," I growled my agreement with the beast inside me and gave over to my climax, my mates gladly following me into euphoria.

CHAPTER 35

JAXON

Patrick tucked his dick away inside his slacks, watching as I pulled out of our female's tight pussy. "Turn around. Let me see you," he told her.

Prim sighed and did as told, putty in his hands as he grasped her hips and lifted her ass into the air. He sank to his knees, and her sweet scent filled my nose as Patrick leaned forward to lick her clean. The musky tingling of my cum mixed with her tang of release made me crave his, but Prim had swallowed every drop he'd nutted into her mouth.

Grinning like a goddamn fool, I clasped my hands behind my head and leaned against the headboard, wondering at the lack of sting from last night's belt lashings on my backside while my alpha tongued deep into her, his desperation for more almost laughable. The mighty Doctor Macaire, needy as a kid in a candy store, always driven to get exactly what he wanted. "Does my spunk taste good, Doc?"

He shot me a glare over her ass, his tongue working to make her squeaky clean.

"Kind of cool seeing you on your knees, desperate for my nut."

"Go to hell, kid." He stood, his lips glistening, his gaze hard. "Or keep up the arrogant attitude and pay for it later."

My grin widened as my dragon groaned at the dark thoughts flooding Patrick's mind. "In that case, I hope my cum lingers on your tongue all damn day and you jerk off in that office of yours while thinking about sucking my dick."

Patrick's gaze narrowed, need unfurling in my stomach, but he turned to Prim, who lay sprawled along the foot of his —*our*—bed. He didn't argue with the thought in my head, thank fuck. "Jaxon is going to work later this morning, but we'll be back," he promised Prim. "Do not under *any* circumstances come to Lockwood. Understand?"

"Yes, my alpha." Prim's smile dazzled him, and he clenched his jaw and turned away before acting on the lust once more tingling through his balls.

Fuck, I wished he had stayed. Let me get a mouthful of his cum, too.

He swore before slamming our bedroom door behind him, making my grin widen.

Prim curled up against my side, content and happy, and we listened as Patrick went down the stairs and eventually let himself out the garage door—taking his energy and the purr of his satisfied dragon along with him.

Smiling, I closed my eyes, unbothered by the lack of his busy thoughts that tended to jumble in mine. I could sense the hint of peace he'd found, the acceptance gained by giving in to his beast and mates countless times throughout the early morning hours.

"He's still worried."

My eyelids popped open, and my smile faded. While I'd sensed a hint of unrest in Patrick, it hadn't compared to the negative energy I'd felt radiating off him before we'd bonded. Seemed a minuscule thing after the emotion our mating had infused through us.

"And that worries *you*." No use in asking what I could feel radiating off Primrose. I trailed my fingertips down her arm, hoping to inject her with my passivity toward the situation since I felt sure Doc would become as addicted to us as we were to him.

"Yes, it does, and I think you should be a little more concerned." She sat up, causing my hand to fall away from her, legs crossing beneath her. "Patrick has shown his ability to master his dragon, going so far as to completely shut him out."

"But we're bonded. Completely, and there's no reversing that. Right?"

Prim chewed her lower lip, her gaze flitting to the window and the overcast sky beyond as though inwardly searching for the connection between us that our alpha had created. "From what I've read, there should be *no* doubt or lingering questions once the bonding has occurred."

I shrugged, even though her words kicked up anxiety in my guts. "There's nothing else we can do, Prim. We'll show him our devotion, our submission—since that's what he seems to crave—and he'll eventually accept our fate for what it is. Come here." I tugged her arm, pulling her soft body across mine, relaxing once more as her soft curves fit against me.

"I'm not going to let anything ruin what we have worked hard for, Prim," I whispered against her hair, my brow furrowed at the resolve inside me to do just that. "I'll rip this fucking earth to shreds to keep us together, to make you happy. He might be driven to prove himself sane, but that beast inside him is as stubborn and as desperate for us as we are for it. It's going to be okay. I promise."

Her sweet sigh should have erased every doubt, like I'd intended for my words to do, but that underlying bullshit refused to dissolve, making me fear for our future.

PRIMROSE

I took a long, hot shower after Jaxon caught the bus for work, hating how incomplete I felt inside. Both of my mates had gone far enough away their thoughts and beasts no longer communicated with me. Heaviness settled in my mind as I slipped one of Patrick's dress shirts over my nakedness. Even though my inner dragon purred with contentment at his scent surrounding us, I didn't know how to deal with my unrest, the sudden silence after hours of constant communication with the two who owned me, heart, body, and soul.

The stillness, the absence of noise in my head and ears, reminded me too much of the early days after my grandmother's death. She'd left me alone, and it had been years before I'd come to accept the loneliness that had attempted to crush my mind.

I'd been alone.

Isolated deep in the Tetons without a connection to fill my emptiness.

Swallowing hard, I set off to familiarize myself with my

new home, quiet as it was, to pass the hours until their return.

Hints of feminine perfume and something sour teased my nose in various rooms, causing my beast to growl with discontentment atop my blues. Ugliness stirred in my belly as I realized I knew nothing about my alpha's past—who he had let inside this dwelling that belonged to me and my mates.

Restlessness roused in my limbs, and I set my focus on scrubbing every remnant of whoever *she* was from my alpha's domain and keeping busy until my two lovers were once more in my arms.

Cleaning the kitchen took no time at all since Patrick seemed well adept at taking care of his house. No pets meant no dander or fur to sweep up. No children meant no messes, fingerprints on walls, or sticky spills beneath my bare feet.

The thought of two young ones running around my legs, scrambling up the stairs, and laughing, sent an ache through my heart. All females, once mated, desired offspring, but I pushed the longing to the back of my mind.

Patrick needed to entirely commit to our bonding before we could move forward in fulfilling our destiny—never mind my desire to enjoy my mates to the fullest before a young one and its unruly inner dragon occupied my time and attention. While Blood Born of old might see me as self-ish, I'd lived with enough heartache to deserve the fulfill-ment of those things I wanted before setting myself aside to breed and bring another dragonblood to life inside my womb.

I scrubbed the bathroom even though it didn't need it. I scoured the stove, wiped down the woodwork.

Still restless, house spotless and smelling much better without the stench of *her*, I stood out on the porch, eyeing the yard and quiet street with its large lots of desert-like yards and neighbors' houses. The sky had cleared somewhat, beckoning, causing my shoulders to itch.

Fly.

I went back inside, leaving the door open, stripped out of sight, and cloaked myself. A quick glance around let me know I could close the door behind me without anyone seeing it supposedly shut on its own.

Three running steps down the road—and no thoughts as to where I headed other than upward toward freedom—I shifted, the first flap of our wings lifting pebbles and dust swirls into the air along with our invisible body. Cool wind rushed over our face, and beyond the electrical and telephone lines, we stretched our wings as our dragon filled our lungs, giddy on being set free for a time.

We jetted straight up until the air grew cold enough its chill licked along our scales. Free-falling, wings tucked tight against our body, sent a rush of adrenaline through our system, the heart, beating beneath flesh and bone—racing.

While lazing through the sky, my human half wondered if our mates would ever learn to soar the skies with us. If they might be taught as dragonblood coached their young, same as Grandpapa had done in showing us to cloak ourselves—a physical connection allowing the sharing of learned behavior rather than just knowledge.

A burst of wind carried us southward, away from Lockwood and Patrick's home, and my human half rested within our dragon, allowing instincts to carry us through the air. A short while later, we circled Jaxon's apartment, a deep craving banking us toward his place of work. Patrick had warned me away from Lockwood—but not the grocery store where my beta was. Jaxon's energy tingled over our scales like caressing fingertips, coaxing, drawing us toward the ground.

The store's rear parking lot sat empty, and we landed

with hardly more than a clatter of claws on pavement. Beast gave way to humanity, and I took over, shrinking us back into our smaller form, still hidden from human sight.

Jaxon's pull, the tether of energy linking us together, intensified to the point I could tell exactly where he stood beyond the building's walls. A quick walk took me to the store's front, and I followed a woman through the swished-open doors.

My beta stood to the left, exactly where I'd felt his presence. He shoved a box into a bag, his gaze glued to mine even though his human half couldn't see me. A rush of arousal, hot and wet, swept over me, same as it had that first night I'd seen him in the barred window of his room at Lockwood.

I stalked toward him, nostrils flaring while breathing in his earthy scent, my desire for his touch spurring me forward fast enough I had to skirt around a patron and her carriage who dared attempt to slow my steps.

He tore his focus off me to continue bagging groceries, and I crowded against his back, snaking my arms around him to grab his hard cock. A shudder rippled through him.

"I want you," I whispered in his ear.

Yessss, both he and his dragon agreed through our bond.

I continued to stroke him as he finished bagging for their current customer and followed on his heels after he asked for a quick bathroom break.

He locked the door behind us, but I dropped to my knees before he could grab me and slam me against the wall like he'd planned on doing. I freed his erection and took him into my mouth, and he groaned, his hands holding onto my head.

"Fuck, Prim." He groaned as his cock hit my tonsils.

I peered up at him, still cloaked, and he looked down as I backed off.

He snorted a laugh but shoved back into my throat. "It's like my dick is disappearing into thin air." He pulled out, and

I sucked hard, coating my tongue with pre-cum. "I love your mouth, Prim, but I want your pussy."

I hopped up, my core already throbbing, desperate to be one with him.

"Let me see you, baby."

I shimmered into sight while bending at the waist, planting my hands on the door. "Fill me, beta."

Pants seated just below his ass, Jaxon stepped close and ran the head of his dick up through my soaked folds. "I can feel how much you want me," he said, his voice low and lustful. "I love tasting you in the air."

He hesitated, and the tease of his cock's head tapping against my clit trickled arousal from my slit. I whimpered, wiggling my ass.

Jaxon groaned and slowly pressed into me, my breath catching as our shared desire swept over us both, causing my skin to pebble.

"Goddamn, do I love you." He pulled me upright, wrapped his arms around me, and fucked into me hard and fast, feasting on my neck while slamming into me over and over.

"Needed you," I gasped as he pressed my torso against the door, the metal cool against my heated face and breasts. "Couldn't. Stay. Away."

"Fuck." He clenched his jaw to keep from blowing too soon—he wanted to stay inside me forever, feel my wet heat clamp around him, take him soaring to the stars.

Yes, I told him through our bond as my beast did the same. *Forever.*

The first spurt of his cum against my womb took me over the edge, my climax stealing my breath.

"Jaxon," I breathed his name while arching, desperate for his cock to go deeper, pierce my soul, and flood me with everything he was.

"Prim." He stopped thrusting, his arms squeezing me tight, lips and tongue all over my neck, my jaw, my mouth.

The sweetness of his breath swarmed my taste buds, and I drank him in, knowing I would never get enough. Ever. Staying away would never be an option, and we laughed while discussing future trysts in the store's bathroom before he hurried back to work.

CHAPTER 37
PATRICK

Prim's energy had passed overhead, causing my groin to tingle, but it faded as quickly as it came, triggering a flaring bone-deep ache to radiate through my body before quieting once more. Leaving the two of them behind in my bed had been just as agonizing, but every block I'd driven away from my house earlier that morning had proved easier.

As had pushing the suddenly chatty darkness inside me that had graduated to using manipulative full sentences back behind tenuous walls.

Sitting at my desk with quietness in my head was a welcome respite, and I relaxed for the first time in what seemed like days, rather than hours, since our bonding.

Distance is key to keeping my brain quiet, I told myself while flipping through the files for that day's patients, even though the deepest reaches of me longed to return home, where mental chaos—but also a sense of comfort and fulfillment—awaited me.

My cock swelled regardless of my un-sexual thoughts.

Visions of Jaxon taking Primrose from behind flooded my mind, his steady thrusts pressing her against a door. The scent of their arousal hardened me to the point of pain.

Did they fuck?

Yessss.

I pressed my lips tight as the voice pushed past my defenses. It wasn't jealousy but annoyance that tightened my guts over the fact I wasn't there to watch how he loved her during a stolen moment during his workday. I wanted to be the one orchestrating their movements, my commands entwining their perfect bodies. It should have been my words bringing them to climax and allowing me to thoroughly enjoy a show of my own creation.

I shifted on my chair, focusing more difficult than I'd hoped for with how my mind played out its fantasy. Mere minutes later, elation rolled through me, causing my body to tense, a grunt pulled from my lungs. The scent of cum filled my nose, and somehow, I knew my young mates had found their release while I sat hard and unsatisfied in my office chair.

"Fuck." I scrubbed a hand along my whiskered jaw, shaking my head to rid my mind of their coupling like horny teenagers in a bathroom stall. I cursed again, clenching my jaw as I fought to concentrate on the open file on the desk in front of me.

Prim's energy licked at my skin and faded once more toward the east and our home.

She returned alone.

Probably full of his cum.

Need.

I pinched the bridge of my nose beneath my glasses, fighting my beast's inner push against the void he had willingly tucked himself into after I told him to keep quiet like he'd promised to do. Longing to go to our female and add to the seed our beta had attempted to plant in her womb flooded through me. "I have a job to do," I reminded him, my tone stern, and his petulant whining roused my anger even as my shaft continued to ache with the need to bury deep and breed who we belonged to.

"*I am in control*," I muttered under my breath, flipping open a patient file and setting the others aside while the beast pouted and curled up inside me. Silent, thank fuck.

A knock sounded.

I cleared my throat, glad for my one o'clock appointment arriving and giving me something else to focus on. "Come in, Emelia."

She slipped into my office in the same Hello Kitty robe she'd worn on our first meeting.

The beast inside the vault of my soul pressed for release, wanting to make his presence known to her, but he surprisingly stayed quiet.

Regardless, the second her gaze landed on me, she smiled. "You finally listened to him."

Unsure of what to say or how the fuck she knew the truth, I motioned toward the chair. Same as the first time we'd met, I needed to take caution with the questions I asked and how I responded to her.

"You have claimed your mates?"

"How are you feeling today, Emelia?" I asked rather than answer her.

A frown flitted over her brow when my inner beast didn't communicate with her like he wanted to do. Perhaps the fucker was private when it came to intimacy behind closed doors—

They are *mine*, he finally whispered.

Yep—possessive as fuck.

And zero self-control.

Emelia snickered. "I am well, thank you," she answered me.

Hating how easily the beast had given in to weakness, I asked a few more doctor-like questions of my patient to keep us from meandering off the necessary path of my work.

"You aren't happy." Emelia made a note as soon as our conversation allowed her to change the topic off herself.

I lifted my head, my focus on her face rather than her file. Her dark-as-coal eyes peered across the desk at me, but I shoved the inky blackness of my inner beast behind walls before he could breathe a word to her.

Her frown deepened. "Why don't you allow him freedom?"

I considered her question as the clock on the wall ticked, a variety of responses filling my head.

But uttering a word about the madness inside me would condemn and ruin my life if heard outside these office walls, never mind get me in trouble for the poor choices I'd made in the previous twenty or so hours.

"Are you ashamed?" she pushed when I didn't answer.

Still, I kept my lips pressed tight even though she'd touched on another reason for my silence.

"You *are* Blood Born, Doctor Macaire." Her quiet voice, so childlike, sounded as otherworldly as her question. "The orb told me so when I found it."

I leaned forward at her turn of topic, no longer concerned with the time. "You mentioned finding an orb in our first meeting."

The beast inside me roused to breathe fire against the walls, longing to speak, but my humanity proved stronger without my mates nearby.

"Yes." Emelia continued to study me with spine-tingling

intensity. "In a cavern while hiking in the canyon. It's where our ancestors lived."

I sat back at her statement, but my inner drive for truth wouldn't allow me to do anything but ask more questions. "*Our* ancestors?"

"Yes." A hint of a smile curved her lips as though I'd agreed with her. "We're family, Doctor Macaire. You're a direct descendant of the royal line of our house—which is why both your inner beast and human side are so strong. I am a distant cousin, but we're family, nonetheless. It's a good feeling to know we're not alone, isn't it?"

I found myself nodding, unable to tear my gaze from her face as I fought to process what she claimed. "Who were your parents?" I asked since there wasn't much information listed in her file.

"My mother was a ward of the state who heard voices." Emelia smiled, even though she'd used the past tense in regards to her mother. "My fathers were brothers on vacation from Canada, looking for a place to rest."

My brow furrowed at the plural. "Fathers."

"It takes three dragonblood to procreate."

"Your mother..." I cleared my throat to keep from saying anything about dragon shifters out loud that sounded as though I accepted her words as truth rather than a doctor attempting to root out her mental sickness. "What were your fathers' names?" I asked rather than suggested the woman had been more than human.

"My mother didn't know." Emelia shifted on her chair, her gaze flitting toward my bar-covered window. "They only spent the one night together."

Why didn't they bond?

Wily fucker had taken advantage of my being distracted by this new knowledge. I slammed the weakening wall back up, silencing him once more.

"Because they weren't fated mates," Emelia answered my beast's question when I refused to voice what I also wanted to know.

Glancing at the clock showed our time was up, but I had one last question.

"And where is this…supposed orb now?"

"I assure you, it's very real and in my room. Would you like to see it?"

Yessss.

My dragon slammed against the wall, suddenly desperate to escape, but I held firm in my need to appear sane.

While in my humanity alone, while at Lockwood, while building my own practice.

I cleared my throat, shutting her file. "Next time," I suggested before sending her on her way.

Long after Emelia left, I considered my reality and the possible futures ahead of us.

Owning them had weakened me to the point I'd given in to lust as Doctor Sorino had done.

But even though Jaxon was legal and no grooming had occurred, would I escape ruination if our intimacy was found out? And how long could I continue to hide them when every part of me wanted to claim them publicly because they completed me in ways I'd always longed for?

I didn't *want* to be separated from them, but I'd worked hard to finally open my own clinic—even if I struggled to gain patients enough to hire a secretary or even support *myself,* let alone a family of three. Being offered the temporary position at Lockwood had seemed a godsend, but what if it had been fate leading me toward my destiny rather than the resume of a hardworking man?

Would that destiny also provide a path through the sure scandal ahead of us?

The beast remained silent, and I cursed his absence of

knowledge over humanity and how we could very well be frowned upon.

Or worse, shunned and seen as something evil, worthy only of existing behind lock and key, like I had feared my entire life.

CHAPTER 38

PRIMROSE

I slipped out of the store as easily as I arrived, my body sated for the time being. Flying over Lockwood made me long to do the same with my alpha, but Patrick's command to stay away took me westward.

The second I walked through the door I had left unlocked, I pulled up short, my nostrils flaring at the familiar, disgusting scent I had scrubbed from every surface earlier that morning. Old boots lay discarded by the stairs, too small and feminine to belong to Patrick.

My inner beast hissed her displeasure.

Scowling, I stayed cloaked and moved from room to room on the first floor, noting the purse on the island and the empty beer can alongside. Tilting my head back, I peered up at the ceiling as though I could pinpoint through wood and plaster the intruder in my territory.

The scent of her strengthened as I slipped up the stairs—sour beer and sweat. Unwashed body and a trace of old perfume caused my nose to wrinkle and left a bitter tang on my tongue. The need to spit made my mouth water. A skittering, ant-like feeling crept over my bare flesh, which no amount of rubbing over my forearms erased.

Patrick's bedroom door stood open, a pile of clothing in the middle of the floor, snores coming from a lump under the comforter I slept beneath that morning with my mates. I'd straightened the bedding not an hour earlier, preparing for their return so we might have a repeat of the night before.

Quivers owned my body, and I crept closer, baring my teeth.

The woman hugged Patrick's pillow like she'd done so a thousand times, face relaxed and mouth open in peaceful sleep.

A burning sensation lit in my chest. Pain in the back of my throat made swallowing difficult.

My dragon growled as I glared down at the woman.

A single flame from our lips will incinerate her to ash.

A rumble grew in my chest, sneaking past my clenched teeth, and the woman stirred.

"Patrick?" she slurred his name with a smile, eyes still closed. Her sour breath lashed at my nose as she stretched beneath his blankets. "Mmm. I can smell your cum on our sheets. Wanna taste it on my tongue, baby."

I blinked, my tense shoulders dropping from where they'd hitched near my ears.

Patrick, my alpha, the one meant to look after my heart and mind, had another woman.

Rage should have erupted wings from my back, muscles and bones stretching to give space to my inner beast. A roar should have ripped from my lungs as I tore the woman limb from limb before feasting on her rotten flesh to rid the earth of her intrusive presence.

Tears stung my eyes instead.

My muscles weakened, trembling taking over my body.

I tugged on my hair as a hot flash caused a cold sweat to break over my brow.

I had promised Jaxon I would never run—but I'd made no such vow to my cheating alpha, who'd been coerced by his inner beast to bind us together.

He didn't truly want us.

Never had.

Patrick had someone else, and his human half's strength had allowed him the ability to hide her from us even after he'd been enticed into being a part of a bond he had never desired to begin with.

Spinning on my heel, I set my focus on the open door at my back. The empty hallway…stairs I stumbled down in my haste to escape.

Chest tight and stomach churning, I burst free from the front door, and with a single sob, I gave over to my dragon's need.

Agony ripped through me as I shifted into my true form, unimaginable pain that felt as though the bond between female and alpha tore in two.

We took to the sky, harsh flaps of our wings speeding us away from what we had believed to be our new home, the place of comfort and fulfillment we had been searching for. The connection we'd been desperate to find. The love and belonging we had been so damned desperate to finally experience.

Ignorant fool.

CHAPTER 39

PATRICK

Concern over my future still ate at my guts, regardless of my inner beast's drive to return home to our mates. My dick ached at the thought of Jaxon and Primrose waiting for me. Would they be entwined already? On their knees, ready to drink down my cum?

"Jesus, I'm a mess." I rubbed a hand over my face before gripping my steering wheel once more.

A fight continued inside me: the desire for freedom like Emelia had promised and the fear of losing everything I had fought to prove and attain. While the age difference no longer bothered me as much as it had when I'd first felt the draw to Jaxon, I couldn't reason away his being an ex-patient. Fucking the boy, while fulfilling the parts of me I'd been longing for, could have very well been the biggest mistake of my life.

Hoping I would find my answer while losing myself in both him and Primrose, I sped home. My heartbeat kicked up as I pulled into the garage, and I hurried into the house. I tossed my keys on the island, suddenly realizing the riotous voices were loudly absent and that the energy linking us should have made my skin shiver—but didn't.

My brow furrowed at the purse and empty can on the island, my inner beast growling. "Fuck." I jerked my gaze toward the hallway, seeing the discarded boots by the front door. Every muscle in my body tensed. I strode up the stairs, dread eating at my stomach with each step.

The familiar scent of floral perfume informed me of who had broken into my home, and my heart stumbled—fucking seized in knowing what I would find.

Jessie lay burrowed under my comforter, snoring and reeking of stale beer.

The beast inside me gnashed its teeth, wanting to rip her apart for putting her stink atop the beautiful scents of those I had coaxed from my two young lovers earlier that morning.

"Jessie." Her name coated my tongue like fish oil—gag-worthy. "Jessie!" I raised my voice when she didn't so much as twitch. "Goddamnit—*Jessie!*" I hollered.

She finally stirred, blinking up at me with bloodshot eyes. "Pat. There you are, you sexy beast. Plant your fine ass over here," she said, patting the mattress. "Let's make a mess of these sheets."

I ignored her outstretched hand, grabbed her clothes off the floor, and tossed them at her face. "Put those on and get the *fuck* out of my house."

I stomped out of my bedroom and back downstairs to grab her purse and shoes. Waiting by the front door, I simmered and shook, the need to hurt someone boiling my blood.

I'd been sure Primrose had flown to Jaxon and then returned home during the workday. Had she found Jessie like I did? Comfortable and resting peacefully in our bed like she belonged there?

Lava flowed through my veins.

Primrose's beast side would be instinctive as mine—surely, she would have burned Jessie alive for waltzing in here like she owned the place. Or had Primrose made assumptions that had sent her running back to Jaxon in search of comfort?

Either way, Primrose wasn't where I'd expected and wanted her to be.

Neither was Jaxon, who should have gotten off work two hours ago.

A low growl rumbled in my chest, and Jessie appeared at the top of the stairs in her panties, clothes clutched to her chest. Bloodshot eyes stared at me. "The fuck is wrong with you?"

"*You.*" I held up her purse and shoes, struggling to rein in my inner beast. "You're not welcome here any longer. I thought I made that clear."

Her brow smoothed out, and she sauntered down the stairs. Nothing about her curves or the see-through lace of her panties enticed me to have what I'd already had my fill of.

"Pat." She touched my chest, but I shoved her purse and boots at her, stepping out of reach, hands dropping to fist at my sides.

"Get dressed and get the fuck out, or I'm calling the police," I stated in a low tone through clenched teeth.

"You don't mean it—you left the front door open for me."

Primrose must have when she'd gone to see Jaxon.

I stalked to the kitchen and grabbed my cell off the island. Through the hallway, Jessie eyed me holding the phone aloft a few seconds before cursing me out and tugging on her clothes.

"I don't know what the fuck crawled up your ass, Pat," she said, shoving her feet into her shoes as I once more approached her, "but I'm about done offering you second chances."

"Good." I pulled the door inward and pointed down the road, my glare stating once more what I'd already told her.

My inner beast hissed, clawing for release and the right to rip her to shreds, but I held tight to my control.

Jessie stepped over the threshold, turned, and opened her mouth, but I slammed the door shut in her face and locked the deadbolt.

A few choice curse words made their way past the oak plank between us, but I ignored her ranting and name-calling.

Stomping into the kitchen, I rang the number Jaxon had called me from the night before.

It felt like days had passed rather than hours when I'd first laid eyes on golden scales and amber eyes I'd recognized immediately.

Jaxon didn't answer.

"Jesus fucking Christ," I muttered, grabbing my keys off the island and making my way into the garage. I smashed the button on the wall to put up the door with my fist.

My car roared to life seconds later, and I backed out of the driveway.

Jessie still stood on my porch, and I rolled the passenger window down.

"You try to break in, and I'll press charges for trespassing!" I hollered, pushing the button on my visor to close the garage door again, and took off down the street.

There was only one place the two of them would have gone.

While I might not be ready to claim them publicly and face the consequences, I wanted them back where they belonged, making my head a riotous mess and filling that void of emptiness in my soul.

CHAPTER 40
JAXON

Prim's familiar energy rippled over me again, but instead of adoring arousal like earlier, pain tore through my chest.

My breath ripped from my lungs, and I grunted, curling in on myself as the beast inside me whimpered. Grimacing, I glanced outside the store windows at my back.

What the actual *fuck*?

I stumbled forward, hands resting on cool glass, eyes quickly scanning the area. The parking lot...sidewalk... cloudless sky—no Prim.

Go.

Comfort.

She was here—I could feel her, but she'd cloaked either her dragon form or nakedness.

I flagged my manager down, and he approached, concern lighting his face as he looked me over.

"You okay?" he asked, frowning. "You're white as a ghost."

I clutched my stomach rather than my chest, which ached in agony. "Gotta go," I rasped. "Gonna be sick."

He quickly stepped off to the side, motioning me away

from him. "Take a break. Come back when you're feeling better, and if not, just head home and keep in touch, okay?"

Swallowing audibly, I nodded and hurried out the automatic doors, arm still over my torso as though fending off nausea when it felt like my heart ripped in two.

I stepped outside into the sunlight.

There's another woman in our alpha's bed.

I stiffened suddenly, my vision blurring, my soul ripping to shreds. *What?*

We aren't enough—

Invisible talons wrapped around me, winking me from sight. A blast of wind and sudden change of altitude shot my shattering heart into my toes, and I gasped, surprised by Prim's strength, her ability to rip me off the earth's face when she'd been so sure of being unable to do so without a free fall involved.

Her pain owned her. Gave her strength beyond the beast within.

I clutched at her warm leg, the scales golden and glinting in the sun, visible to my eyes since her gift had cloaked me along with her—we were in a world of our own, but I couldn't dwell on that thought and what it might mean beyond the bond between the two of us.

No fucking way Patrick would replace us so quickly.

Had he been pissed Prim came to see me and that I fucked her in a bathroom stall like she was some whore?

Both of us shivered at my thought, but due to fear over his possible anger, not arousal at the memory of mating in the confined space.

He couldn't possibly know what we were up to, as we were both unaware of his thoughts or feelings due to the distance between us.

Prim's attempt to reassure me did little to ease the unrest inside me. I had no answers, no other questions to help make sense of what she had seen and the resulting emotion now rippling through both of us.

"Thank you for not leaving me," I croaked out what passed through my mind, and her mourning dragon only caused my heart to hurt more.

We landed in the cul-de-sac, and she continued to hold onto me while shifting back to her smaller form. As one, and still invisible to the human eye, we hurried up the stairs, hand-in-hand to my apartment, needing the physical connection between us. She fell apart the second the door closed behind us.

The memory of finding another woman in our bed replayed in her head, filling me in. I pulled her into my arms, lips against her hair, heat rising behind my eyelids.

"That woman means nothing to him." Considering all we had done last night, I refused to believe otherwise. The ancient words and fire. Bonding through blood and mutual pleasure. Gifting each other the life-giving nectar to ensure we lived a full, satisfying existence together.

My declaration I wanted to believe to be true didn't make a difference to either of our tumbling emotions, so I simply held Prim, powerless to ease her suffering. She cried while I tried and failed to fight off crushing disappointment in our alpha—and in myself for believing that sexually submitting myself to Patrick would gain his acceptance and undying affection.

While I wanted to give Patrick the chance to answer for what Prim had seen, I couldn't keep from thinking that he *had* been trying to fuck us out of his system as his thoughts had betrayed him before getting on with his life with whoever the fuck the woman was between his goddamn sheets.

Fuck, this sucked ass—and not in the good way.

I wanted to curl into a fetal position and cry.

Sock my alpha in the goddamned nose and mar his gorgeous face for the pain he'd caused us both.

"Come on." I tugged Prim toward the bed, and we lay down together, clinging to each other. Slow kisses and tender caresses eventually calmed her enough to stop the tears, but the hurt remained.

"I love you so fucking much," I murmured against her lips, breathing her as deep into my lungs as possible. "I'll move mountains to keep you safe and make you happy, sweetheart."

But could I?

Alone, would I be enough to satisfy the cravings of her dragonblood?

No.

Nausea stirred in my guts, and it seemed as though I was collapsing in on myself. My throat tightened, and Prim heaved a sigh, wound her arms around me, and pressed her naked chest against mine.

She also felt inadequate.

What a fucking pair we were.

"Too many clothes," she whispered, tugging on the back of my t-shirt.

I rolled away to rip my clothes off, ready to give my female the world if that was what she requested—

"Just your skin against me, Jaxon," she whispered, nuzzling into my neck. "Need to feel your heart beating in time with mine."

Ignoring both of our arousal from naked close proximity, I tucked her satiny curves against my body and allowed myself to mourn what we had lost.

"Are relationships always like this?" Prim whispered against my neck, her breath warm and sweet. "All this—shit?"

"I'm not any more schooled on relationships than you are, but I'm not so ignorant as to think bad stuff and regrettable days don't happen." I pushed strands of hair from her face, needing her eyes on me even though barriers in communication didn't exist for us.

"I like the good ones better."

"Did you *expect* a bed of roses?" I asked, but not with sarcasm or in an attempt to deepen her pain—I honestly wanted to know what dreams she'd had so I would be better equipped to fulfill them on my own.

My inner beast snorted.

Prim sighed heavily, making me thankful she could feel me—hear my intentions without me having to speak them. "Yes, actually. I believed once we bonded that everything would align—the stars, our hearts and minds…I didn't think there would be any discord or unrest."

I'd had that hope too.

"You're so perfect," she said on a sigh, affection sifting its way through the hurt between us. "Why can't Patrick be more like you?"

"Patrick *is* hot as fuck," I suggested, trying to lighten our mood. "But also a dark, tortured soul who desperately needs your gentleness and my cock."

A hint of amusement lit in her eyes along with her heart. "You're one arrogant man."

"And you love it." I rested my nose against hers, breathing in her exhales, but the tightness in my chest refused to loosen.

CHAPTER 41

PATRICK

I parked along the cul-de-sac, and the second I stepped from my car, the delicious, combined scents of both Jaxon and Primrose flooded my nose. A jumble of emotions reached through the energy linking us that had been absent with the distance between us.

I couldn't make sense of the noise in my head and heart, but one thing I knew for certain. Prim had definitely found Jessie in my bed.

And Jaxon's instincts to protect our female were a beautiful force of nature that made my dick hard.

I climbed the stairs to his apartment's balcony, desperate to ease and quiet the bond among us.

My beta wrenched the door open as I lifted my hand to knock, his fist hitting me at the same time as the full brunt of his anger did.

Stars erupted in my eyesight, pain radiating clear through my head at the inhuman impact against my cheek.

I stumbled backward onto my ass.

"Fucking asshole." Jaxon's growl didn't hide the simmering lust inside him as he towered over me, completely naked, the energy between us vibrating and zapping with electrical charges that caused my hair to stand on end.

The beast inside me slithered in darkness, hissing, curling in readiness to strike—and fuck.

"Jaxon!" Primrose pushed past him. She, too, filled with desire from being close to her alpha, but hurt swirled thick and acidic beneath, making my chest cave in.

"Who the fuck is she, Doc?" Jaxon's anger lay like a black cloud over me, shrouding Prim's more tender emotions as she knelt beside me and gently touched where Jaxon had hit me, uncaring of her own nakedness.

"Ex-girlfriend. She means nothing to me."

"Bullshit."

I stood, Primrose's hands falling away from me.

"You bonded us together, but you're holding back." Jaxon glowered, hands fisted at his sides, the truth of *his* claim one hundred percent true. "Why the fuck should we believe you? Huh? She's closer to your age—fucking *safe* for your upstanding, professional façade of a life. Selfish prick. You don't care about anyone but yourself. Fucking *coward.*"

He knew the truth of what Jessie used to be and no longer was to me.

He could hear my every thought, how his poking at my fears hurt me.

My boy needed an outlet for his anger, and I would give him exactly what he required to make this right.

I leaped forward, barreling into his chest, sending us tumbling through his door and onto the apartment floor. I landed a soft hit to his stomach while burying my face in his neck—goddamn delicious-smelling and bite-able.

"Fuck you, Doc." Jaxon slammed a fist into my side, hating that I was taking it easy on him.

"You want pain?" I yanked his head back by a firm grip on his hair, my breath ripping from my lungs as his fist connected with my gut. I returned the favor, showing my teeth as my inner beast chuckled in delight, driving me toward violence.

I grunted as we rolled, our hard cocks pressed against each other with only my slacks between us, our hips grinding with the desire to fuck even as fists flew. I ended up on top and shoved a thigh between Jaxon's bare legs while grabbing his wrists and pinning them to the floor alongside his head.

Our heated gazes locked.

Arousal thickened the air between us, making breathing difficult. He didn't melt into the floor at my show of dominance, but some of the tightness in his chest that in turn hurt mine eased.

"Keep your hands there," I said with a growl, and he obeyed as I sat on my haunches to free my straining dick. "This what you want, Jaxon?" I slid the mess of leaking pre-cum down over my length.

He glared up at me even as I could feel the moisture flooding his mouth. "Fuck you."

"In your dreams, boy." I huffed, still short of breath.

Lust rocketed among the three of us regardless of my denial of the underlying desire behind his words.

Primrose's whimper behind us was like an accelerant to flame, making me bookmark for later the need to question the claim I made.

Jaxon grinned up at me, anger's fire still bright in his eyes as my dick pulsed pre-cum onto my waiting fingers.

I narrowed my gaze. "This is the only lube you're getting, boy."

"We both know that isn't the punishment you think it is—fucking give it to me." He grabbed the backs of his knees, showing me his little pink pucker. "All at once. I want the pain."

Take.

Own.

I crowded close, holding the tip of my cock to his asshole, too overcome with need to argue with him.

I shoved in, and he gasped, his body tensing.

"You asked for this," I said through clenched teeth, planking over him and pulling out to the head, "so take it." Another thrust buried me in his ass.

"Fuck," he groaned, fingers turning white from how harshly he gripped his thighs.

He was going to need something to focus on in order to survive what I had in store for him.

I slapped his hands away, controlling his thighs, grabbing hold with a firm grip that would leave fingerprints in his skin for me to appreciate later. "Sit on his face, Primrose."

My dragon growled, rumbling my chest as our female obeyed my command, spreading her legs and settling over Jaxon, her wide, golden-eyed gaze latched on my face mere inches from hers, pulse thrumming in her neck.

An audible inhale sounded from Jaxon, and he groaned as the scent of strawberries flooded my nose. "Love your smell, sweetheart."

I clenched my jaw against releasing early while dragging my cock out from the hot clutch of Jaxon's hole.

He clamped his arms around Primrose's thighs, and the second his tongue dove deep into her pussy, her sweet, juicy tang flooded my senses.

All three of us moaned at the same time, a shudder rippling through us like a wave.

Grabbing her flowing hair, I yanked her toward me, taking her mouth in a bruising kiss as I fucked into Jaxon exactly like he needed.

His inner beast begged for more, and the darkness inside me roused in strength as it always did in their presence, but this time, growling with violence, gnashing teeth with desire to tear into flesh.

I slammed into Jaxon, and he grunted a curse against our female's pussy. "Gonna rip this ass in two." I stuffed him full, pulled back, and repeated the motion, slamming my groin against his body.

Lust swelled faster than any rising tide, beasts and humans yearning for completion and the fulfillment we would feel once emotions quieted.

But not yet.

I was in control—this would go my way, end how *I* wished.

I pulled away from Primrose's mouth and sat back, holding Jaxon's thighs wide to the point I could feel his pain, watching my dick disappear into his ass with every forceful stab, my own twitching and tingling.

I'd never seen anything so goddamn sexy. Never heard sounds like those pouring from both of their lips as I speared into my beta's guts over and over again with harsh thrusts that ripped the air from his lungs and almost made me wish I had something up my own ass.

"Oh, fuck, yeah, Patrick," he murmured against Primrose's succulent flesh. "Right the fuck there."

My balls tightened, the base of my spine tingling at the same time as his.

"Fuck." I leaned down, sprawled over Jaxon's chest, trapping his dick between our abs, and shoved my mouth onto Primrose's clit as she rode his face, his tongue flicking up along mine to gather her sweetness and swallow it down.

Our female shuddered, her hands ripping at my hair. "Please...alpha, please. Patrick!"

I plowed into Jaxon hard enough his body slid along the floor, causing a delicious ache through his spine and mine.

Now.

Both of my mates obeyed the command.

Primrose's cream coated our hungry tongues.

Jaxon shot off between our stomachs.

The coaxing pulls of his ring milked my shaft, and my balls erupted, spunk shooting deep into his ass.

Shared gasps and climactic pulses settled that same sense of rightness over all three of us, like when we had bonded. A cocoon of warmth and soothing love flowed through the energy, even as our releases heightened each other's. Dizziness swept through me until I planked over my beta, balls wrung dry. Tingles raced through my blood, and I hung my head, arms shaking to keep me from collapsing.

My inner beast purred, curling up inside the void where I couldn't be bothered to lock him away completely.

Jaxon clenched his hole around me, and my oversensitive dick twitched.

"Fuck." I shuddered, my humanity alone ready to take a belt to his backside.

"Later," he promised, his plan to give me further reason to punish his fine ass simmering in the back of his mind.

My beast's interest piqued, and my dick attempted to revive at the thought of appeasing my sadistic nature now that my beta had learned how to submit to his masochistic side.

A wave of arousal flickered through the bond, but deeper matters tugged at both of my mates' hearts, requiring these animalistic urges to wait.

I lifted my head to focus on Primrose, where she knelt over Jaxon's face, his tongue lazing over her folds with small licks meant to clean, not arouse.

Golden eyes, tear-hazed and aching like her heart, peered into my soul, searching for answers.

Pressing my lips against her palm, I pulled out of our beta, the sight of his abused hole leaking my seed satisfying as fuck. But the smears of his cum over the bumps and valleys along his core made my mouth water.

Mine.

Taste.

I licked up his torso, gathering his life-giving essence on my tongue, holding it there long enough I could enjoy the earthy flavor of him before swallowing it down.

He groaned against Primrose's pussy, his cock thickening, his arousal stirring my own.

I backed away, smacking his ass as I went.

He chuckled, and Primrose curled up beside him on the floor. She reached for his shaft.

"Leave it," I commanded.

She obeyed while Jaxon hissed his displeasure.

I left them for the tiny bathroom and cleaned myself before wetting two towels for them.

Jaxon sprawled unmoved when I returned, eyes closed and brow dented—dick still hard. His restful mind and the purr of his dragon allowed me to attend to our female first since she required the soothing that only a complete story would provide.

"I kicked Jessie out the same day I met Jaxon," I said, kneeling to wipe between Primrose's thighs even though our beta had already cleaned her with his tongue.

A cocky grin curled Jaxon's lips as satisfaction curled deep inside him.

"You had nothing to do with that choice. She was on her way out already." I set him straight, tossing the second towel onto his stomach, deciding his cocky ass could clean up the mess I'd made of his hole.

"I'm not all that?" Jaxon said, using sensual glides of the towel over his abs rather than efficient swipes to rid himself of my cum like I'd intended for him to do.

"You're hot as fuck, and you know it," I muttered, standing over them.

"So are you, old man." He tossed the sticky towel aside, leaving his swollen pucker as-is, sticky and wet from my spend.

I narrowed my gaze, considering everything we needed to discuss, everything I needed answers to. Words in my head warred with the ridiculous, insatiable desire to fuck him again while he slid his tempting cock into our female.

A hint of jealousy lingered within Primrose, so I turned my focus on her, ignoring our insatiable beta.

His needs could wait.

Hers could not.

CHAPTER 42

PRIMROSE

"Jessie was nothing more than a warm body to fill my bed, an attempt to battle the loneliness I'd experienced when I first returned to Arizona. We never connected on an emotional level. There was no…insatiable hunger or possessiveness with her like there is with the two of you," Patrick explained, his desire to ease my jealousy clear.

Jaxon preened some more at that last bit, but I ignored him, my focus on my alpha as I sat, arms around my knees.

I couldn't help the bitterness in my stomach over the fact that I had been driven to save myself for my mates, and Patrick had been fucking women all along—

"Jaxon was hardly celibate." Patrick stared at me, a sliver of annoyance radiating inside him, and our beta's sudden uneasiness rippled through our bond.

He feared my judgment for his promiscuity, which he'd never been bothered by before this conversation.

Lips pursed, I frowned, trying to figure out what exactly I felt, why Jaxon's past didn't bother me as Patrick's did.

"It's not because I'm older and should know better," he said as the thought flitted through my brain.

"But you're the alpha," I said, fighting to put into words my disgust with another female being more familiar with his body than I was.

Patrick spread his arms wide. "You're welcome to your fill, Primrose. Learn what you wish—*take* what you wish."

Jaxon groaned, his unrest from seconds earlier erased by a well of lust in his groin. "Care to make that offer to me?"

Patrick shot a glare at our sprawled beta. "You've already earned another date with my belt—and a whip or cane once I can get my hands on some real toys."

A shudder rippled through Jaxon, and I fought to keep my focus on the conversation that needed to be spoken and put to rest.

My alpha fixed his gaze on me, his dark-blue eyes as intense as the feelings swirling inside him. "You don't trust me."

"I want to," I whispered up at him, not understanding how this hesitation between bonded mates was even possible—

"You can sense everything that I do, Primrose. You can hear my every thought." He grabbed hold of my hand, pulled me to my feet, and pressed his to his chest. "You *know* I speak the truth when I say that the women I fucked in the past didn't own my heart."

He did speak the truth. But the same as he'd done to them, he *had* pushed me away.

Jaxon stood, hovering at my back. "He rejected us both, but that was *before* we bonded." He stated what I needed to be reminded of, even though his words didn't bring any assurance.

"And I've never been more goddamn sorry," Patrick murmured. "But there is no tearing us apart now. Surely, you feel that."

"And yet you still hold a part of yourself separate,

attempting to keep your other half imprisoned," I whispered, as tears laced my voice. "We are not whole."

Disquiet flooded Patrick's mind, and he released his clasp on my hand, stepping away to glance between the two of us. He expelled a breath as heavy as the sudden weight on his chest, running his fingers through his hair. "I was diagnosed with mental illness as a child, and my psychologist taught me how to lock the…dragon away." Eyes closing, he frowned, turbulent disappointment riling throughout him as he fought to keep his thoughts off his doctor.

Something awful had happened, an event that had shattered Patrick. Changed his dreams—

"The need to prove myself sane, worthy of life and love, pushed me to excel," Patrick stated, focused on ridding his mind of the man he'd considered a hero once upon a time. "I was driven to conquer any task in sight. Complete every plan —obtain each goal I set before myself."

"And you succeeded," Jaxon said, his tone low and full of reassurance.

"In most things, yes." Patrick's gaze locked onto him. "But the sexual drive for you, to bring us together time and again…" He glanced at me. "I've never felt anything like it. I want to stay in this bed with the two of you and ignore responsibilities and the possible consequences of being caught with an ex-patient."

His fear overrode all of his senses at his admission, and our hearts beat faster—in sync from shared emotion.

I hugged myself, and both mates reached for me, their warm palms settling on my skin. But the physical contact didn't bring the relief we hoped for.

"You wish to keep us a secret," I stated, my throat growing tight.

"I have no choice."

"What's the worst that could happen?" Jaxon asked him, his brow furrowing.

"If you pressed charges—"

"I would *never*."

"I could face jail time. I would lose my license to practice," Patrick stated.

"Everything you've worked so hard for." I spoke the other thought he didn't voice out loud.

Patrick nodded, his eyes and heart imploring us to understand.

Fate will not allow separation—not even in death.

Both Jaxon's and my inner beast hissed their agreement with our alpha dragon's declaration.

Patrick's eyes slid shut, and he lowered his head.

"What?" Jaxon asked as something niggled in the back of Patrick's mind.

"A patient of mine said that what I've been driven to find my entire life exists in the void I've attempted to imprison inside my soul. She claimed I would never be happy until I became one with that part of me."

"Is she a fortune teller?" Jaxon asked as I sifted through Patrick's words and the reality of the supernatural.

"She's Blood Born," I stated the only truth possible, a conclusion he had come to as well.

"Yes," Patrick said before filling his lungs and heaving another heavy exhale. "But I can't—Jesus fucking Christ, I can't just flip a switch and let this thing inside me have control. It's…weak. Impulsive. So damned…needy."

Jaxon's grimace perfectly portrayed the insecurity slapping his face at our alpha's descriptors, two of which he embodied.

I took his hand in my own. "I love your impulsiveness and how desperate you are for my love and affection."

Patrick enjoyed the second, but the first? Not so much.

"Only because it gets you into trouble," he muttered, trying to reassure our beta.

"There's nothing weak about your other half," I stated firmly. "He is just driven by instinct to fulfill your destiny. The desire for unity with your mates and our responsibility to keep the royal Blood Born line from extinction."

Patrick met my stare as the thoughts that both of us belonged to the ruling lines of old slid through our minds.

She had told him—the patient he'd mentioned.

"I want to meet her," I stated.

"You can't."

I huffed, lips thinning.

Silence descended as a sense of peace over our first...fight as a throuple, drew near its end.

The girl—Emelia, my alpha's dragon supplied—had spoken truth gifted to her by our ancestors. Patrick would not experience true rest or enjoy the fulfillment he'd been searching for until he submitted himself to reality.

But even aware of that truth, his humanity refused to relinquish control.

"I don't know how to," he murmured, eyes closing.

Jaxon and I both wrapped our arms around our alpha, attempting to cocoon him in safety and warmth.

"We don't know shit about relationships," Jaxon said, pretty much what was on my mind, "and while we all have a lot to learn, I promise we're in this for the long haul. We can be patient."

At least, I thought I could be.

"You can't map out your emotional responses in advance of actions or unexpected triggers," Patrick said, nosing over my hair. Need kindled among us as my scent flooded his lungs. "Jesus—will this ever lessen?"

"I've read the instinct to breed will fade a bit, but I'm not sure how long it takes." I frowned, considering my short stay in the Tetons days ago. "When I went back home to see Grandpapa, he, Vanni, and Ashley had been bonded for a few months but were still busy as rabbits."

"Vanni." Patrick's curiosity piqued.

"You know him?"

"Perhaps—Giovanni DiLoreto?"

"Yes."

"Shit." Patrick huffed. "He's a friend of a friend. I was told he'd taken off for Wyoming with a man and woman he claimed were his mates. Giovanni is your grandfather's alpha, I'm assuming, since he is a Dominant."

"Something that annoyed Grandpapa when they'd first met," I supplied. "It was his humanity that denied the destiny his inner beast fought for."

Patrick squeezed me tight and released a long exhale that eased some of the tension riddling his body. "Pack up your things, Jaxon."

"Why?" he asked, already turning away from us to do as his alpha had ordered.

"Because you're coming home with me, where you belong."

Happiness swept through the bond among us, but unease still lay like a cancer inside Patrick's mind. Short of the three of us moving out of state and starting over, I feared his complete submission to fate.

"I'm trying, Primrose," he murmured before pressing a kiss to my hair.

I nodded, wondering why our bonding couldn't just be as easy as flipping a book's pages. Happily ever afters weren't a bed of soft sheets and gentle caresses when hidden thorns prohibited fulfilling rest.

CHAPTER 43

JAXON

I t took fifteen minutes for me to throw my and Prim's stuff into a couple of trash bags. Darkness coated the land when we left my apartment, and Prim once more sat on my lap rather than the back seat as Patrick drove us an hour northward—home to his place.

"Shit," I muttered as reality slid through my mind. "Taking the bus to work every morning is going to suck ass —and not in the good way."

Arousal flickered to life in Patrick's groin, making my own dick twitch.

"Wanna eat my ass, alpha?"

A muscle ticked in his jaw, and I grinned when our dragons hummed their approval in unison.

"Quit and find something closer to home."

The issue of my GED and the possibility of college flickered through my head, and Patrick glanced over at me. "Yes. Finish your education. I will provide for you both until you decide what you want to do with your future."

"We don't need financial help," Primrose told him what she and I had already discussed.

The truth slid through Patrick's mind, and he nodded, shoulders relaxing slightly.

Finances worried him—as did the fact his new practice wasn't exactly flourishing.

But our man was driven to succeed.

"And you will," I stated firmly, which caused a swell of gratitude through our bond.

A sliver of worry still lay in the back of Prim's thoughts, even though she tried to contain her emotions. I had no fucking clue how to change her mind or even soothe the unrest deep inside her. At least her inner beast lay quiet. Content and unbothered now that we were bonded. It was her humanity that responded to our alpha. Both's wounds dictated their thought patterns.

And I was no psychologist.

Simply a horny-as-fuck *boy*—

I side-eyed Patrick, catching the tick in his jaw.

My inner beast snickered and moved around inside me like smoke above roused embers.

Yeah, Patrick wasn't super thrilled about the age difference, but at least that wouldn't get us into any trouble like the other concern he'd brought up. He shoved hard against memories of his past and whoever he'd put up on a pedestal.

This shit train of thought with both of them had to stop.

So, I did what I do best.

Punishment awaited me, and I let that darkness inside me play out possible scenarios in my head, loving that both of my mates would see what I did in my mind's eye. My dick swelled against Prim's ass, and she wiggled against me with a sigh as I buried my face in her soft neck, drawing her sweet scent deep into my lungs.

My alpha would gift me pain, and this lush, delicious woman filling my arms would distract me with pleasure.

Patrick muttered something about me being a brat, even while his groin responded, flooding with blood.

His beast's demands that we fulfill our lust were as loud as my own, whimpering for the same.

My asshole clenched—without a trace of soreness or an ache from the pounding my alpha had given me for landing the first punch to our fight that had led to the best hate fuck of all time.

I grinned, but my smile dissolved as we turned onto Patrick's street, and Primrose's gaze fell on the house.

The memories from earlier in the day rushed through her head, bringing the jealousy and hurt along with them.

I saw the woman in Patrick's bed in a flash, same as she did. Heard the words she'd spoken.

"She's gone," Patrick snipped and hit the button to put up the garage door a little too hard. "Nothing but a memory."

The garage door rattled shut behind us as he turned off the engine.

We climbed out without another word, and I grabbed our bags from the back seat and followed on my mates' heels into the kitchen.

The sour scent of booze and perfume lingered.

Prim's jealousy spiked again, rousing my anger.

"Don't tell us to calm the fuck down," I grumbled before Patrick could speak, dropping our bags on the floor. "How would you feel if another woman's scent lingered on my skin? Traces of another alpha's cum clung to Prim?"

Patrick's dragon growled, rumbling his chest.

"Exactly." I lifted my chin, staring him down, pleased my push toward violence had worked. Maybe coercing his beast to the surface would help Patrick grow more accustomed to and comfortable with his other half.

"Manipulative little shit."

I shot him a toothy grin. "It's what I do best."

Patrick's annoyance rose along with his desire to put me in my place—with force. Pain. Breath-stealing pleasure.

Prim whimpered, the scent of her arousal in the air thickening as quickly as my dick.

The muscle ticked in Patrick's jaw. "Upstairs," he bit out, expecting us both to scurry in our lust for him.

Obey.

Hurry.

I ambled toward the hallway regardless of my hunger for my alpha and my inner dragon pushing me to get my ass in gear.

I yanked my shirt off overhead, dropping it where Patrick would have to step over the mess I made in his house. One kicked-off sneaker lay halfway up the stairs, the other at the landing where I paused.

The sour scent of Patrick's ex intensified here on the second floor, and I scowled, my chest rumbling.

Prim's emotions rolled as she moved up beside me, sliding her hand into mine.

Patrick cursed, stepping around us to rip open the linen closet door. He strode into his room, and we stayed put, allowing him to change the sheets—toss the ones she'd slept on along with the comforter literally out the window. He lit candles to rid the air of her scent.

Prim and I entered our bedroom, one that wouldn't be shared with anyone else. Ever.

Prim hurried to rid herself of clothing, exactly as Patrick wanted, his eyes soaking in every inch of flesh she uncovered to his hungry gaze.

I stayed in place and smirked, waiting for him to glare at me for ignoring his unspoken request.

Prim finished, her breathing and heartbeat heightened.

Our alpha turned his focus on me.

I held Patrick's flinty stare, flicking the button on my

jeans, slowly sliding down the zipper. Took my good old time pushing my jeans to the floor. My dick reached toward him, the slit wet, and I grabbed my base, roughly stroking upward to entice pre-cum to well and drip onto his floor.

He growled, a mix of annoyance and need slithering through the bond.

My backside clenched, and instinct sent me to the foot of the bed faster than Prim, our legs spread and asses in the air. We faced each other, cheeks pressed to the mattress, her pupils huge, the tanginess of her cream-smeared thighs making my mouth water.

I would stab a fucker for even thinking about laying a heavy hand on my female, but she wanted this too. Longed to feel the evidence of our alpha's fierce need for darkness. The only difference was, hers was from true desire, not attempts to entice instincts to the surface that would hopefully overshadow and defeat Patrick's human side.

"Such a good girl," Patrick crooned, but withheld from speaking his thoughts about me and my antics.

Perfect.

Yeah, his dragon half loved me. I preened the slightest bit, wiggling my ass and humping the bed.

Patrick swatted my ass, his palm lingering to squeeze my cheek, intensifying the sting. "None of that," he said, leaning over me, his breath hot on my neck as he jerked his belt loose. "Every inch of you belongs to me. Your climax is mine to command."

"I'll come whenever the fuck I damn well please," I shot back, grinding my dick into the bed, grinning as my declaration caused the darkness to well inside him.

Yessss.

"Goddamn you." Patrick ripped his belt from his slacks, the energy rippling among us vibrating with lust and violence.

Fucking. Bring it.

He let loose, the whoosh sounding a split second before a thousand bees stung my ass. "Fuck!" I jolted, and he gave our sweet Prim what she desired, the impact and pain over her backside searing through our bond.

I growled between clenched teeth, taking pleasure only in the fact our alpha experienced the same ache we did.

The next swat landed even harder, and I cursed Patrick to the fucking stars. His blow on our female's ass didn't hold the same impact.

"You know she feels what you give me," I reminded through gritted teeth, my balls throbbing regardless of the lack of distraction from pain I had needed last time a power play between us had occurred.

Want more.

Yeah, no shit, Sherlock.

Patrick ignored me and the tears on Prim's cheeks, taking out his anger on his mates who willingly submitted to help bring him to his senses and find peace with his beastly half.

He didn't deserve us, or so he thought, but we would do everything within our power to help make him—and us—whole.

Lashes landed, lesser in impact as Patrick found satisfaction in the marks on our skin. Arousal climbed higher among us, our needs feeding off each other. Dragons prowled inside, Prim's closer to the surface, her eyes glowing amber and gold, no longer wet with tears.

I lost myself in her stare, drowning in her desire to be filled by both of us. Her womb would welcome our seed—we would create life as we'd been destined to do.

A low groan rumbled from Patrick, his belt clattering to the hardwood floor. He grabbed hold of our backsides, a palm for each of his mates, fingers digging into heated flesh, intensifying the sting from his lashes.

"Jesus fucking Christ—so good for me." He kneaded our backsides, the scent of his pre-cum making both of us hunger for a taste.

"Such a good little boy and girl." He smacked us both, humming as his dick bucked inside his slacks. "I don't know which one of you I want to sink my cock into first."

A sour scent wafted through our room—

"You sick *fuck!*"

Prim and I both jerked upright, a slew of emotions rushing through the bond. The sting in our backsides connecting with the bed dissolved as adrenaline crashed over us like a wave.

All three inner dragons growled and hissed, but it was Patrick who seemed to grow three feet taller, darkness surrounded him as he spun, hands fisted at his sides. "Jessie," he bit out her name like a curse.

She stood in the open doorway, bloodshot eyes taking in our nudity, a scowl uglying her mouth.

Patrick stepped in front of us to shield his mates from her stare, his muscles quivering. I swore scales covered his back for the span of a heartbeat, midnight blue, shimmery like a rainbow.

Prim whimpered, and I clutched her waist, pulling her tight against me.

"How the *fuck* did you get in here?" Patrick demanded.

"You should be more worried about the fact you're fucking children!" Jessie shrieked, her words slurred.

Patrick vibrated, the clench in his gut causing mine to knot. Tendons stood out in his neck, his pulse throbbing, making mine and Prim's do the same.

I hugged her tighter as images of what could be crashed through our minds.

"You're one sick fuck, Pat," Jessie spat, the scent of booze reaching my nose.

"Out!" he roared with an inhuman voice.

The sound of stumbling footfalls sounded—and Patrick stalked after her, his stomps louder down the stairs in pursuit of his drunk ex.

"Jax…"

I slid Prim onto my lap, wishing I could rid her of the tumbling emotions and thoughts causing her flight instincts to kick in. "I've got you, sweetheart. Stay with me. We'll get this figured out. Everything is going to be fine—we're fated. Nothing can keep us apart."

At least, I hoped for that truth to reign over our destiny.

Patrick hollered for Jessie to get out again, his voice easily reaching through the floor separating us.

"Sick fucking *pedophile!*" Jessie screamed, and a stinging slap sounded.

The anger radiating through the bond spiked, our alpha's growl vibrating through both Prim's and my chest.

Patrick hissed, his humanity slipping toward the edge of losing control to instinct. "Leave before I rip your flesh to shreds."

"Fuck you, Pat!"

Another slap sounded.

Prim's silent urge to not uncover the truth of our species snagged Patrick's focus enough he held control over the claws attempting to elongate from his fingertips.

He growled again before sudden, tense silence caused our ears to ring.

All three dragons hovered like stalking prey, deadly quiet.

I could feel Patrick's spine straighten as though it were my own.

"The fuck are you doing?" he asked, alarm skittering over all three of us.

"Fucking pedophile—calling the cops!" Jessie barked, her tone half-hysterical. "What else would I be doing?"

Fear speared through Patrick's mind, piercing through the bond and stealing our breath. His cold sweat broke out on my forehead.

I clutched Prim tighter, mouth dry, heart in my throat.

The front door yanked open—a quick scuffle sounded—and the door slammed shut.

"Get dressed and get your asses down here!" Patrick hollered up the stairs even as Prim and I reached for our clothing.

"What's going to happen?" Prim asked me, her voice small, heart like a hummingbird's wings inside her chest.

"Don't fucking know." I yanked my jeans up and grabbed her hand. "Let's go."

CHAPTER 44

PATRICK

J essie stood outside on the porch, her drunken rant about the mighty Doctor Macaire fucking children reaching my ears as my mates' anxiety to be by my side spurred them toward obedience.

Bile rose up the back of my throat as the thirst for blood and violence pushed to own my soul. Needing to keep my fucking hands busy—ward off the itch for something more to take over—I slammed open a cabinet, nearly dropping three glasses as I retrieved them.

Flared nostrils couldn't help but drag in a lungful of Jessie's lingering stench as I grew desperate to rid myself of her presence. I ground my teeth, muscles quivering, on the verge of exploding. Thickening. Lengthening.

The beast inside me was a force to be reckoned with.

Protective and possessive, neither trait carried negativity in my human mind. He was gut instinct—had seen me through my lifetime even without my knowing. It was him driving me home to stay where fate had intended me to be. Dragonblood had always held dominion over my destiny.

And in fear of being seen as insane, my humanity had attempted to do the same to my other half.

Primrose clung to Jaxon when they entered the kitchen, both of them struggling to make sense of the thoughts and jumbled memories of my past, attempting to align my humanity with the beast inside.

Jaxon squeezed her hand and motioned toward a chair at the table.

Legs weak, she sank down, a slight sting in her backside reminding us of what had been interrupted. A sinking sense of dread from her swamped whatever arousal might have attempted to rekindle among us.

"What's going to happen?" she asked, worry eating like a cancer at her insides.

My brow furrowed at all the possible outcomes as Jaxon sat beside her.

"It's not a big deal," he said.

I glared, my spine straightening at his attempts to brush off our situation as nothing.

"What?" Jaxon shot at me, stare unwavering. "Enjoying a little kinky action and threesomes isn't illegal."

"No, but this town is conservative enough that my career could be ruined," I hissed.

"Who gives a flying fuck what people think about you?" Jax grumbled beneath his breath.

"I do! Do you know how hard I've fought to hold onto my sanity, study the human brain, so I could prove myself of sound mind to myself and help others who struggle? Do you have any goddamn idea the emotional turmoil I've dealt with over the years?"

The ache in my chest knifed Primrose's, and a sob caught in her throat.

"You're not the only one dealing with emotional turmoil, *Doc.*"

Primrose's thoughts shut down, overrun by anxiety. She slumped, heaviness owning her limbs. Chest sinking in, she hung her head and closed her eyes…her longing for reality to dissipate sweeping through me.

"Fuck." I pulled her up into my arms and hugged her tight against me. "I'm so goddamn sorry, Primrose."

Affection and the desire to ease her despair leaked warmth through our bond, attempting to break through the coldness closing her off.

Jaxon threw his arms around both of us. The intangible parts of our bond could only go so far in reminding us of how our souls had been brought together, but the physical connection among all three of us? As mates, we couldn't become any more real to solidify the truth in my mind I had been on the verge of submitting to mere moments earlier.

Primrose sagged against me, the slowing of my heartbeat causing hers to sync with mine.

"We're going to figure this out," I stated, even though unrest over the confrontation ahead of us lay at the back of my mind.

Shift.

Take our mates from this mess we created.

"We didn't create it, Prim," Jax argued out loud with her inner beast attempting to sway her into shifting to her true form and stealing us away. "That bitch did."

"And I can't flee from my responsibilities," I added. Fate had brought me back to Arizona—and not just to meet my mates. A deeper need to accomplish…something *more* seemed to root my feet in this dry soil where beauty abounded. "Arizona, this land, is our home."

My beast purred in pleasure, curling up in contentment where I used to imprison him, but no more.

Primrose peered up at me, hope swelling over the last barrier that had kept us apart.

A siren sounded in the distance, not allowing for further reflection or conversation. "The cops are going to want proof you're over the age of consent—please tell me you have IDs," I said.

"Yeah—I'll grab them." Jaxon left us for the trash bags lying beside the garage door.

"When I turned sixteen, my grandmother insisted I get my license to drive our old truck down out of the mountain," Prim said as memories flitted through her mind, flooding me with her thankfulness and lingering grief.

I had so much to learn about my two young lovers—and I wanted their every joy and heartache to become my own.

Tears welled in Primrose's eyes, and I rubbed my nose over hers, eyes closing briefly.

"Cops are coming, you sick fuck!" Jessie hollered through the front door, seeming pleased with herself, but I couldn't be bothered to look away from amber eyes that overflowed with love when my gaze met Primrose's once more.

Car doors slammed.

Jessie hollered more nonsense.

Regardless of the ruckus growing outside, our heartbeats slowed, love and passion swelling between us.

"Bring it—" Someone pounded on the door, cutting off Jaxon's statement, loaded with dual meaning and cooling the instinctive need within us to mate.

"We *are* consenting adults," I stated, setting Prim on her feet.

"Let's go take care of this shit so we can get back to what that bitch so rudely interrupted." Jaxon's attempt at lightness fell short, but I ordered them to the living room and made for the front door.

A young cop stood on the porch, Jessie shrieking at the elder of the two officers who held her arm, escorting her down the stairs toward the cruiser with flashing lights in front of my house.

"Patrick Macaire?"

I stepped away, motioning the blond man inside.

"Sorry for the intrusion," he said, stepping past me and peering deeper into the house. "Your neighbor called about a disturbance, along with another call from whom I assume is your ex?"

"Yes." I led him toward the living room, wanting to get this over with.

Jaxon and Primrose sat side by side on the couch, gazes flicking from me to the man stepping into the room behind me.

Dragonblood.

Brow furrowed, I struggled to make sense of what Primrose whispered through the bond and how it roused the quiet darkness inside me.

My beast growled with clear intent as the cop introduced himself—Officer Ayling.

His explanation of why they were making a house call went in one ear and out the other as I attempted to sync my humanity with the beast inside me, allowing his instincts to make sense in my brain. Fucker was quiet, merely simmering, heating my blood like lava.

"Nothing wrong with a little kink," Jaxon said with a flirty tone that caught my attention. I glared at him, a rumble growing in my chest. "Especially when all three are consenting adults."

Officer Ayling fought a smirk, blind to the danger at his elbow as his gaze ate my beta the fuck up.

My cocky boy preened—until the officer turned his focus on our female. Jaxon's eyes narrowed, eyes filling with blue-green fire.

Both of our dragons hissed.

"Can I see your IDs?" Officer Ayling asked, still clueless as he stood between two predators who wouldn't think twice about tearing his head from his body.

As one, my mates lifted what they had in their hands, not tightly clasped between them.

He took Jaxon's, checked the date of birth, and immediately handed it back, fingers brushing over my beta's.

"They're both legal." I struggled to keep from growling as the cop checked Primrose's ID, lucky for him, without touching her skin. "They're also *mine*."

Arousal burst through the bond at my verbal claiming.

Jaxon snickered, leaning back enough to adjust his bulge. He smirked up at the officer. "There's just something about a man in uniform…"

I hissed.

Little cocksucker winked at me and proceeded to lick over his bottom lip while holding my gaze.

I'll suck your cock any day of the week. Always hungry for your spunk, alpha, he assured me.

I hoped the brat realized he was in for it.

Jaxon choked on a groan, and the cop cleared his throat.

"Your ex is beyond drunk and claims to be tired of giving you second chances," Officer Ayling told me, his gaze flitting over my blatantly sexual beta and flushed female before turning to face me. "If her being upset over your *legal* partners taking her place continues, might I suggest a restraining order?"

Dragonblood, Primrose whispered again.

And I got it.

The inky ugliness of my jealousy and possessiveness slid from my mind, and I peered into the officer's brilliant blue eyes, straining to hear or see for myself what Primrose did. "Do you know a young woman named Emelia?" I asked the cop, wishing my royal blood had gifted me such insight as it had my female.

His brow furrowed for a moment, but he shook his head. "Should I?"

I considered explaining, but my gut instinct urged me to keep my silence—for now. Finally recognizing and trusting my inner beast's leading, I shrugged a shoulder and motioned toward the front door. "Never mind. You'll be removing Jessie from my property?"

"Public intoxication, disturbing the peace…seems enough to give you three a quiet rest of the evening."

"I appreciate it." I opened the door, taking note of my ex in the back of the cruiser, the other cop striding toward us. He paused on the walkway, his gaze meeting Officer Ayling's as he stepped out onto my front porch.

"All set?" the elder asked.

Office Ayling nodded and stuck out his hand to me as his partner returned to the cruiser. Our shake was firm. Bold, but not threatening on either side.

"Enjoy the rest of your night," he encouraged me, eyes twinkling with a knowing look.

"I plan on it."

Chuckling, he strode down the stairs, unaware of the flare of lust through my groin over the hours to come and how my mates responded in kind.

I noted my neighbor on her porch and, teeth gritted, offered a forced, polite smile and small wave.

Nothing to see here.

The cops drove off, and I shut my front door, headed straight for the stairs.

Primrose and Jaxon scrambled to hurry after me.

CHAPTER 45

JAXON

Even though violence still heated Patrick's blood, he no longer wished to inflict pain. With acceptance of our bond solidified in his mind, our alpha wanted to taste us, drink in our essence from the source. Imprint our scent and flavor in his senses.

Both Prim and I whimpered as we stepped into our bedroom.

"On the bed, my sweet love."

An ache slid through Prim's chest at the pet name, and she obeyed, laying herself out, thighs spread for her alpha.

I sat beside her, reaching for my straining dick.

"That's mine," Patrick stated, his tone firm, and I lusted to have his mouth on me more than I wanted punishment for disobeying.

I fisted my hands at my sides.

"Good boy," he murmured.

I expected him to go for Prim—she would *always* come first, but he paused, gaze settling on my straining dick.

A slow smile curled his lips, one that promised agony—

"Oh fuck." I croaked, lying back and pulling my knees to my chest.

Prim settled in for the show, the scent of her arousal flooding my nose.

Strong hands grasped my ass cheeks and harshly pulled them farther apart as though attempting to rip my pucker in two.

Patrick was going to eat my ass—

"Fuck!" I jolted in his firm hold as his nose slid through my crack, lewd sniffing noises making my dick buck and filling my senses with my own musk. "Oh, God—Jesus, fucking hell."

He licked from my hole to my taint, midnight eyes glowing with fire as our gazes met.

Delicious.

My cock throbbed with the need for friction, pre-cum dripping onto my belly.

Patrick shifted his hips up, prohibiting his own shaft from rubbing against the mattress.

"Bastard." I huffed, and he chuckled before flicking his tongue over my hole with teasing caresses that made more wetness trickle from Prim's pussy. Curses spilled from me as I stared at my alpha worshiping my ass, taint, and balls. "Please," I begged for what he already knew I wanted—and I was well aware he had zero intention of giving in.

My dick ached from the lack of friction, but I would gift my alpha what he desired. What I loved.

Coming untouched.

The out-of-control agony of my taint pulsing, shooting spunk up my shaft—

I gasped, swallowing hard, fighting to keep my eyes on Patrick's as he made a meal of me and waiting for his permission to come.

Pleasure rippled through him, far beyond the sexual gratification my body offered him.

Your submission allows me the control I need. His thought echoed through my head, causing what I expected love would feel like to swell in my chest. *The trust you offer me. The acceptance of my darkness—the longing for it.*

Swallowing hard, I nodded.

All of my life, my parents couldn't be bothered with me. They'd sent me away when I became too much. I'd acted out in desperation for attention—for discipline that showed they cared. Patrick went far beyond giving me what I required, setting me straight when necessary.

Even though he secretly got off on my brattiness.

He growled against my slack hole, nibbling on my sensitive flesh.

"Please…"

My alpha shoved two fingers up my hole. Curled them inside my ass, searching—

"Fuck!" I jolted, my hold clutching at the backs of my knees, writhing against him. My dick throbbed in pure agony, my balls tight, ready to seize. "Patrick—fuck! *Please!*"

Prim whimpered, fighting to stop herself from reaching between her thighs.

"Come, boy."

I hollered as spunk shot up my shaft, splattering over my chest and chin in endless spurts. I fought to hold his gaze, crying out again as he grabbed the base of his own shaft to keep from joining me in my release that seemed to go on forever.

Heaving for breath, I went lax with the last dribble of seed from my slit. I'd come my brains out but was hardly satisfied.

Prim's shudder rippled through all of us, pebbling my skin.

A low hum of approval, of pure pleasure, rumbled in Patrick's chest as he released his hold on my ass and straightened my legs around where he knelt between my thighs. He dragged a finger up over my torso, smearing my cum while the need to mix his own into the mess tempted him to jerk off.

But he wasn't done.

He bent, licking up my flaccid shaft, leaving a wet trail of saliva over my abs. He gathered my spunk from my chest on his tongue, swallowing me down. More sounds of satisfaction escaped his throat, and he lapped and sucked, cleaning me of every last trace of my release.

Prim's mouth watered, but she held still beside me, a vibrating bundle of need.

"Such a salty snack," Patrick said, smacking his lips. "But now I'm hungry for something sweet."

"Yes," Prim whispered, whining deep in her chest when Patrick climbed over to settle between her thighs.

He buried in her pubis, breathing her in like he'd done with me. Both of us groaned over the scent of strawberries flooding our noses.

I grunted at the zing of lust stirring again in my groin.

Patrick liked my body's response. Had planned on it. He would make me ache before giving us all the shared climax we lusted for.

As Prim had done, I settled in to watch our alpha fill his senses with her, sharing them with me through our bond.

He slid his hands beneath her backside to lift her pussy toward his waiting mouth. "So sweet."

The pulse through her core made my groin tighten, the strands of his hair seeming to tangle in my fingers as they did Prim's.

He licked her, and I tasted her on my tongue, moaning as she did.

"Oh, fuck." I tipped my head back and watched through lowered eyelids as my alpha devoured our female.

Their yearning swirled through my mind, but needing more, I slid my hand over Prim's heaving chest. Skin to skin allowed me the experience of their desire feeding off each other, and I groaned, soaking in emotion and pleasure until I felt like I would combust.

"You're killing me," I croaked, and Patrick hummed while slurping at Prim's core.

She clutched at his hair, the slight sting causing my scalp to tingle.

The supernatural fucking rocked.

Yessss.

Our beasts hissed their desire as one voice, and Prim came on our alpha's tongue, crying out his name.

Sweetness swamped my mouth, and I swallowed…nothing, jealous Patrick enjoyed sustenance while I'd been teased.

That was the end of my punishment, I realized as he slid up her body, shaft spearing into her throbbing pussy, filling her with one thrust.

She clutched at his shoulders, still coming, and he rolled before she finished, settling her atop him.

Hands on her ass cheeks, he showed me her pink, spasming hole.

Groaning, I got on my knees, hand in a death grip around my granite-like dick.

"Please," Prim begged, face buried in Patrick's neck.

I gathered my pre-cum, smearing it over her back hole as she finally settled from her climax, sated and blissed out.

But still wanting.

Yessss.

There was no need for orders, no commands given.

Patrick pulled from her core, and I took hold of his soaked shaft, milking him until I had a handful of his pre-cum. He eased into her pussy again, Prim's shudder skittering along my spine.

"Fuck, yeah," I muttered, smearing Patrick's slickness over her asshole, rubbing at her pucker until she softened while he gently rutted into her.

Beta.

I lifted my head to find Patrick's passion-hazed focus on me. Fire burned bright in his eyes, his control slipping. "Take her, boy."

Holding his gaze, I slid two fingers past her ring, rubbing along Patrick's length as he backed out of her wet heat.

He groaned while pushing in again, a mere membrane of our female between us.

"Need you both," Prim begged, and I used my other hand to palm Patrick's dick as he slid from her tight sheath.

"Fuck." He clenched his jaw as I gathered their combined arousal off his shaft to slicken my dick.

Need swelled through the bond among the three of us to the point I couldn't tell one's thoughts from the others', or whose inner beast whimpered for release the loudest.

Everything but my alpha and female disappeared from my head. Yearning to give of myself overwhelmed me—or perhaps it was Patrick's heightening mine—and I positioned the head of my dick against Prim.

She pressed back, and I slid in halfway, planking on my palms, snuggling Prim between us. I held still, studying Patrick's swirling dark pupils, Prim's parted lips as she panted against his neck. The energy rippling among us was like a living thing, full of love—and acceptance.

Nothing mattered in that moment but being one, our hearts beating in time, alpha to female to beta. No outside force, no human or dragonblood could break what our alpha had bonded together.

We were bonded.

Completely.

Never to be separated again.

I pushed into Prim's tight heat, my balls resting against Patrick's as he buried deep inside her pussy. "You belong to us," I whispered, going onto my elbows, one hand against his cheek, the other closing over his in Prim's hair, none of us caring that the stickiness of our need coated my fingers.

"Yes."

"Show her how much you mean that, Doc," I said, my voice ragged at the consent—the love—shining through the energy ebbing among us.

He reached up to grab my nape and turned his head, taking her mouth.

I backed out, Prim's ass hot and tight around my dick. The second I pressed in, Patrick pulled from her clasp, and Prim whimpered into his mouth, both of their flavors—male and ripe strawberries—flooding my senses, swirling inside me like fuel.

"So sorry," Patrick whispered against Prim's mouth as his length slid along the underside of mine. "I'll make it up to you both. I promise."

The truth of his words, his desire to shower us with love and appreciation, swelled inside me until tears pricked my eyes.

Staring at each other, we fucked in and out of our female, slow enough I clenched my jaw to keep from begging him to move faster. As though he had all the time in the world, Patrick licked her mouth and tasted her tongue, his fingers digging into the back of my neck, holding me close and trapping her to him.

The second he pulled his mouth off hers, I dove in, claiming his swollen lips. The taste of Prim clung to him and dizzied me, and I shoved my tongue into his mouth, desperate for more.

Prim whimpered between us, teetering on the edge of climax again, her pants, her pulse thrumming in my ears.

Come.

My body responded in agonizing sweetness at my alpha's command, and Prim sobbed between us, her core clenching around us in pulsing waves. A maelstrom of passion and release swept over us.

One heart.

Shared emotion and love aligned perfectly as both Prim and I had wished.

I finished first, a sweaty, sated mess slumped over my mates who could easily handle my weight.

I'd always told myself I wasn't right in the head, but…

"I'm goddamned perfect," I murmured against Patrick's shoulder.

Neither snickered but agreed in their minds, still too cum drunk to voice how awesome I truly was in being everything they needed.

"I love me," I supplied for them. "I'm worthy of your adoration."

Yessss.

Grinning, I wiggled a little bit, settling in for a good rest right the fuck where I was—where I belonged.

CHAPTER 46
PRIMROSE

My alpha's warmth and strength were the foundation beneath me, my beta's heat a protective heat over my back.

Our heartbeats slowed, emotions settling. Silence owned the room and our thoughts, but the feelings among us floated as though on a gentle wave, through one and into the other in a never-ending circle. Comforting in a way I had hoped for but never expected due to our rocky beginning.

Unrest in the atmosphere brought healing rain, sustenance to grow things. Working through the turmoil, and sometimes pain, was part of the process.

I now realized that truth while resting between my mates, our entire beings known to each other without hindrance or second-guessing.

Had our finding one another been easy, our connecting accomplished without effort, there would be no reward. Yes, our inner beasts would have connected without issue, but my human half wouldn't have held appreciation in my heart if this bond hadn't been earned.

"You, my sweet love, are perfect too," Patrick murmured, his chest rumbling against mine.

I smiled, a heavy sigh relaxing me further.

"Your drive to find us and the hard choices you made in seeking out your mates are admirable. Your vast knowledge of the half of me that I'm ready to explore and understand…" Patrick swallowed hard as tears laced his voice. His warm palms slid along my thighs bracketing his torso. "I'm thankful that you opened up this part of me that fills what I'd always seen as an empty void in my soul."

"But you made the choice to claim us," Jaxon pushed for our alpha to understand that none of us were better than the other, that we all had areas we needed to grow in.

Patrick's humanity had aligned with his inner beast, and as one, they *had* staked their claim before another dragonblood. He'd spoken what had solidified in his mind without manipulation or coercion, gifting me the fulfillment I had dreamed of since childhood.

I had found my mates, and we were bonded in every way until we rested among the stars.

Peace sank into my bones.

I woke to bright sunlight—and Jaxon's face buried between my thighs. Lifting onto my elbows, I blinked, glancing around to find Patrick and all trace of his energy gone. What would have sent my anxiety through the roof twelve hours earlier didn't even prick at my emotions since the question of Patrick committing to us fully had been eradicated the night before.

Smiling, I lay back, stretching, my pussy growing wet beneath Jaxon's loving licks and nibbles.

"I want you to come all over my mouth, baby," he said, his voice muffled by my slickened labia.

"Mmm." Still smiling, I grabbed hold of his hair and shifted my hips to meet his hungry mouth.

"Did you like having our dicks inside you last night?" he asked, pressing a finger into my core and lifting his head. Sleepy, blue-green, and full of lust, his eyes swallowed me up the second our gazes caught.

"Yes."

He pulled his finger from my pussy and slid it down over my asshole, pressing until he slipped past the ring of muscle. Holding my gaze, he flicked his tongue out, up and over my clit while fucking my ass with his finger.

"More," I said, my heartbeat kicking up, leaving me breathless.

Laid out flat on the bed, he pressed two fingers from his other hand into my pussy.

I groaned and tipped my head back, my thighs clutching at his head while our memories relived our coming together last night.

Every inch of my body begged for release, and my unselfish beta returned his focus on making me come twice, both times crying out his name.

"What about Patrick?" he asked with a teasing tone once I lay spent and lax beneath him.

"I'll call out his name when our alpha comes home from work and gives me pleasure while you watch," I said exactly what went through my beta's mind.

"Mmm." Jaxon lay beside me, cupping my cheek to angle my head toward him. "He loves us. Completely. You felt that last night, didn't you?"

A burst of sunshine lit my soul, radiating between us.

"Yes," I simply stated what he already knew to be true, my

smile a warmth my beta adored. "I didn't take note of what the turning point was, though."

"When that dragonblood cop checked us out. Didn't you feel him go all alpha and shit?"

He had been flooded with jealousy, indignation that another Blood Born dared to look at what belonged to him. Warmth roused in my core at the memory, a reminder that newly bonded mates were insatiable for one another.

How had he found the strength to leave us this morning?

His drive amazed me, his stubbornness something to be admired.

But I longed for him, yearned to feel the completion he'd gifted us the night before.

"Let's go see him," I suggested, a vision of what I wanted causing Jaxon to groan.

"He told me to stay away from Lockwood when he left this morning. If we go, he'll beat our asses."

"And?" I pushed, snickering when he hopped out of bed as quickly as I did.

We'd never gotten to finish that spanking scene, and visiting our alpha at his place of work ensured he would follow through with punishment this time.

We quickly dressed and hurried out the door, driven by the dragonblood rushing through our veins, spurred on by the beasts prowling beneath our skin.

Hand-in-hand and invisible to the human eye, we approached Lockwood on foot, adrenaline causing both of our heart rates to thrum.

Patrick wouldn't be pleased to feel us draw closer, but Jaxon looked forward to our alpha watching his dick disappear into our cloaked mouths one after the other. Invisible lips, tongues, and teeth taking him to the point he fed us his cum, ordering us to swallow it down.

A shiver rippled over my beta, and I giggled under my breath.

The second his energy rippled through us, I second-guessed my choice to sneak into his office.

"You're crazy enough *you* belong in there," Jaxon whispered as we drew alongside the fence across from the third wing.

"The first time I ever climaxed was right here," I told him, drawing up beside the chain-link fence.

Both of our gazes locked onto the barred window.

"I couldn't see you, but I sure as fuck felt you."

"I watched you masturbate," I murmured as the memory fed my libido, readying me for mating.

"Do you regret anything?" he asked suddenly, turning and grasping my face in his hands.

"Not one moment—even the bad times. We've had a hard-earned happily ever after, but it's been so worth the effort. Wouldn't you agree?"

Jaxon hummed, gave me a quick peck on the lips, and once more laced his fingers through mine. "You might regret going in there right now, though."

My smile warmed him clear to his toes in his sneakers. "Never." It was my turn to place a chaste kiss on his bowed upper lip. "Pain, pleasure," I murmured against his mouth, "I want it all. With both of you."

"Forever?"

"Forever," I vowed.

PATRICK

Energy licked over my skin, causing goose bumps to break out and my groin to tighten.

Instinct demanded I close my eyes and breathe deeply in hopes of catching the scent of my mates. I had warned Jaxon to stay away before leaving for work, but if he and Prim experienced half of the pain I did in being separated from them, I expected their resolve to waver.

With it being Jaxon's day off and Prim not working, they would fuck themselves into a stupor and eventually realize they needed me in order to feel truly sated.

I was just as arrogant as my boy, who had chosen disobedience and dragged our female into his plans.

Lips pressed into a line, I glanced at the clock on my office wall to see how much time I could afford them—not much.

I could taste their hunger, my mouth watering along with theirs.

Oh, they had plans, all right, and there would be no better sense available for denying their desire.

Damn them.

I settled my gaze on my office door while pushing my chair back from my desk.

Seconds later, the handle twisted, the door pushing inward as though on its own.

Brave little mates.

The earthiness of Jaxon and the sweetness of our female flooded my office, and I inhaled until my lungs ached, lust simmering through every cell of my body as our cravings fed off each other's. The door clicked shut, appearing to leave me alone, but my gaze became glued to where the energy radiated from—a shimmer and bend of light revealed my mates for a moment.

I freed my dick without a word, shoving my slacks to my shins and widening my thighs.

They knelt before me, and I pushed down on my dick, pointing it toward them.

Warmth brushed against my legs, both bodies crowding in close and completing the physical circle that made us one in heart and mind.

Wet heat slid down over my length—my cock disappearing before my eyes.

"Goddamn," I groaned as similar warmth closed over my balls. I grabbed hold of both of their heads, fists tangling in hair, and tipped my head back against my chair, stars dotting my vision as they worshiped their alpha.

They suckled, licked, and kissed along my length, taking turns lapping at my pre-cum, shoving their tongues into my slit in search of more until I panted, my sac tight and ready to explode.

I grabbed the base of my dick to keep from coming. "Let me see you," I growled through clenched teeth.

As one, they shimmered into sight, Primrose's dark pupils fastened on my face, and Jaxon's lust-filled eyes stared up at me, both of their lips reddened and swollen from enticing me to give them what they craved.

"Open your mouths."

They obeyed, their eagerness for my cum sending the first spurt out of the tip of my dick before I jerked myself.

"Fuck." The next rope landed on Jaxon's tongue, and he grasped my thighs, his tongue licking at the smear on his chin.

A deep groan rose from my chest as the next shot landed on Primrose's face, her pink tongue darting out to capture my essence.

I grabbed Jaxon's head and yanked him down over my pulsing shaft, gifting him the rest of my cum.

"You're going to pay for this," I promised as the last bit spurted into his throat. "Going to redden your ass, boy."

"It was my idea," Primrose whispered, her light brown eyes luminous and full of need for me.

"Then I'll bend you over my lap and spank your gorgeous ass—"

A knock sounded, and I cursed, yanking up my slacks and shoving my dick away. Primrose grabbed Jaxon's hand, and they disappeared from sight in the blink of an eye.

"One moment!" I called, glowering at the clock.

She was five minutes early.

"You two need to get the hell out of here," I whispered harshly.

Dragonblood, Prim whispered.

Emelia, I supplied through our bond.

Either the young woman heard me say her name or decided she didn't want to wait for permission to enter. The door pushed inward. Wrapped in that tattered robe, she stepped into my office, her cheeks pink, eyes widened as she quickly scanned the office.

"Where are they?" she squealed, and I heaved a breath, clenching my eyes shut for a second.

"Shut the door, Emelia."

She did as told and quickly sat across from me, small body practically vibrating. "I know they're here," she said, still smiling and glancing around the room. "I can hear their dragons—and yours." She turned her focus on me, her dark eyes peering into mine as she stilled momentarily. "You're happy."

"Not right at this moment," I said, my voice low as both my mates' joy radiated what resided in my heart.

Emelia's grin lit the darkness of her eyes, like stars in the night sky.

Primrose's dragon whispered a word I didn't understand but felt I ought to. Energy rippled from her as she quickly stood and shimmered into sight, leaving Jaxon de-cloaked and scrambling to his feet on my other side.

Thank fuck they were both clothed.

Primrose faced Emelia, wariness and excitement rising in her mind even though red flushed her face. "You know the word my dragon spoke," she said rather than asked.

Emelia's eyes widened, and she blinked, staring up at my golden goddess, who dwarfed her small stature. "Yes."

Golden beams of fire licked at Primrose's legs as a shiver slid over her body. "Who were your fathers?"

"C-Canadian brothers," Emelia whispered, also rising to her feet, her smile widening.

"*French* Canadians," Primrose said with a light laugh, her disbelief whipping my focus between the two young women. "Twin brothers."

Emelia's head jerked up and down, and they both let out a shriek, rushing to embrace each other.

Sisters.

I glanced up at Jaxon, and grinning, he shrugged.

Enticing Primrose to leave her newly found little sister proved near impossible. Jaxon sat against the wall while the two girls chatted the entire allotted hour away.

Fucking dragonblood everywhere.

Jaxon huffed a laugh, and I glanced over at him. "You two have to go home."

"Home." His eyes lit with amusement and love. "I like the sound of that."

"Good." I shot a glare at Primrose, hoping she would finally pay attention to my annoyance and concern over the fact my next appointment would show up any second.

"My grumpy alpha needs his space," she whispered to Emelia, laughter in her eyes as she glanced over her shoulder at me.

"I have no wish to lose my *job*," I said, my voice stern, my inner thoughts telling her to obey me or else.

"You'll be leaving Lockwood on your own soon, anyway," Emelia said with a smile. "You don't have anything to fear." She glanced at my mates. "Some will not understand and judge who you've partnered with, but your reputation will not be ruined." Her steady gaze returned to my face. "Your business will grow."

Yessss.

While a few weeks prior I never would have trusted her mutterings or the voice inside me, my eyes had been opened to a truth far beyond what most of humanity would grasp, let alone consider to be true.

Shoulders relaxing slightly, I studied her for a moment longer, wondering how I hadn't seen the resemblance between the two women before. Although her eyes were dark as coal while Primrose's were golden brown, the same slant angled the corners. They both had high cheekbones, generous mouths, and thick hair with a natural wave and part on the right side.

Emelia stood a good five inches shorter than Primrose and didn't have nearly the womanly curves as my female.

I cleared my throat and tipped my head toward the door. "Please go. I trust Emelia's words about my future, but I'd rather not have to explain visitors who snuck in without passes," I said, motioning at Primrose and Jaxon.

"I'll come back to visit," Primrose promised Emelia, hugging her tight.

"How about I help her get discharged instead," I said as the thought entered my head, rising to my feet, "so I won't have to worry myself sick over revealing what we are to the world?"

Jaxon pushed up from the floor where he'd been lounging and sauntered to Primrose's side. "Let's go, Prim. We got what we wanted." Cocky boy winked at me. "And the promise of punishment."

"Jaxon." I growled in my chest, and both Emelia and Primrose's faces flushed.

"See you, Doctor Macaire," Emelia said, scampering toward the door. She flashed a smile at Primrose. "See you, Sis."

"Cloak yourselves," I ordered the second the door closed behind her, "and get the hell out of here."

Hands clasped and both grinning, my mates shimmered out of sight.

Weak with desire, I left work early. Again.

Primrose's moan hit my ears at the same time the scent of their fucking did—the second I walked in my door. I shed my clothes while hurrying up the stairs, the slap of skin and grunts of my beta heightening my blood.

My dick jerked in my hand as I crossed the threshold.

Our female rode my beta, sweat glistening over her body in the afternoon sunlight shining through my open bedroom window. Golden hair shimmered like a sunrise but fell in a cascade around her and Jaxon as she lay over his chest.

Need, all three inner beasts moaned as one.

Jaxon rolled them, pinning Primrose beneath him. He fucked into her hard and fast, the scent of the slickness between them coating my mouth with drool and making my dick leak in readiness.

I climbed between Jaxon's spread thighs and stilled him with a hand to his lower back. He arched like a good boy, dragging his dick out of Prim, barely notched inside her dripping pussy.

I'm ready—stuff me full of your cock, his humanity spoke without words.

A stronger alpha would have denied his desire. Whipped his ass until he begged for mercy—and to come.

But I longed to be inside him, physically connected in more intimate ways than thought and emotion.

I smeared my pre-cum down my length, using my other hand to spread his cheeks. Lube glistened around his hole.

He'd prepared himself for me.

"Such a good boy," I murmured while rubbing my leaking head over his slack pucker.

Own.

Groaning, I pushed in until my groin sat flush against his backside, both of us feeling deliciously full.

Yessss.

I shoved harder, forcing him back into Primrose.

Electrical currents shot through me, all three of us

moaning in our shared longing for connection with our mates.

Heat swept through me. Passion flooded my chest.

My disobedient mates' desire to experience how we had bonded—but this time with no barriers between hearts and souls—spurred me to give them better memories.

I rocked into my beta with slow, slickened glides, every shudder, whimper, and moan creating the most beautiful music to caress my ears. Their scents swarmed my nose, the feel of muscle and soft flesh cradling every inch of my body.

We thirst.

Overridden with shared senses, I latched my teeth onto the base of my beta's neck, same as he did to our female.

Euphoria shot us into weightlessness.

Complete satiated bliss.

EPILOGUE - PRIMROSE
TWO MONTHS LATER

We banked, flying low back the way we had come through the starlit night, our joy unspeakable, our dragon halves' desire to roar in victory barely reined in. The energy of our mates rippled behind us with the same excitement, and we glanced over our shoulder, dragon sight allowing us a glimpse of midnight blue and shimmering blue-green scales and wings flapping haphazardly in an attempt to keep up with us.

We shot upward with a gracefulness our mates lacked, the rushing wind stretching our grin wider.

Show-off. Jaxon's humanity grumbled through our bond while Patrick's focus, his drive to succeed, honed his thoughts on staying in flight and not nose-diving into the ground like he'd done a half hour earlier.

Laughing internally, we spiraled down to earth, a flap of wings pulling us up before we smashed into rock. Our claws rested on the ledge in the Grand Canyon's northern wilderness, where we had been visiting the previous couple of weeks to practice our mates' shifting into their true forms.

We tracked my mates through the air as they banked and headed our way.

Gentle, we warned through our bond.

Jaxon's beast landed—on his feet, pride and cockiness flickering through us, causing our own chest to swell.

Well done, beta.

He preened.

Patrick followed in a scatter of stones, his backside hitting the ground.

Jaxon's and my humanity shared a snicker, but our amusement turned to purring as both of my mates' dragons blanketed me, their long tongues lashing at my face. Need to release the adrenaline from their first flight flooded through our bond, and we obeyed our alpha without a word having to be spoken.

I shifted to human form, my hands on their scaled flanks. "Focus—allow your instincts to gift you what you desire."

Jaxon did as told, his beast's stubbornness over finally having been given freedom to *fly,* causing muscle and bone to shrink slowly.

And rather than listen to his female, Patrick's dragon snaked his long, forked tongue between my thighs.

Wet.

"Mmm," I agreed, widening my stance.

He licked my slit from ass to clit before dipping into my core with his long tongue, probing deep against my womb.

My knees went weak. "Need you, Patrick—please shift," I whispered, grabbing hold of his scaled jowls.

Jaxon pressed against my back, his arms wrapping around my waist as a shuddered sigh rippled through him. "The things I do for you, woman."

I chuckled, experiencing his disappointment at having to return to the earth and tuck those glorious wings beneath his skin.

Our alpha's desire sent us both to the ground, Jaxon beneath me, my back tight against his chest. His hard cock lined my ass crack, and I scooted higher, needing him inside me.

Patrick struggled to take on his human form, his aggravation and desire to mate making it that much more difficult.

Relax, I told him. *Focus on regaining your arms and legs, not my emptiness or Jaxon's seed.*

A huff of hot dragon breath, sweet as sugar yet full of brimstone and smoke, wafted over us both—and Jaxon slid me onto his shaft.

I arched against him, gasping at the sudden fullness. "Patrick," I groaned, reaching for him.

His curses slid through my mind, but he appeared in human form a heartbeat later, longer hair mussed as though blown in the wind, eyes dark in the night but glowing with an inner blue light.

He crawled atop me on hands and knees, claiming my mouth, tongue sliding between my lips to curl with mine.

Jaxon moved in and out of me with slow, gyrating thrusts, causing my body to heat.

Breed, Patrick ordered through the bond as he had been doing on a daily basis—sometimes twice a day. As the alpha, he was driven to fulfill our destiny, and even though I had claimed I wanted to live for a while before being tied down with offspring, the deepest parts of me longed for the same as my mates.

With every passing day, both his and Jaxon's dragons had grown stronger from our bonding, from the sustenance they gave each other. Our connection of shared hearts and minds solidified our unity, and while Patrick sometimes needed space, he never stayed away for very long.

Our need for one another was too great.

"Let us give you a child, my sweet love," Patrick

murmured, lifting from my mouth, his cock sliding up over my clit with every thrust from Jaxon beneath us.

Our beta shuddered, grasped my hips, and held still inside me as he drew too near to flooding me with his release.

"Prim—sweetheart," he murmured against my ear, his breath warm. A vision of my belly swollen with their offspring flitted through the bond, and my eyes stung as their shared desire welled.

"You can say no," Patrick said, his eyes burning bright while staring into mine.

Jaxon silently agreed.

But it was time—I could feel it deep in my bones. This is what we had been meant for, the reason for my existence.

Yessss.

All six parts of us hissed in agreement, but I nodded my consent for my mates to take me as one.

Patrick groaned and grabbed the base of his shaft, sliding it along Jaxon's as he pulled out, coating them both in the slickness necessary to ease their attempts to breed me. He ensnared my gaze, his lips parted, emotion pouring through our bond as Jaxon sank into my core.

None of us had yet declared the word with one another, but evidence of our love was portrayed in how we touched, edified, and nurtured each other.

Still, deep need required I gift my mates my vow spoken out loud.

"I love you, Patrick, my alpha," I stated, cupping his whiskered cheek in my palm. "And you, Jaxon, my perfect, sexy beta." I laced my fingers through his atop my thigh.

Emotion radiated among us, but both men's throats had closed off, keeping them from vocalizing the sentiment echoing through my head.

Holding my gaze with tear-glazed eyes, Patrick pressed against the back of Jaxon's length and pushed forward.

"Oh!" I gasped, the initial sting, the burn of being stretched by two cocks in my pussy, caught my breath.

"Breathe, baby," Jaxon whispered against my ear, his voice strained, free hand sliding over my taut stomach. "Relax and let him in."

I exhaled, forcing my muscles to do as he'd said.

The discomfort shimmered away like a shadow upon the sun's rising.

"More." I whimpered, and I relaxed completely, entrusted in Jaxon's hold and opening to our alpha.

Planked over us, Patrick worked his way into my body, inch by inch, sharing space with our young lover.

"Fucking hell, old man—be careful but hurry the fuck up," Jaxon groaned between clenched teeth, determined to withhold from climaxing too soon.

A shared exhale emptied our lungs as Patrick bottomed out against my womb alongside our beta's throbbing shaft.

"Oh, holy fucking *hell*," Jaxon croaked, and our alpha's eyes blazed, fire burning deep inside him.

Heat rushed through us, singeing and glorious.

"Love me," I whispered, drawing Patrick's head down so I could own his mouth and swallow his cries when they filled me with their life-giving seed.

EPILOGUE - PATRICK

I could feel the pebbles biting into Jaxon's spine and the overwhelming fullness Prim experienced having us both inside her tight sheath, nudging in and out in a gentle, synchronized rhythm. Jaxon's resoluteness to keep from blowing his load matched my own, his teeth gritted and sweat beading his brow from holding back until my command.

Our female attempted to writhe between our arms, which were bands of steel, clutching her in place to gift her what I'd been dreaming about every night since bonding.

I wanted her swollen with our child, glowing and filled with evidence of our love and commitment that radiated through our bond every moment of the day while in close proximity—my favorite place to be.

"Yes." She moaned, her sweet breath ghosting over my mouth as our foreheads rested together.

"So good, Prim." Jaxon groaned, his lips against her ear. "Perfect in every way. So soft and warm." Hissing, he pressed in deep, his stomach muscles clenching, fingers digging into my hips as silent pleadings for me to give him permission to come flooded my head.

Primrose would receive her pleasure first—every single time.

She moaned between us, sweat slickening our skin as we pleasured each other, her hands grasping at my shoulders. "Patrick," she begged, her need rousing a growl inside my chest.

Instinct drove me forward, and I slammed into Primrose, pulling a grunt from both of my mates.

Jaxon responded in kind, giving our female exactly what her inner desire called out for.

"Harder," she vocalized her need, breath loud in my ear as I hugged her tight, giving her everything I had, encouraging Jaxon through our bond to do the same.

"Come for me, my sweet love," I said on a grunt while burying against the softened opening of her womb.

She shrieked, her core clamping around our shafts.

"Fuck!" Jaxon's cock throbbed against mine, shots of cum spurting deep inside our female in perfectly synced euphoria.

Her inner walls contracted around our pulsing shafts, her body milking us, sucking every drop from our balls into her womb. I could sense the flood, the mixing of seed, rushing toward where fate dictated.

Heaving for breath, I held myself on my elbows, not wishing to crush either of my precious mates I had been gifted and sometimes didn't believe I deserved. They had set their sights on me, had been driven to make me see the truth.

And I'd never been more grateful for anything in my life.

A well of emotion flooded through our bond, reassurance of acceptance, unconditional love, and thankfulness.

But.

Jaxon groaned, his hold on my hips loosening, without a doubt leaving bruises behind. "Fucking rock in my shoulder blade," he grumbled, and I rolled to my side, taking my mates with me.

We remained buried together inside Primrose, all three of us silent beneath the stars—our ancestors and others watching over us as our hearts slowed to beat as one.

For the first time in weeks, I was at rest. Tension no longer rode my shoulders or burdened my mind. The three of us had walked through fire, coming through turmoil, refined and stronger as individuals and a throuple.

Jessie had spewed shit about us upon her release from the holding cell she'd been in, and while I'd had to get a court order to keep her away from us, her defamation hadn't caused any serious damage to my reputation like I had feared.

Officer Ayling had referred the Chief of Police to my office when he mentioned wanting to talk to a therapist. The following week, the chief's sister had booked her first session at my office on Main Street, where Jaxon now worked as my assistant—he hated the word secretary.

"Still do," he muttered, and I chuckled, rubbing my fingertips down his spine.

A shiver slid through him, and both of my mates sighed in unison.

"The mayor's wife enjoyed chatting with you, but I hate the vibes you got from her," Primrose muttered what she'd already informed me of. Twice.

I kissed my female's lips. "And men don't drink in their fill of your beauty whenever you walk down the street?"

She huffed. "You're mine."

"Indeed, I am," I reassured her with words even though she didn't need to hear them from my lips.

Considering we couldn't hide our thoughts, I had needed to have a serious sit-down conversation with my mates, discussing the confidentiality of my patients and how they couldn't share whatever they heard in my head. Jaxon especially, since his office lay beyond my door, our proximity allowing him full access to my brain's workings. I trusted they would protect those who came to me for help as determinedly as they would me.

I'd given my two weeks' notice at Lockwood and left with an excellent referral should I need one in the future—exactly as Emelia had claimed.

Primrose visited with her sister a few times a week, and even though we offered help getting her released, she rested in believing she was exactly where she needed to be for now.

Jaxon let out a sigh and snuck his arm between Primrose and me, laying his hand on her lower abdomen. "Do you think it worked?" he asked, reining all of our thoughts back to the present.

I closed my eyes, searching through the three of us, wondering. Hoping, while caressing Prim's cheek with my thumb.

"Yes," Primrose whispered, grasping my hand on her face and sliding it down atop Jaxon's.

Three hands—four heartbeats.

"Shit…" Jaxon laughed as I grinned. "Already?" he asked, pulling out of Primrose and leaving me feeling bereft. He rolled her between us, causing my spent cock to slip from her body and releasing a rush of cum to drip from her core. His gaze plastered to her belly and our clasped hands atop.

An ancient word whispered through my sweet love's mind, and she sighed. "Stars help us."

"Why?" I asked, still smiling and not understanding.

She slid my hand beneath hers to rest directly against her skin.

Five heartbeats.

"Shit." I jerked my head up. "Twins?"

Her laughter echoed her joy inside, but underlying fear

and anxiety rose. "They can hear us, you know, so no cursing."

I grumbled another curse.

"You wanted this, so pull up your big boy panties," she said, biting back a laugh.

"I don't wear panties—or briefs," I reminded her, my brow furrowing. Hell, when we were at home, none of us wore a stitch of clothing.

"Well, if I'm this fertile—" she giggled enough that lightness filled my chest, "you might want to start—and never remove them."

"Nope." I crawled over her on hands and knees—fuck the goddamn pebbles—to reach Jaxon. "I'll just fuck our beta."

"Mmm." Primrose slid her hand between her legs and ran her fingers through fresh arousal trickling from her pussy. "If that thought wasn't so hot and didn't burn Jaxon up, I'd complain."

I claimed Jaxon's mouth, our dicks swelling between us as Primrose moaned her approval over how our tongues dueled for dominance.

"Love you both so much," she murmured on a sigh, her heart overflowing.

As one, Jaxon and I turned our attack on our female, her squeals and giggles lighting up every corner of my soul—and Jaxon's—as we pressed in close against her.

"Let's show her how much we love her, beta," I said, pausing in my devouring of her breasts, her furled nipples that tasted of strawberries. "You opened our hearts, Primrose."

Yes, Jaxon agreed through our bond as he licked the saltiness of drying sweat off the back of her neck.

"You've given us everything," I stated, peering into her golden-brown eyes a man could drown in.

"Yes." She huffed a laugh, caressing her belly. "Twice over."

"So much more than twins, Prim." Jaxon roamed his hand between me and Primrose again, rubbing over her belly. "Unconditional love and acceptance and a family of our own."

Primrose's fear over the future rose once more as the twins' hearts beat stronger in time with ours, but she turned full-on to face our beta, gifting me the privilege of pressing my groin against her plump backside. "It was *you* who brought us together, Jax," she murmured, cupping his cheek. "Without your strength and encouragement, I would have given up on us."

"You're a good man, Jaxon," I said in agreement of her feelings while catching his gaze over her shoulder.

"Nah." He grinned. "I'm just a horny bastard who believed in fate enough to accept you both, flaws and all."

"I hope like hell neither of these two takes after their beta father," I said with a grimace, the heartbeats strengthening against my palm.

Jaxon chuckled while Primrose groaned. "We're in trouble," she mumbled.

"We'll be fine." I snuggled against her back, uncaring of the rock digging into my hip. "We'll handle it."

"Together," Jaxon said, sandwiching her tightly between us.

Together. Always, I told them through our bond, and their echoed love and commitment filled my heart, my mind, and I knew I had found what I'd been driven to accomplish my entire life.

THE END

About the Author

Spicy romance author Lynn Burke believes everyone deserves healing and a happily ever after. She loves writing hot, inclusive stories of various pairings or triplings and creates characters who will steal your heart.

She is a USA Today Bestselling author, a wrangler of her three spawn, and a farmer's daughter who grows organic food. To escape reality, she hides in a quiet corner with her nose in a book.

You can find more about Lynn at her website: www.authorlynnburke.com

Also by Lynn Burke

Abel's Obsession

Divulging Secrets

Healing Storms

In Between

Reluctant Lumberjack

Resisting his Mate

Billion Dollar Love Anthology

Blood Born Series

Bonds of Worship Series

Dark Leopards MC

Darkest Desires Series

Devil's Outlaws MC

Elite Escort Series

Elite Escorts MM Series

Fallen Gliders MC

Forbidden Obsession Duet

Found by Fate Series

Midnight Sun Series

Missing Link Series

Pippen Creek Series

Risso Family Series

Sandy Ridge Series

Sinful Nature Series

Vicious Vipers MC